One night in paradise. . . .

Caroline and Charlie vowed no one would ever know the truth about what really happened that night in the vault. But now, Caroline could no longer deny the truth—the truth that soon everyone would know: in less than nine months, she was going to give birth to a living reminder of the night of passion she'd spent in the arms of wisecracking, insufferable Charlie Donohue.

Caroline wanted a baby. She wanted to hug it, love it, give it the best of everything. She just wasn't too sure about its father. . . .

Charlie and Caroline were blue jeans and haute couture, nachos and pâté. Not only didn't he fit her upscale image, he happened to drive her crazy. But Charlie had to be told.

His reaction floored Caroline: "A kid's parents ought to be married," he said.

Who could argue with that?

ABOUT THE AUTHOR

Barbara Bretton's published works range from stories in Katy Keene comic books—written when she was ten years old—to articles in the *New York Times,* to contemporary and historical romances. The author of over a score of novels, Barbara is a favorite of American Romance readers for her unique talent of creating characters whom we care about and laugh with. And we surely will, with the oil-and-water combination of Charlie and Caroline in this book. Barbara makes her home in suburban New Jersey with her husband.

Books by Barbara Bretton
HARLEQUIN AMERICAN ROMANCE

193–PLAYING FOR TIME
211–SECOND HARMONY
230–NOBODY'S BABY
251–HONEYMOON HOTEL
274–A FINE MADNESS
305–MOTHER KNOWS BEST
322–MRS. SCROOGE
355–ALL WE KNOW OF HEAVEN
365–SENTIMENTAL JOURNEY
369–STRANGER IN PARADISE

Don't miss any of our special offers. Write to us at the following address for information on our newest releases.

Harlequin Reader Service
P.O. Box 1397, Buffalo, NY 14240
Canadian address: P.O. Box 603,
Fort Erie, Ont. L2A 5X3

BARBARA BRETTON

BUNDLE OF JOY

Harlequin Books

TORONTO • NEW YORK • LONDON
AMSTERDAM • PARIS • SYDNEY • HAMBURG
STOCKHOLM • ATHENS • TOKYO • MILAN

Published June 1991

ISBN 0-373-16393-2

BUNDLE OF JOY

The Beginning

i

It was commonly understood around O'Rourke's Bar and Grill that Charlie Donohue and Caroline Bradley were just not meant for each other. Like oil and water or chalk and cheese, the ex-Navy cook and the beautiful entrepreneur were a bad match, and although O'Rourke's was filled with inveterate matchmakers, even the most determined of the lot had to admit this was one match that would never happen.

Not that they hadn't tried to bring the two together. Dinner invitations. Extra tickets to a Princeton theater production. Cookouts and charity balls and all manner of obviously phony reasons designed to bring a reluctant man and an unwilling woman into close proximity.

Nothing worked. Months passed and, one by one, the matchmakers at O'Rourke's threw their hands up into the air and admitted defeat. "Opposites don't always attract," said Professor Scotty MacTavish, the wisest of the group. "It would serve us well to remember that."

And so the notion of Caroline Bradley and Charlie Donohue becoming Caroline-and-Charlie faded away, and the two very single adults settled into an adversarial relationship that suited them both—if not the rest of the group at O'Rourke's.

Not that Caroline willingly spent a great deal of time at O'Rourke's, mind you. If it weren't for the fact that her best friend Samantha had married the owner's son, she wouldn't be caught dead parking her Maud Frizon pumps under one of the scarred pine tables scattered around the smoke-filled tavern. Caroline liked champagne and strawberries; O'Rourke's offered beer and peanuts. Her idea of stimulating conversation ran more toward Louis Malle movies, while the "A" topic at O'Rourke's was whether the Giants would go all the way to the Super Bowl.

On that fateful afternoon in the first week of June when it all began, Caroline was perched on the edge of a rickety wooden chair with her elbows resting lightly on the sticky tabletop, doing her best not to notice the noise and the smoke and the general air of good-natured pandemonium that was the hallmark of the bar and grill. One thing she couldn't help but notice was that most of the pandemonium seemed to center around the brawny figure of Charlie Donohue. He'd spent the better part of the last hour lugging beer kegs down to the basement while the silver-haired clientele cheerfully offered suggestions on how to lighten his load. Charlie Donohue was proportioned on a heroic scale: tall, with wide shoulders and narrow hips, he hoisted those beer kegs as if they were down-filled pillows. It wasn't that she'd been paying a great deal of attention to the short-order cook, but it was a trifle difficult to ignore six feet three of rippling masculinity on parade. When he caught her looking at him, his impertinent wink made her remember why she didn't like him in the first place.

She cleared her throat and turned her attention to her best friend. Across the table, Sam was nursing a large glass of iced water and lecturing Caroline on the miracle of childbirth for the thousandth time in the past eight and one-half months.

"It's a whole other world out there," Sam expounded. "When I had Patty twelve years ago, they still treated you as if you were sick, not pregnant. Why, except for this gigantic belly and breasts the size of the Twin Towers, I'm as healthy as a horse."

Caroline feigned a swoon. "Enough of that medical talk. I'm the one who passed out when Lucy gave birth to Little Ricky."

"That was a rerun," Sam said, laughing. "Little Ricky must be thirty-five years old by now and losing his hair."

"It's the principle of the thing. I firmly believe childbirth should be left to those best suited for it."

"You have the equipment," Sam pointed out.

"I have the equipment to run the New York Marathon, too, but you don't see me lacing up my running shoes and heading for the starting line."

"You're a terrific godmother, Caroline. I know you'd be even more terrific at the real thing."

Sam's blue eyes went misty, and Caroline reminded herself that hormones were powerful things; Sam couldn't be held responsible for taking it upon herself to promote the joys of marriage and motherhood. Caroline liked men just fine, thank you, but she didn't want to own one. Why that should bother so many people was entirely beyond her.

"Remember who you're talking to?" she asked, summoning up her best dumb-blond voice—the one men seemed to love. "I went from diapers to dinners à deux with no stops in between."

"You're terrible," Sam said with a laugh. "I seem to remember a bout with braces and skinned knees—"

"Shh!" Caroline ordered as Charlie Donohue walked past their table. "I have a reputation to uphold." She'd worked hard to create the image of a beautiful and pampered woman with nary a care in the world. That very image was responsible for making Twice Over Lightly, her rent-a-designer-dress boutique in Princeton, the phenomenal success that it was. Lacroix fantasies, Karl Lagerfeld extravaganzas and Chanel originals like the one she was wearing all vied for attention in her elegant shop. Somehow she had managed to bridge the gap between middleclass pocketbooks and aristocratic tastes, making her clientele feel special the moment they walked through the door—even if they could only be Cinderella for one night.

Sam grinned as Charlie stripped off his work shirt and, muscles rippling in his white cotton T-shirt, hoisted another keg of beer. "Impressive, isn't he?" The look she cast Caroline was pointed.

Caroline shrugged, almost as if male pulchritude made no difference at all. "Denim work shirts are simply too *outré* for words."

Sam groaned and took another sip of water from her icy beer mug. "No French words today, please. It's too hot. Charlie may not be a *GQ* cover boy, but he's a damned good cook. My father-in-law's lucky to have him here."

"I think I liked you better before you got pregnant," Caroline observed, fanning herself with her latest copy of *Vogue*. "You've become entirely too domesticated, if you ask me."

"I haven't asked you. Besides, you have no one to blame but yourself for my condition."

Caroline arched one pale blond brow. "Really, Samantha?" she drawled. "Perhaps you should sit in on one of your daughter's hygiene classes."

Of course, Caroline knew exactly what her oldest and dearest friend was talking about. Caroline and her goddaughter, Patty, claimed full credit for bringing Sam and Murphy—the reluctant caterer and the intrepid reporter—together. Today, however, she felt like being difficult. "I have retired from the matchmaking business," she declared with a wave of her manicured hand, "and I advise you to do the same."

Sam's dark blue eyes widened in mock surprise. "Match make? Whatever do you mean?"

Even in French Caroline's comment carried an earthy punch. "The music teacher, for one."

"He asked for your phone number, Caroline. I didn't volunteer it."

"I choose my own male companions, thank you very much."

"Like that snooty professor?" Sam wrinkled her nose.

"Alfred is a lovely man. Is it my fault you prefer jocks to intellectuals?"

Sam's laugh bounced off the walls of the dimly lit bar. "You may be able to fool the others with that line, Caroline, but I've known you way too long to let you get away with it. That soap opera star you dated last winter had his doctorate in hairspray not quantum physics."

"So I'm a sucker for a pretty face. Is it a crime?"

Sam angled her head toward the bar where Charlie Donohue was talking to the afternoon bartender. "Charlie's not half bad."

Caroline shuddered. "I may be a world-class flirt, but I do have my standards." They watched as he shrugged into his shirt, laughing as he talked to the afternoon bartender. It wasn't that Donohue was bad-looking. Quite the contrary. There was something so brazenly male about him that she half-expected he would start beating his chest and drag off the next available woman to his cave. She preferred men whose appeal was a bit more subtle. And yet even Caroline's breath caught as his powerful back muscles strained against the confines of the T-shirt, and she coughed to cover the moment.

Unfortunately, Sam knew her too well. "Denim doesn't look so bad all of a sudden, does it?"

Caroline hid her grin behind her glass of iced tea. "I'll admit he has a certain rough charm but he's not my type at all." And Charlie's type, she was sure, wore spandex dresses and stiletto heels and looked up to Madonna as a cultural icon.

Sam leaned back in her seat and glanced at the wall clock near the jukebox. "Murphy's late. Is that going to throw a monkey wrench in your plans?"

"Not a major one." Sam's husband had volunteered, after some not-so-subtle urging, to help Caroline move a truckload of "gently used" designer dresses into the storage room of her shop. She pushed back her chair and stood up, smoothing the sleek skirt of her raspberry silk Donna Karan. "Why don't I go back to the store and get started? You can send Murphy over when he gets home."

Sam looked from Caroline to Charlie and again at Caroline. A sly smile darted across her face.

Had Caroline seen that smile, she might have had a chance to change things, but the smile disappeared before Caroline noticed it, and her fate was sealed.

CHARLIE DONOHUE rarely did anything he didn't want to do, so when Samantha O'Rourke asked him to pitch in and lend a hand to her pal Caroline, the word no was on his lips before Sam had finished her sentence.

"No?" Sam's dark blue eyes narrowed. "You said no?"

He tempered his lack of enthusiasm admirably. "It's not that I don't want to help out, but it's happy hour. I've got to man the skillet and start turning out the burgers for the hungry hordes."

"I'm sure Bill wouldn't mind if you took a few hours off, would you, Bill?" She aimed her smile at her father-in-law and Charlie watched, amazed, as his crusty employer crumpled before his eyes. "See?" She sounded triumphant. "Murphy was going to help Caroline with the coats, but he's been delayed, and besides, I was hoping he'd be around tonight." She patted her belly absently then launched her final salvo. "You never know. Junior might decide to make a surprise appearance."

Bull's-eye. Charlie could say no to just about anything, but he couldn't say no to a pregnant woman who apparently was ready to deliver her baby any moment. To his dismay, he found himself agreeing to drive over to Caroline Bradley's hotshot boutique and help the small blond whirlwind unload a truckful of mink coats.

"You're a doll, Charlie." Sam planted a kiss on his cheek. "Caroline will be so pleased."

"Not when she sees me, she won't be."

"Of course she will," Sam protested a shade too vigorously. "She's just so absorbed with her business that she hasn't had time to get to know you."

"Yeah," said Charlie. "Right." If you asked him, Caroline Bradley was a cross between Scarlett O'Hara and Donald Trump in the body of a petite Marilyn Monroe. She was opinionated, flirtatious, with a spun-sugar face and an acid-etched tongue that she didn't hesitate to use on anyone who didn't see the world through the same pair of rose-colored glasses she did.

He remembered the first time he saw her. He wasn't due to start work for a couple of days, but he'd decided to stop in the bar and get to know some of the regulars. O'Rourke's had struck him as a *man's* kind of place. Lots of dead fish hanging on the walls, plenty of smoke, a wall-mounted TV permanently set to the sports channel. A place where a man could relax. Forget about his troubles. Enjoy a brew and a ball game.

He pushed open the door and stopped dead in his tracks. There, perched atop an old piano like Michelle Pfeiffer in *The Fabulous Baker Boys,* was the most beautiful woman he'd ever seen. She wore a black dress that clung to her small but curvy body. Her hair was pinned atop her head, tendrils curling around her elegant cheekbones.

She was exactly the kind of woman he dreamed about regularly but made a point to avoid. He ambled over to the bar, steering a wide path past the piano. Bill O'Rourke was behind the bar.

"Something, isn't she?" Bill pushed a draft toward him.

"Do they always crowd around her like that?" From the stool where he sat only her shiny blond head was visible in the crowd that surrounded her.

"Always." Bill explained that the vision was Caroline Bradley, best friend of his daughter-in-law, Sam.

"What is she, a singer?"

"She runs a dress shop."

Charlie angled another look in her direction. For some strange reason he was beginning to feel angry with the woman. "Is she going with one of those old-timers?"

Bill chuckled. "I don't know who she's going with. All I know is those guys would do anything for her."

"She hang out here a lot?"

"Only when she drops in with my daughter-in-law, but when she does, watch out! She takes over the piano and before you know it, every man in the place is in love with her."

What in hell was a looker like the beauteous Ms. Bradley doing wasting her time flirting with the over-the-hill gang? She hadn't so much as given Charlie a second glance, and he was closer to her age by a good fifty years.

"Want an introduction?" asked Bill, eyes twinkling with mischief.

"Forget it. She's not my type."

Bill's laugh was loud and boisterous. "Pal, she's any man's type."

"Not mine."

"Yeah," said Bill, refilling Charlie's beer mug. "Right."

Charlie wasn't lying. He had no use for women who collect men's hearts like charms on a bracelet. You'd have to be blind to miss what she was up to over there, fawning all over the old men. Practicing her skills. Sharpening her weapons. Killing time until better prey came along. Everything about her looked expensive, from her hair to her fingernails to the pale suede shoes on her small feet. A man could go broke trying to keep her in panty hose.

Yeah, Caroline was beautiful—you'd have to be a fool not to notice—but Charlie never much cared for women who fancied themselves as southern belles. Especially not when the southern belle in question lived in central New Jersey.

He had to hand it to her, though, he thought as he drove the back roads from Rocky Hill to Princeton. She had the old geezers at O'Rourke's eating out of the palm of her hand. Scotty almost fell over his orthopedic shoes every time she swept into the bar in one of those idiotic rented outfits of hers, smelling like expensive perfume and dripping sugary compliments. Even Bill O'Rourke, who was about as hard-boiled as you could get outside of Charlie himself, turned to geriatric mush when she batted her false eyelashes in his direction.

Not that Caroline Bradley spent any time batting her eyelashes in Donohue's direction. She still didn't like him any more than he liked her, and that was just fine with Charlie. He'd bumped into her once over at the Princeton Marketfair movie complex. He and a friend were waiting in line to see Schwarzenegger's latest when Caroline and her boyfriend of the moment came sweeping out of the newest foreign flick. Charlie had raised his bag of popcorn in salute, and it was clear by the horrified expression on her face that she wished he was invisible—or, at least, dressed in something preppie and safe like her pal. A Coors T-shirt seemed okay to Charlie but then there was no accounting for taste, especially not around Princeton. The geek she was with was a case in point.

So there he was on his way over to her precious secondhand dress shop. If she'd looked horrified that evening at the movies, he could only imagine how she'd look when he showed up on her doorstep, ready to manhandle all those frilly ball gowns or whatever the hell it was she'd made her fortune hawking.

Most of the rush hour traffic had disappeared by the time Charlie turned onto Nassau Street and made his way to the shop. The late afternoon sun was strong and he slipped his sunglasses on, still squinting behind the dark lenses. A few aging prep school grads strolled down the street toward Palmer Square, still lean and tan in their tennis whites. The hell with old soldiers never dying, he thought with a shake of his head. Preppies seemed to go on forever.

He stopped for a light across the street from Micawber's bookstore, tapping his broad fingers against the wheel. Too damn crowded in town, if you asked him. In the two years since he'd breezed into the area, he'd seen a change. Condos springing up everywhere. New construction where old farms used to be. The hand of progress everywhere you looked, generally gumming up the works and pushing civilization where it had no business going.

The light changed to green, and he shifted his truck into gear.

Not that he was a crusader or anything like that. He pretty much took life as he found it, not taking the problems too seriously, not letting the good times slip away from him. His years in the Navy had given him a hatred of bureaucracy and a love of freedom, two attributes that made it hard for a thirty-five-year-old man to make it big in the United States in the 1990s.

He made a left at the next corner and angled into a parking spot behind the U-Haul van parked in front of Caroline Bradley's shop. Not for him the seven-day workweek, busting his behind so secretaries could dress up like socialites. Whatever it was driving Bradley on, it had paid off in spades. Even secondhand, you didn't buy the clothes she hung on her curvy little body with peanuts and, if he had any real estate smarts at all, this Princeton address came with a pricey monthly rent attached to it.

The door to Twice Over Lightly was open. He stepped inside the quiet shop and was hit immediately with a gentle wave of perfumed air. Yeah, she had bucks, no doubt about it. Big bucks. The walls were washed a smooth ivory color with a wallpaper border in some fussy, female print. Pots of flowers, all pinks and violets, rested on odd tables scattered around the room, tables that sat next to chairs so delicate they looked as if they'd collapse if a hummingbird perched on one of them. He could easily imagine Caroline in one of those chairs, one leg crossed over the other, as perfectly suited to her dress shop in Princeton as he was to the bar in Rocky Hill. He fingered a gold mesh gown on one of the skinny mannequins near the door. He had seen spiderwebs thicker than the silky threads that kept that dress together. Hell, this was probably the kind of getup the perfect Miss Bradley wore to unload a truck. It was hard to imagine her getting her manicured hands dirty. He doubted if she'd ever worked up a sweat in her entire pampered life.

"Anybody here?" he called out. His voice sounded like a foghorn in the hushed, female stillness of the empty shop. He cleared his throat and tried again. "Hey! Someone could walk out with a mink coat."

"I wouldn't try it."

He turned in the direction of the steely, silk-coated voice. It sounded like Caroline Bradley, but that was where all resemblance ended. "Caroline?"

"Who did you expect?" Her tone was edgy. "This *is* my store."

He couldn't believe he was looking at the same ultrachic woman who'd been sitting in O'Rourke's less than an hour ago. Instead of an upswept hairdo, she wore a ponytail. The high heels and sheer hose had been replaced by bare feet, and the designer dress had given way to shorts and a T-shirt. He couldn't have been more surprised if she'd appeared in a gorilla suit.

"Close your mouth," she snapped. "Haven't you ever seen a woman in shorts before?"

"Not on you." Not bad, he thought, gaze roaming the surprising length of her slender legs. Some interesting surprises had been hidden by those high-fashion duds she usually wore.

She ignored the quasi-compliment and peered out at the street. "Where's Murphy?"

"The A-Team's busy," Charlie said. "If you don't need the help, say the word and I'm out of here." He sure as hell didn't want to be where he wasn't wanted. He noted with pleasure the way her chiseled cheekbones reddened. Score one for the blue-collar worker.

"I need the help." She gestured toward some huge white boxes stacked ceiling-high in the corner of the store. "The fur coats have to be put in storage in the back."

"What do you have back there, a big closet or something?"

She pushed her pale hair off her face with impatient, stabbing motions and sighed theatrically. "An air-conditioned storeroom."

He glanced at the stacks of boxes. "Must be a pretty big room to fit all of them inside."

"And there are more where those came from," she said. "Look, if you don't think you're up to it, Donohue, I'll ask the teenage boy down the block to help me. I hear he lifts weights."

Now that stung. The quickest way to a man's ego was through his masculinity. He swung one of the boxes onto his shoulder. "Which way?" he said, his voice more a growl than anything human.

She pointed toward a long hallway at the rear of the store. "Straight through. Last door on the right." Her eyes lingered on his bare arms. "It's freezing in the storeroom. Maybe you should put on a sweater."

"Worry about yourself," he said, heading toward the storeroom. He doubted if anything could be colder than her attitude.

The phrase "bull in a china shop" leaped out at Caroline as she watched Charlie Donohue make his way down the pink hallway. She closed and locked the front door and hung up the embroidered Closed sign. Not that there was any crime to speak of in Princeton, but when you had an inventory like hers, it paid to be careful. If only she'd thought to lock the door before Donohue showed up....

"I'm going to kill you, Samantha," she said aloud, reaching for the telephone. She dialed Sam's number, waited, then slammed the receiver into its cradle. Busy. Sam was probably on the telephone with Scotty, crowing about sending Donohue in Murphy's place. Of all the outrageous, idiotic stunts! She hoped Sam was enjoying her victory because Caroline intended to prove that victory Pyrrhic the first chance she got.

"This wasn't my idea," she said when Donohue came into the front room and hefted another stack of boxed fur coats.

He cast her a perfunctory glance over one brawny shoulder. "Who said it was?"

She straightened her shoulders. "It needed to be said."

The perfunctory glance turned curious. "Why?"

"That should be obvious."

"The only obvious thing in this room is the fact that we both want to get this over with as fast as possible."

Caroline wasn't used to being dismissed quite so nonchalantly and she bristled. "Look, why don't we just call it a day? I'll phone Sam and—"

"Forget it," he broke in. "I gave her my word."

"You don't have to look as if you promised to walk naked through a hailstorm."

"If you're giving me a choice, I'll take the hailstorm."

She bit her lip. What on earth was the matter with her, wanting to smile when she'd been insulted? "I'm sure Murphy wouldn't mind helping me out tomorrow."

He stacked a third box in his arms. "Sam's nine months pregnant. Why don't we humor her? When her hormones are running normally again, she'll forget all about this matchmaking stuff."

"That's disgusting."

His thick dark brows lifted. "Hormones?"

"Your attitude. That has to be the most sexist remark I've heard in years."

"Fact of life, Bradley. You're ruled by hormones from the day you're born until the day you die. Especially when you're pregnant."

"Right. And I suppose you're an expert in pregnancy."

"Doesn't take an MD to see what's what."

"Ridiculous! We're ruled by our intellect. Our sense of reason. Our—"

He was still laughing as he disappeared down the hallway once again. Caroline barely restrained herself from tossing an antique vase at his head. The fact that she had been guilty of a similar notion about Sam's pregnancy earlier that afternoon didn't absolve him of his guilt. Of all the idiotic, outdated notions, his statement about hormones took the cake. Sure, Sam was a touch more weepy than usual these days, but this wasn't the Dark Ages, for heaven's sake.

Grabbing two fox capes from a chair near her Louis XIV desk, she hurried toward the storeroom. He was bent over a stack of coats by the door to the store's tiny bathroom, an impulsive afterthought she'd had added to the storage area when she renovated the building last year. "I suppose you also think women should be kept barefoot and pregnant."

"Don't put words in my mouth." He rose slowly, unfolding inch by powerful inch, until he towered over her. Dear God, he was enormous. He certainly had never looked so...so *imposing* at O'Rourke's Bar and Grill.

Why couldn't he at least have the decency to be less aggressively male, surrounded by fur coats and fancy dresses?

He looked absolutely ridiculous standing there in his close-fitting T-shirt and even closer-fitting jeans with the hole in the right knee. Oh, Caroline knew plenty of men with holes in the knees of their jeans, but those men had bought said jeans complete with fashionable holes scattered hither and yon. She had no doubt Charlie Donohue's had come by his state of disrepair honestly.

"I know all about your type," she said, living dangerously.

"Yeah?" He took a step forward.

She said a prayer and held her ground.

"I could tell you a few things about your type, too, lady."

"Oh, really?" She drew herself up to her full five feet one inch. "I'm sure I'd love to hear."

"You're some rich guy's spoiled little daughter who has some time on her hands between dates so Daddy bought you a store to keep you busy until he hands you off to some poor human bank account you'll call a husband."

"You're more perceptive than I would ever have imagined," she drawled in her best spoiled-little-rich-girl's voice. She'd tried for many years to cultivate her to-the-manner-born persona, and it was gratifying to know how well she'd succeeded. "Now if you don't mind, it's been lovely but I think we should say good-night."

"That's it?" He looked almost disappointed. "I cut you down to size and you stand there like Princess Diana, saying thank you and good-night?"

"I could recite the preamble to the Constitution, if you like, but that won't change things. This was a rotten idea of Sam's, and we'd be smart to cut our losses before there's bloodshed."

She headed toward the big metal fire door that separated the storage room from the rest of the store, but Donohue stepped in her way. "Not so fast."

"Joke's over, Donohue," she said, heart beating faster. "Let me pass."

"You're making me feel like a louse," he continued. "Go ahead. I'll give you one free insult and we'll call it even."

"I don't make it a habit to insult people, *Mr.* Donohue."

"I've watched you shoot down guys at the bar, Bradley. Your mouth should be declared a lethal weapon."

She ducked around him and was practically at the door when, to her horror, he gave it a push and it clanged shut. The sound rang in her ears.

"You idiot!" She forgot to modulate her voice as she pounded on the door with her fists. "Have you lost your mind?"

"Idiot," he repeated with a grin as he leaned against the door. "Not bad, but you can do better. One good insult and I'll open the door and—"

She whirled to face him, eyes blazing with fury, fists aching. "Don't you understand?"

"Unlock the door." He looked at her. "You *do* have the key, don't you?"

"There *is* no key, you fool! We're on a timer."

"You have a phone in here?"

"So the minks can call their mothers? Get real, Donohue! Face it, we're locked in here until tomorrow morning."

ii

"I have to hand it to you," said Donohue. "You had me going there for a minute." Locked in the fur vault with the enemy until nine o'clock the next morning. Talk about unjust punishment. "Now open up."

She swung on him with all the self-righteous fury of the condemned. Her delicate fist landed a punch right in the middle of his solar plexus, and he ducked one to his jaw. He grabbed her wrists; he could encircle both with one hand. Under different circumstances, that might have given him a rush of pleasure. At the moment, however, he was more interested in self-preservation. If he wasn't careful, he could end up a castrato.

"Do something!" she cried. "I'll go crazy if I'm stuck in here with you."

"You're not exactly my idea of a swell evening yourself, lady," he muttered, dropping her hands and stepping out of reach. He glanced at his watch. Six o'clock.

Fifteen hours until the door opened in the morning.

Fifteen *long* hours alone with a crazy woman.

And he'd thought combat in Nam was scary.

Charlie pounded on the door, aimed karate chops at the lock and searched in vain for a window or an emergency switch—anything that would get them the hell out of that fur-lined icebox. He turned himself into a human projectile aimed at the door hinges but no dice.

"They told me the security system was foolproof," said Caroline, voice trembling.

"They were right," Charlie growled. "Fort Knox doesn't have a security system like this son of a bitch."

"Must you?" she asked automatically. "It's bad enough we're locked in here together. You don't have to be crude on top of it."

"Crude?" His laugh made her want to punch him again. "I haven't begun to get crude."

"Keep it to yourself then. I don't need a barroom vocabulary lesson, thank you." She knew all the words; she'd even used a few of them herself on occasion. However she wasn't about to grant him so much as an inch. If she let down her guard for an instant, he would be running roughshod over her as if *he* owned the place.

He muttered something about "ice princess" and she murmured "simple-minded cretin," then they both fell silent. What was there left to say, when you came down to it? She was certain her vocabulary of insults paled compared to his. Besides, there was the matter of her image to be considered, although how she would maintain her cool, calm and collected persona for the next fifteen hours was beyond her.

She glanced around the room, cursing herself for not having the presence of mind to put in a skylight at the very least. But, no. She had to listen to the experts who told her that sunlight was the archenemy of fine fabrics. "No windows, Ms. Bradley, and plenty of air-conditioning year round. Fur vaults must be cool and dark," she'd been told. "Think hibernation!" Great for grizzlies, but not exactly optimal conditions for two adults trapped together against their wills.

If only there were some way out of this mess. Her gaze fell upon Donohue, who was pacing the length of the room like a caged beast. He was big and strong. Why couldn't he fling himself at the door just one more time? Surely the locks, wonderful though they were, couldn't withstand another assault from all that coiled male outrage. She opened her mouth to tell him so, but the look he shot in her direction convinced her to keep her own counsel, at least for the moment.

His jet-black brows seemed permanently knotted over the bridge of his nose, and his jaw was set in granite. She'd already pummeled him once and gotten away with it. From the expression in his eyes, she doubted if she would get away with a similar stunt again.

No, she thought, sitting on a box in the far corner of the room, right near the sables and minks. *The thing to do is concentrate.* She'd never once met a problem she couldn't solve with her wits, and she'd be damned if she let this one get the better of her. There was no way she would spend the next fifteen hours alone with only Charlie Donohue for company.

Absolutely no way on earth.

THE FIRST SIXTY MINUTES of the captivity of Charlie and Caroline ticked away with the slow and deliberate rhythm of a funeral dirge. Caroline felt a scream lodged somewhere deep in her chest. Charlie wanted to see if he could pull a Rambo and blast through the walls with fists instead of an Uzi. The incessant hum of the air conditioner made it seem even colder than it was—and that was saying something.

"Moron," muttered Caroline from the safety of her spot near the fur coats.

"Ditzy blonde," growled Charlie from his position by the door.

Neither acknowledged the other's words or, for that matter, the other's presence in the growing-smaller-every-minute storeroom. The clock on the wall showed 6:59. And then it showed 7:00.

"I feel like I've been here for eons," said Caroline, more loudly this time.

"Solitary confinement would be easier than this," said Charlie, equally loud.

"A sophisticated adult would have inquired about a timed lock system."

"Bull," said Charlie, determined to let her know exactly how he felt about sophisticated adults. "Anybody with a brain would have a fail-safe system for emergencies."

Caroline lifted a patrician brow in his direction. "And, pray tell, how many emergencies does one encounter in a fur vault?"

"Can the Princetonese, Bradley, and give me a hand." He hunkered down and began prying away at the base of one of the door hinges.

"You'll never be able to move it like that," said Caroline, glancing at her brand-new French manicure. Thirty dollars about to go down the drain. "You need tools."

"Right," said Charlie, "and I'm using the ones I have." He waved those big hands of his in her face, and Caroline gulped at the sheer power they represented. "Now give me some help." He paused, his gaze resting on her perfect fingernails. "That is, unless you'd rather spend the night with me."

"Move over," said Caroline, "and let's get this damn door open."

SEVEN O'CLOCK became eight.

Eight o'clock gave way to nine.

And by nine-fifteen it had become crystal clear to even the most pigheaded of optimists that an escape was just not in the cards.

Charlie sank to the ground and held his head in his hands. Caroline thought his posture a bit extreme but then who was she to talk? The notion of spending the next twelve hours in his company had her teetering on the verge of tears.

"This is terrible," she said, her voice breaking on the last word. "We're trapped and it's all because of you...."

Charlie looked up, about to fire off a wisecrack in his defense, when he caught the glisten of tears in her eyes. She looked so pathetic standing there next to him. So delicate. So *female*.

Now hold on a minute. That was dangerous thinking. She might look like a porcelain doll, but she packed one hell of a wallop. *Remember that,* he warned himself. Even if she was remarkably curvy beneath her T-shirt and shorts. Even if her big cornflower-blue eyes looked wide and vulnerable.

Even if he felt an answering stir deep inside him, that primitive male urge to comfort and protect.

Just remember that the ultrafeminine, extremely pretty Caroline Bradley swung her fists first and asked questions later.

Still, it took Donohue until nearly ten o'clock to convince himself to stay on his side of the makeshift fur vault.

AND AS FOR Caroline, she was deeply immersed in self-pity, wondering what sin she'd committed to deserve a fate like this. In her darkest nightmares, she'd never imagined anything as dreadful as being locked in her own store with Charlie Donohue for company. That is, if you wanted to consider his presence as company. The two of them hadn't exchanged a civil word since he walked through her front door. If only Sam had kept her matchmaking nose out of Caroline's life and let Murphy help unload the furs. Only a crazy person would have thought putting Caroline and O'Rourke's short-order cook together alone in close quarters was a stroke of romantic genius. Not that Sam had intended for them to be locked together like this, but sometimes fate had plans that mere mortals would never understand.

Caroline cast another surreptitious look in Donohue's direction, doing her best not to notice the interesting play of muscles along his back and biceps.

Come to think of it, Donohue *was* behaving awfully well, considering the circumstances. Another man might have taken advantage of the situation, dousing the overhead light and turning the storage room into a wolf's lair with Caroline as the lamb on her way to the slaughter. There were advantages to being trapped with a man who didn't find you the least bit attractive, even if that fact stung her ego.

Donohue, through pacing for the moment, sat down on a crate near a collection of beaded Arnold Scaasi gowns and broke the silence. "I'd kill for a burger and fries," he said.

Caroline, stomach rumbling at the thought, sighed. "One of Sam's *torta rusticas*."

"*Torta rustica?*" asked Donohue. "What's that?"

"Meat loaf," she mumbled.

"You're kidding."

"A very *fancy* meat loaf," she said, trying not to smile. "Not the usual fare by any means."

"Meat loaf is meat loaf."

"That's like saying wine is wine."

"You took the words right out of my mouth." He looked as if he were holding back a grin and not altogether succeeding at it.

"There's a world of difference between Thunderbird and Pouilly-Fuisse."

"Like the difference between the two of us," he observed.

Ah, there it was: the killer grin a weaker woman would gladly die for. Caroline was glad she was above such obvious temptations. "Exactly," she said coolly. "Like the two of us."

"I'd still kill for a burger."

Suddenly Caroline leaped to her feet. "It's not a burger with fries, but I have something that'll do in a pinch." She hurried to the far corner of the room, pushed aside two fur coats and uncovered a grocery bag from Food Town. "Cheese, stone wheat crackers and champagne." She raised the bottle in a gesture of triumph. "And what do you think of that, Charles?"

He hadn't been called Charles since before he joined the Navy, but the name sounded kind of nice rolling off her elegant and eminently kissable lips. "Better than C rations," he said with the right note of casual interest. "You make a habit of storing midnight snacks in here?"

"I had to pick up a few things this afternoon," she said with a self-conscious laugh. "This seemed as good a place as any to stash them."

A smile tugged at the corners of his mouth. "Your date must be wondering where you are."

Was it her imagination or did she detect more than a slight note of curiosity in his voice? "I don't have a date tonight, Charles."

He looked at the Brie, the fancy crackers and the champagne. "You bought all this stuff just for you?"

She nodded, busying herself with opening the package of crackers. "I believe in surrounding myself with the finer things in life." She paused, then looked at him. "Go ahead. You're about to laugh at me, aren't you?"

He filched a cracker and made short work of it. "Why do you say that?"

Why, indeed. "Because men like you usually think the finer things in life are an extra six-pack and a corned beef sandwich."

"Nothing wrong with that."

"Nothing particularly right about it, either."

"You really are a snob, aren't you, Bradley?"

"The name's Caroline, and yes, I suppose I am." She'd worked hard to acquire the accoutrements of the good life and wasn't about to make light of any of them. Especially not to a man like Donohue.

"Some women would take a burger and a ball game over dinner at the Ritz any day."

"And they're welcome to both," said Caroline magnanimously. "I, however, shall stick with the Ritz."

Donohue took the bottle of champagne and wedged it between his knees. "Bet they don't do it like this at the Ritz," he said, proceeding to pop the cork.

"I wager you're right," she said, wishing they had some glasses. It was hard to imagine an elegant maître d' with a bottle between his knees.

Her mouth dropped open in amazement as Donohue took a swig right from the bottle. "Good stuff."

She was speechless as he handed her the champagne.

"Try it," he said.

Gingerly she wiped the mouth of the bottle with the back of her hand, ignoring his low, masculine chuckle. Tipping her head back she brought it to her lips the way she used to drink Pepsi when she was a kid. The bubbles filled her mouth and throat and she sputtered then swallowed. "Delicious," she said, aware of the golden liquid trickling down her chin and onto her T-shirt. She extended the bottle toward him. He didn't move. What on earth was the matter with him?

THE DROPLETS of champagne were beaded along the curve of her mouth, her delectable chin, spotting the rounded upper slope of her breasts. He wanted to lick them off her, drop by drop, until he tasted nothing but her rosy skin beneath his tongue.

"Charles?" She extended the bottle toward him again. "Is something wrong?"

Get a grip on yourself, man. He blinked hard, grabbed the bottle and took another long swig. "Drinking on an empty stomach's a killer." He motioned toward the cheese and crackers with the half-empty champagne bottle. "We'd better eat something."

"Can't hold your liquor, is it?" she asked, taking the bottle and indulging in another dainty sip. And then another. "You surprise me, Charles, being a bartender and all."

"Cook," he said, tearing his gaze away from the subtle rise and fall of her chest in that snug T-shirt. "I'm a cook."

"Well, this may not be up to your professional standards, but help yourself to cheese and crackers."

He did, with gusto. A long time ago he'd learned about something called sublimation. It seemed that this was a case in point, substituting the taste of champagne and crackers for the taste of her mouth beneath his.

She brushed a stray lock of blond hair off her cheek with a carelessly graceful gesture that seemed to pierce his heart with its beauty. Champagne was dangerous stuff, to turn a practical, hard-hearted man like him into a poet. But then she was the stuff of which poetry was made—all delicate, shimmering loveliness with the hidden sparkle and strength of a diamond.

Geez.

He grabbed for the bottle.

CAROLINE DIDN'T KNOW what she was enjoying most: the champagne, the Brie or staring into Donohue's green eyes.

Of course, green was too vague a term to describe the amazing color. Charlie's eyes weren't emerald or jade, but the deep, luminous green of a forest shot through with sunlight. Thickly fringed with lashes of the darkest jet, his eyes seemed to blaze with heat that found its target somewhere deep inside the pit of her stomach.

She giggled, a most unlikely sound coming from the so-phisticated Caroline Bradley of Princeton. "I, for one, can hold my champagne quite well, thank you very much." She took a dainty sip right from the bottle, and this time she didn't bother to wipe it first. "I wish we had utensils," she said. "Utensils are what separate men from animals. Did you know that one of the first steps in human evolution was learning how to use eating utensils?"

He started to laugh, the sound beginning somewhere around his feet and moving upward, gathering in volume. "Where the hell did you go to school? The Shirley Mac-Laine University of Advanced Crystal Reading?"

She drew herself up with as much dignity as she could muster given the circumstances. Good Lord, but he was an attractive man. Words she never used, like "hunk" and "stud muffin," popped into her mind and out again. "Forks and spoons are responsible for Western civiliza-tion as we know it," she said, making it up from whole cloth as she went along. "If it weren't for cutlery, we'd still be baying at the moon."

He started to say something both profound and witty but instead found himself staring at the dimple in her right cheek. Funny thing. He'd seen her a score of times before tonight but never once noticed that incredible dimple be-fore. That dimple was a work of art in the perfect canvas of her face. *In vino veritas,* the saying went. It suddenly seemed to Charlie that not only truth was found in the grape, but madness as well.

He took another sip and gave her a loopy smile. Not even the fact he was turning into a human icicle bothered him. Who would have imagined madness could feel so terrific?

CAROLINE DIDN'T notice the loopy smile or the Arctic temperature. She'd been happily occupied with the task of memorizing the impressive muscles barely hidden beneath his T-shirt. Why had she never noticed how silky and thick his jet black mustache was, or just how dazzlingly white his teeth were? She prided herself on being an observant person, and it boggled the mind that such important details had somehow slipped by her.

"Aren't these crackers wonderful?" she asked, crackers being an infinitely safer topic of conversation than anything else she could come up with.

"Delicious," he said, his gaze lingering on her mouth.

They ate in silence except for the crunch of crackers and the last gasping bubble of champagne. Yet, it wasn't a silence like the one earlier, a silence fraught with anger and mistrust. This silence resonated with something else, an emotion infinitely more dangerous had either one of them been able to recognize it for what it was.

But then, how many people actually recognized their future even when it was staring them right in the face? Oh, somewhere down the road a man and a woman could usually pinpoint that moment in time when the gods smiled upon them, but that realization usually came after many years and many, many tellings of the story of how they met and fell in love.

This was all too new for Caroline and Charlie. They had no common history, no shared memories except of brief greetings at O'Rourke's Bar and Grill and of a general lack of interest. The magic between them was as new as the moment, as real as the beating of their hearts. And it went far deeper than the hazy glow of champagne would lead either one of them to think later on.

iii

They finished their impromptu picnic supper a little after eleven. A wave of drowsiness washed over Caroline, and she stifled a yawn. Her lids, however, were half-lowered, and Charlie thought he'd never seen a woman look sexier or more vulnerable in his life. The combination was lethal. He had to find a physical outlet for his volatile emotions, and fast.

He got up and started unpacking the fur coats from their boxes, hefting minks and sables over his arms as if they were a pile of sweatshirts. "Might as well get some work done," he said. "Where do you want these?"

She got to her feet with a motion so graceful and feminine that a lump formed in his throat and he looked away. The cold air must be affecting his thinking.

"This way." She led him past racks of dazzling dresses resplendent with sequins and beads and needlework so amazing that even Charlie could recognize how special it was. "Over here with the foxes."

He found himself eyeball to eyeball with a fox fling. "I had an aunt who used to wear stuff like this," he said, handing Caroline one of the coats so she could slip it onto a cedar hanger. "I hated it then and I hate it now."

"Mercifully outdated," said Caroline, draping a square of muslin over the poor fox's face. "Thank God you don't see things like this very often these days."

He handed her another coat. "Something pretty outdated about wearing dead animals on your back, don't you think?"

She gave him a glance that he couldn't quite read. "That's why I have so many of them, Charles. Few people wear fur these days. They're giving them away and taking a tax write-off."

"But people still rent them?" Charlie saw the world in black and white. Gray areas of moral ambiguity never ceased to puzzle him, like the difference between buying a fur coat and renting one for the night.

Caroline made room on the rack for the next pile of coats. "For your information, I'm not planning to rent these to anyone. I'm donating them to a women's shelter in October. Not that it's any of your business, you understand, but that smug look on your face is beginning to get on my nerves."

"Good for you, Bradley," he said, ignoring the jab. "I wouldn't have figured you for the charitable type."

"And I wouldn't have figured you for the type who cared one way or the other about much of anything."

"By the time the night's over, we should know everything there is to know about each other."

She gave a mock shudder in response, but he couldn't help noticing the twinkle in her eyes and the way her lush mouth tilted with a smile. "Heaven forbid! Proximity does not a friendship make, Charles. Remember that."

She has a sense of humor, Donohue noted with surprise.

He's a lot smarter than I thought, Caroline was pleased to realize. Who would have figured rough-and-tumble Charlie Donohue would care one way or the other about the fate of furry creatures? It was a side of him she liked a great deal. Perhaps it was the champagne at work, but she found herself wondering what other surprises were hidden beneath his macho exterior.

Charlie feigned a matador's pass with a ranch mink stole, and Caroline chuckled as he parodied a close call with an angry bull.

I like her laugh, he thought as she rescued the stole from him. He especially liked her mouth, all soft and inviting and female. Definitely female.

I wonder if he's a good kisser, she mused. Again and again her eyes were drawn to his mouth, his lips firm and enticing, made even more so by contrast with the jet black mustache that was practically an invitation.

By ten after midnight they had emptied all the boxes in the room and put all the furs safely away. Then they polished off the rest of the champagne and crackers, even though the temperature in the vault seemed to be plummeting with each second.

"Geez, it's freezing in here," said Donohue.

Caroline pointed to the wall-to-wall furs. "Grab a coat, Charles. That's what they're made for."

He scowled at the lush silk-lined coats. "They're for women."

"Suit yourself." Caroline got up and chose a gorgeous full-length sable. Under normal circumstances, she didn't believe in wearing fur, but this was definitely an extraordinary situation. "I didn't know freezing to death was a sign of virility."

He mumbled something vaguely incendiary but she chose to ignore it. A few hours ago she would have flown into battle, all flags flying. Now it was enough to watch the goose bumps break out all over his manly arms as he tried to pretend the numbing cold wasn't really bothering him.

He paced.

He jogged in place.

He even resorted to push-ups.

Burrowed deep inside her sable, Caroline couldn't resist a gentle barb. "There's a very masculine ranch mink back there," she said, stressing the word *ranch*. "I won't tell anyone, if that's what's worrying you."

"Nothing's worrying me," he lied. "I like to keep in shape."

"I've noticed." The words were out before she knew it, and she pushed her face more deeply into the luxuriant fur, praying he hadn't heard.

He had. Not that he said anything, mind you, but Caroline could tell by the glint in his eyes, the swagger in his step, that he enjoyed the fact that she'd noticed his body and liked what she'd seen. A little voice inside her wondered, *What does he think of me?* but she firmly allowed it no quarter. Little voices like that had a way of getting you in trouble.

The overhead lamp flickered then went out, leaving only a pale wash of light from the minuscule bathroom that illuminated the far corner of the room.

"It got colder," said Donohue.

"I know," said Caroline. It had also gotten darker, scarier and a great deal more intimate. She wished he would sit down somewhere—anywhere!—and not loom over her, all huge and shadowy and imposing.

The minutes ticked away while the mercury continued its downward slide. Finally, Donohue gave in to the inevitable and let Caroline retrieve the masculine mink she'd told him about. She struggled to keep a straight face as the extremely macho Charlie Donohue draped the coat around his torso sideways, just so no one could accuse him of wearing women's clothing.

"I wish I had a camera," said Caroline, teeth chattering. "You are certainly a sight."

"There's one good thing about having no lights. The less you can see, the luckier I am." He sat down next to her and extended his right hand. "A pact," he said. "Nothing said or done in here tonight goes beyond these four walls."

Caroline groaned comically. "Not even you in that fur coat?"

"Especially not me in this fur."

Solemnly they shook on it, Caroline's hand swallowed up in his larger one. His palm was warm, surprisingly so, and his warmth registered itself against her skin in a way both pleasurable and sensual.

"Sam and Murphy would love to see you in that coat," she said, trying to break the spell his touch had somehow woven around her. Her teeth were chattering, and her words took on a staccato rhythm.

"Speaking of coats, I think you need another over you. You're shaking, Caroline."

Caroline didn't argue. *Caroline.* He'd called her Caroline. She'd been "Bradley" and "lady," but never Caroline. The sound of her name on his tongue sent a shiver up her spine that had little to do with the polar temperature in the storeroom. Rising to her feet, she led the way through the darkened room toward the furs, and they quickly undid all their hard work of a few hours ago. Together they made a soft pallet of minks to sit on, then Donohue covered them both with a foot-high blanket of chinchillas with a few sables tossed in for good measure.

The furs tickled her bare legs, but it was more a seductive sensation than a comical one. There was something almost unbearably erotic about the feel of the sleek soft furs against her skin. It made her think of how his mustache would feel against the curve of her breast...or of how his broad and furry chest would feel against her lips or....

"You okay?" asked Donohue, peering into her eyes.

"F-fine," she managed. "I think the cold air is robbing me of brain cells."

"Come here," he said, pulling her closer to him. "You're shaking like a leaf."

"That's all right. I'm fine."

"You're not fine. You're a human icicle. Let's get a little body heat going."

"Charles!" *Oh, Lord. You don't sound terribly disturbed by the suggestion, do you?* What she sounded was flirtatious, intrigued and altogether too willing. "We'll add another layer of fur coats to the pile."

"That's not going to do it."

"I know." Her voice was a whisper. She slid a few inches closer to him.

He laughed and pulled her right against him, then rearranged the fur coats until they were practically skin to skin. Their thin T-shirts provided virtually no barriers, and Caroline was certain she could feel the springy hairs on his chest right through the cloth.

"I feel warmer already," said Donohue.

She looked up in time to see the lecherous twinkle in his eyes. "I should have known!" She struggled to pull away but he held her fast. She would have been disappointed had he done anything else. "You can let me go now, Charles. I doubt if we're in danger of freezing to death in here."

"You never know," said Donohue. "I wouldn't want to take the chance."

His heart was pounding beneath her ear, a steady soothing rhythm that made it hard for her to remember why she'd ever thought this whole arrangement was dangerous.

"Think of it this way," he continued. "Can you imagine the gossip if Sam and Murphy found our dead bodies in here?"

"It would serve them right," Caroline said, chuckling. "It's their fault we're in this predicament to begin with."

"I thought it was my fault. You had some choice words for me when I tripped the automatic lock a few hours ago."

A few of those choice words brought a blush to Caroline's cheeks. "You wouldn't have tripped the lock if Sam hadn't engineered this whole thing to begin with. Our deaths would be on her hands." She was proud of how gracious she sounded.

"We'd be the talk of Princeton."

"Yes," said Caroline, "but we wouldn't be around to enjoy all the attention. If I'm going to be the center of a scandal, I want to be able to read the headlines for myself."

The light in the bathroom blew, and Caroline started in surprise as the room was plunged into total darkness. Donohue's arm went around her shoulder, and she moved closer to him, heart pounding.

"Afraid of the dark?" His voice was low, intimate.

"Yes, but don't tell anyone." She struggled for a casual tone but failed miserably.

"Cross my heart," said Donohue. "We made a pact, remember? Nothing that happens here tonight goes beyond these four walls."

"You mean I could tell you my middle name is Letitia and you wouldn't embarrass me in front of your pals at O'Rourke's?"

"Not if you didn't tell anyone my middle name is Aloysius."

She crossed her heart beneath the layers of fur coats. "Promise."

He moved his hand toward his heart as Caroline leaned forward to rearrange a sable wrap. His fingers brushed against the fullness of her breasts, and time stopped for both of them.

He hesitated, drawn toward her softness and warmth.

She held her breath, praying he wouldn't draw away.

His hands slid beneath her breasts. He savored their weight for an endless moment, then drew his palms across her nipples, smiling into the darkness as they grew taut and demanding.

Fire. She was on fire. From her breasts to her belly to the juncture of her thighs, she was pure flame. Never had she felt anything like this wave of heat that seemed part of her blood and bone. She placed her hands against his chest, tugging gently at the neckline of his T-shirt until her palms rested flat against his warm skin. His chest hair was thick, altogether delightful, and she barely fought down the urge to taste him with her tongue. She wanted him, wanted him more than she'd wanted anybody or anything in her life. She was out of control, beyond reason, intoxicated with desire.

Charlie was half out of his mind with wanting her. Her smell, her satiny skin, the soft moans from deep in her throat—all calculated to take a man past the point of no return. And she was willing. His fingers toyed at the hem of her T-shirt, easing it slowly up over her midriff. Her body was warm and pliable in his arms, his for the asking.

"Caroline?"

"Yes," she breathed, moving against him. Knowing what he asked. "Oh, yes...."

The word was unnecessary but the sound of it, soft and sibilant, shimmered in the air between them. Her hands dropped from his shoulders, her palms slowly drawing over the hard muscles of his chest as she memorized the feel of his body in the welcoming darkness.

"I wish I could see you," Donohue murmured against her hair as he lifted her T-shirt over her head.

She moaned as his lips found the curve of her breast. She was glad she had the cover of darkness to hide the look of naked desire she knew must be in her eyes. Her stomach muscles rippled with pleasure as he stripped her of her shorts and panties. The sensation of sable against her bare skin was almost too pleasurable, too exquisite to bear.

She heard the sound of cloth ripping as he literally tore the shirt from his body and tossed it aside. He raised his hips and unzipped his jeans, and the next instant he was naked beside her on their pallet of fur, their bodies pressed close together, yearning, aching to be joined.

It took every ounce of self-control Charlie had at his command to keep from taking her right then. No preliminaries. No soft word and softer touches. What he felt was urgent. So hot and primal and undeniable.

Somewhere deep inside his psyche, in that place where reason gave way to primitive emotion, he recognized the rightness of what they were doing. He felt invincible with Caroline in his arms.

She felt simply splendid.

He tilted his head. She lifted her chin. His mouth sought hers, and she parted her lips for him. He stroked the fullness of her lower lip with the demanding tip of his tongue, teasing, anticipating, making promises she knew he would keep. A voluptuous sigh of pleasure rose from deep inside her, and he used that moment to claim her mouth for his own. Their kiss was pagan, abandoned, so powerfully sensual that she thought she would go up in flames from the sheer heat of it.

He tasted of champagne. She found herself growing dizzy from that marvelous taste. His mustache was as silky against her skin as she'd imagined; she couldn't resist stroking it lightly with the tip of her finger.

Charlie was drowning in the smell of her perfume. Light, sweet, laced with a hint of the exotic. He couldn't put a name to the scent, but it seemed to him as he held her in his arms that it was the very essence of Caroline. He wanted to taste her essence, fill his brain with her smell and feel.

She moved restlessly on their bed of furs as he stroked her inner thighs. He found her with his hand, pressing his palm against her moist heat. She melted against him, open and ready for him.

Caroline gasped as he rolled onto his back and pulled her on top of him. His large hands held her waist and he positioned her above him as easily as if she weighed nothing at all. He was in control, in every way possible, a man who knew what he wanted—and that she wanted it as much as he did.

Gently, so gently, he brought her lower until he pressed against her soft and tender flesh. Moaning, she drew her knees closer to the heat of his body, blessing the darkness that hid her fever from his eyes.

"Oh, Charlie," she whispered, giving herself up to the fever. "Don't make me wait."

His low and primitive cry was all she needed to hear.

They came together with a swiftness born of need. There was no time for questions or answers, for declarations or promises. Only the sweet and quick joining of two very different people whose lives should never have intertwined.

The benevolent darkness cradled them as they made love, binding them in an intimacy impossible in the unforgiving light of day. She recognized his tenderness and power. He understood her vulnerability and strength. If either had been asked to explain how it was that they knew these things, they would have been at a loss, for logic has no place in matters of the heart.

Together they rode wave after wave of passion, discovering new ways to bring pleasure to one another as dawn approached. They spoke little, except for words of praise or wonderment. The language of lovers since time began.

"I wish it never had to end," he said as the clock struck seven.

Caroline reached for her shoe and tossed it in the general direction of the clock. "I wish I never learned how to tell time."

"You were wonderful," he said, nuzzling against her neck.

She giggled—a strange sound from the sophisticated Caroline—and trailed a finger along the miraculous planes of his taut abdomen. "You were pretty splendid yourself."

"This is the last thing I expected."

She pressed a kiss to his shoulder. "Last night this was the last thing I wanted."

He cupped her breasts in his huge hands, gently teasing her nipples with the flat of his thumbs. She felt his touch from her breasts to her belly to the place between her thighs where her fever still raged.

"We should be exhausted," she said.

"I've never felt better."

"Me neither."

"We have two hours until the lock opens."

"I know," said Caroline with a seductive smile. "I wonder how we'll pass the time."

"I have a few ideas," said Charlie.

"You must tell me about them," said Caroline as she moved into his arms and lifted her mouth for his kiss.

NINE O'CLOCK CAME all too soon, and with it came an end to magic.

"Oh my God!" said Caroline, scurrying to gather up her clothing. "The store will open any minute. If Rhonda and Denise so much as suspect I'll—" She couldn't even finish the sentence. The thought was too terrible to contemplate. Wrapped in a sable and clutching her shorts and T-shirt, she wheeled around to face Charlie. "Please," she said, "promise me you won't tell a soul."

Charlie's expression was impassive. "Don't worry," he said in a laconic tone. "I won't embarrass you."

"It's not that I'd be embarrassed." *Well, not exactly.* She fumbled for the right words. "I mean, it's just that I try to keep my private life and my professional life separate."

He laughed out loud. "You can do better than that, Bradley. I've heard all about your fancy parties."

"You know what I'm talking about," she snapped, horrified to discover that she was on the verge of tears. "We made a promise last night, and I trust you'll keep it."

He crossed his arms over his muscular chest, and the mischievous light in his eyes went out. "Don't worry," he said. "I'm not exactly proud of what happened last night, either."

His words found their mark inside her heart, and she swallowed hard. "Well, at least we're in agreement."

"Yeah," said Charlie as she headed toward the bathroom. "We're in agreement."

Last night was last night. It was over. Everything about Caroline told him so. The way her arms were wrapped around her midsection. The tilt of her chin. The fact that she wouldn't meet his eyes. He'd been relegated to the blue-collar world, locked out of her world as surely as they'd been locked in together the night before.

She wanted him out of there, and she wanted him out of there as fast as humanly possible.

8:58.

8:59.

9:00 a.m.

It was over.

The lock clicked open, and Caroline swung the door wide.

"I'd better shove off." He headed for the front of the store. "There'll be hell to pay at the bar."

She followed him toward the outer door. "You—you won't tell anyone about what happened, will you?" She hated herself for sounding so plaintive but it couldn't be helped.

"I already told you I won't," he said, not turning to look at her. He didn't want to see the look of relief on her beautiful face that her interlude with the working classes would remain their secret. "As far as I'm concerned, last night never happened."

"Good," said Caroline, opening the door for him.

"Good," said Charlie, heading out to his car.

"We'll never talk about it again," said Caroline.

"Damn straight," said Charlie.

"Last night was nothing special," said Caroline.

"See you around," said Charlie, climbing into his car.

"Yes," said Caroline, stepping into her shop. "See you around."

The whole affair was over and done with, and neither one of them would utter a word about it ever again. Caroline would refuse to think about the warmth and security of his arms. Charlie wouldn't waste a second dwelling on the way she'd made him feel as if he could conquer the world.

They would do their best to pretend nothing had changed between them, that he was still just Donohue the short-order cook and she was Caroline the snob from Princeton and that their lives had never come together, not even for one magical night in June.

Fortunately for them, fate had other plans.

The First Trimester

i

The hottest June on record slid into the hottest July.

Life in Princeton and Rocky Hill slowed to a standstill. "Damn heat wave," said the regulars at O'Rourke's Bar and Grill as they ordered another pitcher of draft. "Can't even think, it's so hot."

Which was fine with Charlie Donohue. Last thing he wanted to do was think, because whenever he did, he invariably found himself thinking about Caroline Bradley. He'd see a woman with blond hair in line at the supermarket and remember the way Caroline's hair felt against his face. Or he'd catch a scent like perfumed sunshine and that unbelievable night in her shop would come back to him in all its technicolor glory.

"Food's not up to your usual high standards, Charlie," said his boss after a few weeks of this. "Something on your mind?"

Charlie shook his head. "Nothing I can't handle."

O'Rourke was about to launch into another one of his patented what-you-need-is-a-good-woman lectures when the phone rang. It was Murphy, sounding manic, terrified and ecstatic all at once.

"This is it," said Murphy, as Charlie took the phone from his boss who was racing for the door. "They're taking Sam to the labor room now."

"Your old man's going to break every speed limit between here and the hospital," said Charlie. "Better pray the cops aren't out in force tonight."

"Watch the place for him, will you? Sam says this won't take long, but I…" His voice trailed off. Charlie waited for him to finish the sentence, but apparently Murphy was beyond coherent speech.

"Tell your old man not to worry, Murph. I've got everything under control."

At a few minutes past midnight on Independence Day, Samantha Dean O'Rourke gave birth to a strapping baby boy. The gang at the bar went nuts. Charlie's culinary shortcomings were forgotten, and he was allowed to wallow in saccharine daydreams while everyone else went berserk over the news.

And all this for a baby. There wasn't a regular at that bar who Charlie'd figure would give two hoots for babies or children, but they were a surprising bunch. Most of them were grandfathers many times over; the rest of them were putting their kids through college or shelling out money for a daughter's wedding. Not one of them had reached Charlie's advanced age of thirty-five without at least one wife and child firmly in tow.

For a man who saw life in black and white, this full-color explosion of joy over the baby's birth was a mystery. Wouldn't you think they would have hinted at this suppressed paternal instinct at least once in the past two years?

Little James Andrew O'Rourke's arrival into the world was greeted with the same enthusiasm that the bar crowd reserved for the winning touchdown with one minute left on the clock. Charlie was happy for Murphy and Sam, but he wasn't envious. Truth was, Charlie hadn't given a hell of a lot of thought to children. He'd been too busy, first with the Navy, then bumming around, then settling down in Rocky Hill. There'd been women, sure, but never one woman who made him think of white picket fences and bundles of joy.

He wasn't looking for one, either, because as far as Charlie was concerned, you couldn't miss what you'd never had. Besides, he liked his life the way it was.

Why rock the boat?

TO EVERYONE'S SURPRISE, Caroline became a fixture in the maternity ward at the Princeton Medical Center. She was one of the first to see the new baby and had begged Sam to let her hold him for a few moments. She popped up at Sam's bedside morning, afternoon, and night and never seemed to get enough of the sight and smell of that tiny little person bundled in blue.

"I don't know what on earth is the matter with me," Caroline said, dabbing at her eyes with a pastel blue tissue. "I've never been the sentimental type."

"Babies bring out the best in everyone," said Sam as she put her son to her breast.

"You know I've never been one to get all misty over infants," Caroline continued, still sniffling with emotion. "Why, Patty was the only child I ever understood." Sam's daughter, Patty, was a bona fide genius whose infectious sense of humor had delighted Caroline from her very first word.

"Maybe you're growing up," Sam said with a wink. "It happens to all of us sooner or later."

Of course they both knew that Caroline had done her growing up a long time ago. She'd never had any choice in the matter.

"It could be the ticking of your biological clock," Sam offered up.

"I doubt that," said Caroline, laughing. "I pressed the snooze alarm awhile back and haven't heard anything from it since." She blew her nose then checked her makeup in a hand mirror. "I've been working too hard, that's all. Too many trips into Manhattan for new dresses. All that commuting takes its toll."

"I've been meaning to tell you that you look like hell."
Caroline opened her mouth to protest but Sam wouldn't
give her the chance. "Of course, that means you still look
ten times better than the average woman, but you do look
a little green around the gills, kiddo. Anything wrong?"

"Nothing twelve hours' sleep won't cure."

"Go home," said Sam, moving her infant son to her
other breast. "Sleep for both of us. I'm afraid my days of
sleeping in are over for awhile."

Caroline kissed both her friend and her godson. "Thanks
for the advice. I'm going to take you up on it."

A rush of air conditioning hit her as she exited the elevator and she shivered. The last time she'd been this cold
was that night in the storage room with Charlie Donohue,
but they had found a way to stay warm. Oh, yes. The
memories sizzled through her as she crossed the lobby, and
she struggled to push them back into her subconscious
where they belonged. After all, they'd only seen each other
once since that night, an awkward meeting the night of
Sam's baby shower when they'd said little more than hello.

What a fool she'd made of herself, all tongue-tied and
adolescent, unable to meet his eyes without remembering
the feel of his body against hers in vivid and erotic detail.
She pushed open the door and exited to the street. A wall
of heat pushed in at her, taking her breath away. A wave of
dizziness rippled through her and she sank to the steps,
clinging to the railing.

"At least you're at the right place."

Swallowing hard, she looked up to see Charlie Donohue. "What—what're you doing here?"

He waved a big bouquet of flowers. "Same thing you
are. Come to see the heir apparent."

The ground seemed to lift at a forty-five-degree angle.

"Put your head between your knees."

"This isn't a plane crash," she said between attacks of
nausea.

"Do it." He put his hand on the back of her neck and pushed her head down. "Now take a few deep breaths."

"Do I have a choice?" she muttered, then did as he instructed. The world came back into focus. Her stomach resumed its normal position.

"Better?"

She nodded. "Much." She met his eyes. "Thank you."

He bent forward and studied her face. "You look lousy."

He, however, looked splendid. She rose to her feet. "Thank you again."

"So what's wrong? Summer cold?"

"Overwork."

"You should slow down. Get some more sleep."

Conversation ground to a halt. What, after all, was there to say? It was patently obvious he had managed to consign the memory of their night together to some dim corner of his mind. Irrationally she wished it had been harder for him to forget her. She'd believed herself too sophisticated, too self-possessed, to turn to jelly in front of a man she barely knew—yet knew intimately.

"Visiting hours are almost over. If you want to see Sam and the baby, you'd better go."

"I'll walk you to your car."

"No." Her vehemence surprised them both. "I mean, thanks for the offer, but I'm fine." She moved away from him, backing toward the parking lot. "Good to see you, Charles."

"Take care of yourself, Caroline."

He went his way and she went hers and, once again, it was as if that magical night had never happened.

Caroline sighed as she climbed behind the steering wheel of her car. "Who knows?" she said as she turned the ignition key. "Maybe it never did."

CAROLINE CONTINUED to feel under the weather. Rhonda and Denise, her sales assistants, looked at each other, wide-eyed and confused, each time their boss burst into tears at the drop of a hemline or lost her temper over a wrong number. The weeks passed slowly and for the most part Caroline felt as if she were moving through molasses. Her thoughts were fuzzy, her body exhausted. No matter how much sleep she managed to get, she woke up each morning craving still more.

At first she was confused by her condition, then frightened; but, on the morning of July thirty-first, as she checked the slender vial of fluid, she finally understood. A big black plus sign shimmied at the bottom. *Congratulations!* read the enclosed brochure. *You're pregnant!*

"Congratulations?" she asked the terrified-looking woman in the mirror. No husband. No plans for the future. No thoughts of home and hearth or any of the things important for a baby's upbringing. She didn't know the first thing about breast-feeding or toilet training or how to kiss away a child's tears. Suddenly it seemed as if she knew nothing at all, as if the simplest task required Herculean effort.

Fortunately, although her brain shut down, routine took over. She brushed her teeth, did her hair and makeup, then dressed in her favorite pale blue Ralph Lauren.

She'd go to the store. She'd throw herself into her work and put all thoughts of motherhood from her mind. Maybe the test was wrong. After all, it was only a ten-dollar box of chemicals. Certainly there was room for error, wasn't there? Maybe she wasn't pregnant at all. Maybe she was run-down, anemic, overstressed and overtired. There had to be another reason for the way she'd been feeling, and sooner or later that reason would come to her. In the meantime, she was going to the store, the one place where she was in absolute control of things.

"She doesn't look very well," Caroline overheard one of her assistants saying later that morning. "Do you think it's PMS?"

Caroline tossed down her tenth soda cracker and stormed into the showroom. "It is *not* PMS," she said, voice shrill. "And it's not a broken heart, business losses or bad karma. Understood?"

Grabbing her purse and car keys, she raced from the store as if the hounds of hell were at her heels. "PMS," she muttered as she started her new silver-colored sports car. *If only*...

Ten minutes later she burst into Sam's bedroom in Rocky Hill, threw herself across the O'Rourkes' queen-size bed, then broke into tears.

Sam, who was nursing baby James, looked up in surprise. "What on earth is the matter?" Her brow furrowed. "Dear God, did someone die?"

"You could say that," Caroline managed through uncharacteristic sobs. "The rabbit did."

Sam stared at her for a long moment as comprehension dawned.

"You're—"

"Pregnant," said Caroline with a strangled laugh. "With child. *Enceinte.* The ever-popular knocked up."

Sam's gaze went from her baby to her best friend then once again to her baby. "A baby." She glanced at Caroline's belly. "You can't be far along."

"Six and a half weeks. Not that I'm counting."

Sam shifted the baby to her other breast, and Caroline experienced an odd blend of longing and terror. She sat up, hung her legs over the side of the bed and put her head between her knees the way Donohue had instructed her that evening a few weeks ago at the hospital. Funny how handy his instructions had become these few weeks past.

"Poor Sam," she said, swallowing hard against a wave of nausea. "You look shocked."

Sam did her best to compose herself but her amazement was impossible to hide. "I—I didn't know you were seeing anyone special."

Caroline met her eyes. "I wasn't."

Her friend's high cheekbones blazed with color. "I'm sorry, I'm sorry. I shouldn't have asked. It's none of my business."

"It was just one time," said Caroline, unable to stop herself. "It just...happened."

Sam, whose daughter had been born out of wedlock when Sam was only a teenager, nodded. "I understand. Really I do. You don't have to tell me anything about it."

"No, you don't understand." Sam had been deeply in love with Patty's father. The two teenagers had been planning to get married, but his father had had other ideas. Ideas that had torn the young lovers apart forever. "He wasn't some stranger I picked up in a bar."

"I never thought he was."

"Oh, come on, Sam. I'd be wondering the same thing if the situation was reversed."

Sam bristled. "Thanks a lot, kiddo. It's nice to know what you really think of my moral fiber."

"Damn it," said Caroline. "It was Charlie Donohue."

"Look, I said you didn't have to tell me who the father is and I meant it."

"It's Charlie Donohue."

"I don't understand why you're being so arrogant, Caroline. If you don't want to tell me, don't tell me. I've already said it's none of my business."

Caroline glared at her best friend then reached over and clamped her hand over Sam's mouth. Her words were both measured and deadly serious. "The—father—is—Charlie—Donohue. I'm not teasing. I'm not lying. I'm not happy." Sam struggled to speak but Caroline was unrelenting. "I am pregnant by Charlie Donohue. Do you understand?"

Sam nodded and Caroline uncovered her mouth.

"Wow!" said Sam, dark blue eyes wide with disbelief. "I didn't even know you liked him."

"I don't—I mean, I didn't." She buried her face in a pillow. "Oh, hell. I don't know what I mean."

"You and Charlie," said Sam, a smile spreading across her face. "No wonder you two were so adamantly opposed to our matchmaking attempts. You were already having an affair and you wanted to keep it a secret." Sam's laugh was altogether too triumphant for Caroline's taste. "You sly thing, you."

"We were not having an affair."

"Oh, your breakup is only temporary," Sam said with the assurance of a very married woman. "Once you tell him about the baby, your problems will disappear."

Caroline wondered how her once cynical single friend had turned into this contented matron who believed in fairy-tale happy endings. "We're not broken up," she said, battling down a wave of nausea. "We were never together to begin with."

"You were together at least once."

"You're making this difficult, Sam." Caroline paused, struggling with the facts. "There's nothing between us. Nothing at all."

Sam's dark brows lifted. "I'd say there was something very important between the two of you." She kissed her son atop his downy head. "There's a child."

"Somehow I doubt if Charles would find that notion terribly compelling."

"You *are* going to tell him about the baby, aren't you?"

Caroline's eyes filled once again with tears. "I'm not certain I'm going to tell *anyone* about the baby." Until that morning she hadn't been entirely certain there was a baby.

"He has a right to know," Sam pointed out. "Hell, he has a responsibility to both of you."

The thought of her future and Charlie Donohue's intertwining on a long-range basis made her feel both horrified and secretly elated. That combination did nothing to quell her queasy stomach. "Maybe I'll go to Europe for the next eight months," she said with a hysterical laugh. "We can tell everyone I'm searching for designer clothes for the shop."

This time it was Sam's eyes that filled with tears, and it was almost Caroline's undoing.

"Don't look at me that way, Sam."

"Tell him." Sam leaned forward, baby at her breast, and touched Caroline's hand. "You owe it to the both of you."

Caroline tugged at her jacket and smoothed her skirt. "Can't you just imagine me waltzing into O'Rourke's one night in some dreadful maternity frock?" She stood and mimicked the walk of an exceedingly pregnant woman. "I'll take a glass of milk, Charles," she said in a falsely hearty voice. "By the way, how do you feel about fatherhood?"

"Call him at home," Sam suggested.

Caroline's laugh grew even more hysterical. "I don't even know where home is. I don't know one single thing about him." Only that she had felt more protected, more secure in his arms that magical night than she had ever felt in her entire life. "For all I know he has a string of ex-wives trailing behind him and ten kids he doesn't care about."

"No wives. No kids. Charlie's a free agent."

Caroline sank down onto the bed. "I suppose you could give me his phone number."

"I can do better than that," said Sam. "He'll be at the christening tomorrow. Tell him you two need to talk."

"Maybe I'll write him a letter."

Sam's expression was one of such compassion that Caroline broke into tears once more. "You'll do what's right, Caroline," she said, voice soft. "You'll do what's right for the baby."

THE CHRISTENING the next morning went off without a hitch. Caroline had carried along a packet of water crackers in her handbag, just in case, but fortunately her morning sickness was taking an unexpected holiday.

The church with its vaulted roof and stained glass windows rang out with the baby's cries as the holy water was sprinkled on him. The church also rang out with Caroline's sniffling tears, for she proved to be an exceptionally sentimental godmother. Her voice shook when she made her pledge to watch over little James Andrew O'Rourke for all the days of his life. One month ago the meaning of those words wouldn't have had quite the resonance they had now that a new life was growing within her. Twice she had caught Charles looking at her as she stood at the baptismal font with the godfather, Sam's brother, and twice she had felt a telltale crimson blush stain her cheeks.

A terrible thought burst into her mind like an explosion. *He probably thinks I'm some slut who sleeps with any man who stumbles into my fur vault.* The passion they'd shared that night in the storage room had been as incendiary as it was unexpected. Why on earth would a man like Charles Donohue believe it to be an uncommon occurrence when she had spent so much time and energy building her reputation as a sophisticated world-class flirt? Sometimes she found her relentless celibacy hard to believe herself.

The church ceremony was only the beginning. Sam, whose upscale catering service was the rage of Princetonian commuters, had decided to avail herself of her own talents and invite everyone to the house for an old-fashioned outdoor celebration. Murphy strutted around the backyard like a peacock, impossibly proud of his new baby boy. Patty, Sam's first-born, was equally proud of her brother and her status as older sister.

It should be like this for everyone, thought Caroline, eyes once again misting with tears. A baby should be wanted. Welcomed. Loved wholeheartedly with no reservations and no uncertainties. Sam had been ecstatic the day she discovered her pregnancy with James, not sniffling into her grape juice as Caroline was. Even as an unmarried teenager, Sam had carried Patty with joy despite the difficult situation.

This should be one of the happiest days of Caroline's life, yet there she was wishing she could blink her eyes and make reality disappear. Gently she touched her still flat stomach with the palm of her hand and sighed. One thing was certain: with every second reality became just a little bit harder to ignore.

AS FOR CHARLIE, he couldn't take his eyes off Caroline—and it wasn't for lack of trying. *Something's different,* he thought, studying her delicate face and form. The angles of her cheekbones were softer somehow; the swell of her breasts more rounded. There was a more womanly aspect to her that he couldn't quite define except to chalk it up to the fact she was holding Sam and Murphy's son in her arms. Even if a man spent about as much time thinking about children as he spent thinking about soufflé pans, which added up to exactly no time at all.

But even a man like Charlie had to admit there was something downright dangerous about the sight of a beautiful woman with an infant in her arms. It conjured up thoughts of sunny kitchens and home-baked bread and gingham curtains at the windows, none of which were likely to appeal to Caroline Bradley.

Although she seemed as enamored of the infant as everyone else, Charlie suspected Caroline wasn't exactly mother-of-the-year material. You didn't walk around in perfectly tailored white linen suits if you expected to spend much time with small-fry. He grinned at the thought of sticky peanut-butter-and-jelly fingerprints on her pristine skirt.

No, she was probably a hell of a lot like he was. A loner. Someone who made friends easily but kept most of those friends at arm's length. He'd sensed that about her the night in the fur vault. Vulnerable. Lonely. Sweet and passionate and—

Forget it, Donohue. He was certain she already had put it from her mind. Other than a pleasant smile and nod of her head, the elegant Ms. Bradley hadn't so much as acknowledged that they'd ever done more than shake hands. He tried not to, but there was still enough of the old double standard alive and well in Charlie to make him resent any and all other men who had ever been lucky enough to share Caroline's bed.

"None of your damn business, Donohue," he mumbled into his glass of punch. She could have dated the entire Sixth Fleet for all it mattered to him.

"Talking to yourself, are you?" The voice at his elbow was light, breezy, just this side of flirtatious. It could only belong to one person. Caroline.

"Some shindig, isn't it?" he asked, aware of the scent of her perfume wafting toward him on the summer breeze.

She nodded, a strand of pale blond hair drifting across her cheek. "Leave it to Sam to throw the world's best christening party."

"She's something, isn't she?"

"She certainly is."

So much for conversation. They stood together in a pool of sunshine and cast about for something to say.

"Guess I'll shove off," said Charlie after a few long moments of silence.

Caroline tilted her head and looked up at him. "I thought O'Rourke's was closed for the day."

"There's more to life than O'Rourke's."

"I didn't mean to imply that there wasn't." *Good going, Caroline, implying he's nothing more than a short-order cook with no life of his own.*

"Actually I was heading down to the shore."

Her words caught in her throat. "How wonderful. I hope you and your date have a wonderful evening."

He barely suppressed a grin. He knew the sound of jealousy when he heard it. *So she hasn't forgotten our night together after all....* "No date."

Caroline busied herself with the lacy edge of her sleeve while she tried to gather her thoughts. "I've always enjoyed the shore." She favored him with her best smile, the one that usually turned men into oatmeal.

Charlie favored her with a grin that was just this side of wise guy and said nothing.

"Have you been to Cape May?" she asked, leaning close enough for him to catch the scent of her perfume.

"Don't like it. All those gingerbread Victorian houses make me feel like I'm stuck inside an exhibit at Disney World."

"You're being awfully difficult," she muttered sotto voce.

"What was that?"

She upped the wattage on her smile. "I said, you probably enjoy Atlantic City."

"Not much."

One more try, Donohue, and then it's every woman for herself. "Springsteen territory then?"

"Now you're talking."

Her smile faltered as she thought about sweaty beer joints, screaming Harleys and heavy metal. "Asbury Park," she said as cheerfully as she could manage. "How exciting."

He grabbed her by the arm and pulled her behind a towering azalea bush. "You and Springsteen? Gimme a break. What in hell's going on here?"

She tossed her hair with a decidedly seductive gesture. "Whatever do you mean?"

"You don't give a damn about where I'm going or who I'm going with and you sure don't feel like going to Asbury Park. You know it and I know it and everybody at this damn christening party knows it. So what's going on?"

"Conversation, Charles. Is that such a foreign notion?"

He was having one hell of a time keeping the lid on his temper. "We've had one conversation in the two years we've known each other and we both know how that ended up. Why the sudden change of heart?" Almost two months had gone by since the night they made love. Almost eight weeks where she barely managed to say hello to him. She was playing some kind of game and he was determined to find out exactly what it was.

This wasn't surface anger on Donohue's part. Caroline could feel waves of it coming from him. Dear God, what a hash she was making of things. Flirtation hadn't worked. Conversation was impossible. The only thing left was the naked truth.

She met his eyes, letting her Caroline-the-flirt persona drop away like an extra sweater. "We need to talk, Charles. Tonight if you can spare the time."

He didn't like the way his stomach knotted up at the somber look in her big blue eyes. "How about right now?"

She inclined her head toward the milling throng. "I'd prefer we speak in private."

He wanted to make a joke about what happened the last time they spoke in private but fortunately reason prevailed. "We could go to O'Rourke's and talk."

She hesitated. "I'd prefer some place a little more—" She started to say neutral but caught herself in time. This wasn't a battle. When it came to the baby growing inside her womb, she and Donohue were—or should be—on the same side.

Sweat broke out on the back of Charlie's neck. The last time sweat had broken out on the back of his neck he'd been in Nam facing the business end of a gun. He named a restaurant two towns over. "Say we meet there in two hours?"

Caroline nodded. The look of relief on her lovely face only added to Charlie's apprehension. "And, Charles?"

Here it comes, he thought. *The ax is about to fall.* He met her eyes.

Her smile was swift, and then it was gone. "I'd be in your debt if you didn't tell anyone we were dining together tonight."

She was *embarrassed?* Amazing how anger could override even primal anxiety. "I'm not looking for bragging rights at the bar, if that's what worries you. If I was, every one of these people would already know about our night in the fur vault."

He turned and walked away before she could say another word.

Sam slipped up beside Caroline and linked an arm through hers. "I take it he's not happy about the baby."

"I didn't tell him."

"You didn't tell him! I saw you whispering over here, looking terribly serious. What on earth were you saying to him?"

Caroline didn't know whether to laugh or cry, so she did both. "We got into an argument."

"About the baby?"

"About dinner."

Even Sam, born-again romantic, was hard-pressed to find the silver lining in this particular stormy cloud.

"You finally settled on a place to meet?"

"I think so. Whether he shows up now is anybody's guess."

"I know Charlie," said Sam with an emphatic shake of her head. "If he said he'd show up, he'll show up. He's a man of his word."

Caroline sighed. "I was afraid of that."

BIGELOW'S WAS a sturdy steak-and-potatoes type of place on the outskirts of Cranbury, a picturesque town whose history predated the American Revolution. Lots of wood paneling, stained glass and chirpy waitresses who liked to point to the chalkboard menu whenever Caroline had a question about the cuisine. Charlie, who had ordered a brew and a twenty-ounce porterhouse, watched with obvious amusement as she ran a perfectly manicured finger down the long list of batter-fried appetizers and ended up ordering a tossed salad, hold the dressing.

"And a steak," said Charlie. "Medium rare."

"No steak," said Caroline, teeth clenched.

The waitress stopped chirping for a moment and looked from one to the other. "Two steaks?"

"One steak," said Caroline.

"That's right," said Charlie. "One for her and one for me."

"I don't eat red meat."

"Have some ribs then. Best baby backs in the state."

The waitress nodded, her French braid bobbing.

"I don't eat pork."

"You Jewish?" asked the waitress.

"This isn't a religious issue," she said, glaring at the nosy waitress, "it's a health issue." She closed the menu and leaned back in her seat. "Not that it's any of your business."

The waitress skulked away, French braid subdued.

"A little rough on her, weren't you?" asked Charlie, offering her a piece of warm bread from the basket in the center of the table.

"I'm not in the habit of defending my food choices to the hired help."

Charlie broke off a piece of bread and deposited it on her bread plate. She looked at it as if it were one of the seven plagues. "Maybe if you'd ever spent time as one of the hired help, you'd take it easy on them."

She started to say she'd spent a hell of a lot of time as hired help in her day but stopped herself just in time. Her past was nobody's business but her own. All that mattered tonight was the future. Correction: the future of her baby. "I'm not terribly hungry tonight," she said instead. "I overate at the party."

Charlie had noticed every morsel that she didn't put into her mouth at the party. He'd known parakeets who ate more than Caroline had today. He also knew when to keep his observations to himself. He poured himself a brew and took a pull. "So," he said after the waitress deposited a dish of celery and olives then sprinted for the safety of the kitchen, "what's this all about?"

Caroline folded her hands in her lap and took a deep, calming breath. "This isn't easy, Charles." She laughed nervously. "I thought I had this well planned but..." Her voice trailed away.

"Just spit it out," Charlie advised, in his inimitable fashion. "Get it out on the table."

The mental picture his words conjured up made her stomach lurch, but a sip of ice water calmed her rebellious stomach. "I—I assume you remember that night we spent...umm, the night we were stranded together—"

"The night we made love."

"Yes." She cleared her throat. "Yes. The night we made love."

His expression was as dark as the hair falling across his forehead. Had she really ever felt comfortable enough with him to gently smooth it back and feel it, like ebony silk, beneath her fingertips? To think that mouth, that dark mustache, had moved across her—

"I remember," he said, voice bland.

"Well, I realize we didn't plan to get stuck together in my storage room. I mean, it wasn't anybody's fault that you tripped the lock."

"Right," he said. "Just like it wasn't anybody's fault that you didn't have a back-up system in case of emergencies."

"Please." She touched the back of his hand to silence him, then withdrew as if she'd somehow violated his space. Ridiculous thought, all things considered, but there it was just the same. "Well, I'm afraid there's been a . . . complication."

His dark brows lifted. "Insurance problems? I can swear I didn't fence any foxtails."

A strangled laugh threatened the last of her composure. "Charles, I'm pregnant."

The waitress nearly fell into the lazy susan of salad dressings she'd deposited.

"You want to run that by me again?" Charlie asked as soon as the wide-eyed girl had backed away from the table.

"I'm pregnant."

"With my baby?"

She nodded. "With your baby."

"You're sure you're pregnant?"

"Positive." Another wild giggle. "Get it? Positively positive."

She braced herself for a continuation of the paternity issue but it never came. She would always be grateful to him for that. At least there was that much of a connection between them that he knew she was telling the truth.

"So what are we going to do?" he asked.

Her heart was warmed by the word "we" and she blinked back still more tears. "I don't know, Charles." She looked down at her place setting. "I just don't know." There were many alternatives these days, some acceptable to her and some not.

"You're not going to have an abortion, are you?" His voice was gruff, his words rushed.

She shook her head. "No, I'm not. That much I'm sure of."

"I'm glad." The relief on his handsome face stunned her. "I know it's your body and all that, but it's my kid, too."

Her eyes widened. "You want children?"

"Not that I ever thought about." He met her gaze. "You?"

"Same thing here. I always saw myself more as the Auntie Mame type."

"Looks like it's not our choice anymore, doesn't it?"

Something about his words made her spine stiffen. "Listen, Charles, I don't expect anything from you. It's my decision to have this baby and I'm fortunate not to need anybody's help." She had a house and a business, good friends and a great income. She could manage on her own.

"Great," he said, not cracking a smile, "but that still doesn't change the fact that a kid's parents should be married."

ii

Caroline didn't miss a beat. "Don't be ridiculous. This isn't the 1950s, Charles. You don't have to make an honest woman of me."

"I'm not thinking of you. I'm thinking about my kid."

"*Our* kid," she snapped. "Our child. I'll thank you to remember that."

He had the good grace to look abashed. It was the least he could do. "I want him to have my name."

Caroline narrowed her eyes. "I don't think *she* would fare too badly with mine."

"You know what I'm talking about."

"The concept of illegitimacy is an outdated one," she persisted. "In case you haven't noticed, the world's changed a great deal."

"Right, and that's why adults are out there searching for their parents."

"You're talking about adoptions. This is entirely different."

"The principle's the same. People want to know where they come from. It's about blood."

She looked at him strangely. This was the last thing she'd expected to hear from his mouth.

"You'd still be the child's father, Charles, whether or not we were married. You wouldn't be locked out of the baby's life. I don't understand the difference."

"Kids have enough to fight growing up these days. Why give ours anything more to explain or wonder about?"

She paused, struck by his words. With his statement, Donohue had neatly summed up the basic difference between men and women. Caroline could only think of the fetus curled inside her womb, of the baby who would nurse at her breast. And yet there was Donohue, considering the feelings of the child who would venture out on his or her own.

"I—I hadn't thought of it quite that way." Although why she hadn't was beyond her. Hadn't she helped her god-daughter, Patty, search for a father not even two years ago? Patty had wanted a daddy more than anything in the world, despite Sam's best efforts to be mother and father to her little girl. Sam and Patty had been happy as a family of two, but that happiness had truly soared when Murphy O'Rourke came onto the scene.

The waitress, blatantly curious, deposited Caroline's dinner salad and Donohue's side of beef. The porterhouse was rare, just the way he'd ordered it, and Caroline watched a thin trickle of pink juice ooze from the steak where he pierced it with his knife.

"Excuse me." She scraped back her chair and rose, unsteady, to her feet.

"You don't look too good," said Charlie, pushing his own chair back and getting to his feet.

"Eat," she said, praying her stomach would stay where nature had intended it to stay. "One of us might as well."

CHARLIE WATCHED as she disappeared down the hallway in search of the ladies' room. *Green,* he thought, reclaiming his chair. He'd never actually seen anyone turn green before but damned if the beautiful Ms. Bradley hadn't turned a chartreuse right before his eyes.

"Everything okay, sir?"

He looked up at the perky waitress with the intricate braid, who had obviously waited for Caroline to disappear before she dared approach the table again.

"Great," he said, cutting a slab of steak. "Couldn't be better."

"The lady..." The waitress paused delicately. "Is something wrong with her salad?"

"Salad's great. Everything's fine."

The waitress didn't look as if she believed him. Reluctantly she returned to her post near the kitchen, casting a watchful eye for Caroline's return.

"Right," he said into his beer. "Everything's fine."

He'd walked into that restaurant a happy-go-lucky bachelor with nothing on his mind except tomorrow's Yankees game. Ten minutes later he was an expectant father. He knew he should be thinking profound thoughts about the future, about immortality, about having someone to carry on his name, but his mind had gone blank. Things that had seemed so clear when he looked into Caroline's huge blue eyes no longer seemed clear at all. Suddenly he felt as if someone had dropped anchor on him without his knowledge, weighing him down with responsibilities he hadn't wanted or asked for.

But then, neither had she asked for those responsibilities. What had happened between them in the fur storage vault had been a mutual coming together of two adults. Unfortunately neither of those two adults had had brains enough to give even lip service to birth control.

He pushed his plate away and stared blankly at Caroline's empty chair. One night. That was all it took. A few hours and life as he knew it had vanished right before his eyes, and he had no one but himself to blame.

Caroline, paper-white now instead of pale green, crossed the room toward her chair. He stood up and went around the table to hold it for her.

"Feeling better?"

She nodded. "Much."

He motioned for the waitress to clear the table.

"You didn't eat your steak," said Caroline.

He shrugged. "Lost my appetite."

Her smile was gently sardonic. "Morning sickness?"

"Shock."

She closed her eyes for a moment, looking delicate and wan and terribly appealing. Too damn appealing, if you asked Charlie. "I know what you mean."

"Have you seen a doctor?"

"Not yet." She folded then refolded the pale rose linen napkin at her place.

"Is there—I mean, could there be a chance you're not really pregnant?"

Those beautiful blue eyes turned cold as the North Sea. "Wishful thinking, is it, Charles?"

"Practical thinking," he shot back. "I can't believe those home pregnancy kits are foolproof."

"They're not." Her gaze lowered to her breasts, fuller even to his untrained eyes. "Some things, however, are dead giveaways."

"You need a doctor," he said. "Someone to make it official."

She wanted to say that spending her mornings in an intimate relationship with the underside of her toilet bowl was official enough for her but she didn't have the energy. "I'm not going to hold you to that proposal of marriage, if that's what you're worried about, Charles," she said in a weary voice.

He wanted to say that the proposal still held, that he'd meant every word he'd said, that he would embrace the prospect of a child wholeheartedly, but Charlie Donohue wasn't a very good liar and so he said nothing at all.

CAROLINE MADE an appointment with her gynecologist for the next afternoon. The heat wave had finally broken and with it came a rush of cool air that promised an autumn filled with splendor. There were so many wonderful things Caroline loved about the autumn. Gorgeous suedes the color of fine sherry. Sleek evening clothes in drop-dead black and siren red. The parties Princeton was known for kept Twice Over Lightly in business, and provided Caroline with a social life beyond compare.

And that social life was important. Many of Caroline's best customers were found at cocktail parties or gala balls. Young wives on a tight budget, businesswomen with more savvy than cash, they all found their way to Caroline's shop to rent the absolutely perfect dress for that once-in-a-lifetime occasion.

Oh, how the questions would fly the day she showed up in maternity clothes for the first time. She dreaded those questions, the teasing, the defiantly independent stance she knew she would adopt. How much easier it would be if she had a husband....

She pushed the thought from her mind as if it were treasonous. Never once, not even as a little girl, had she daydreamed about weddings and babies. Why on earth at thirty-one was she suddenly thinking about marriage?

The answer, of course, was obvious.

"Yes," she told Charlie from the pay phone in the lobby of the professional building near the hospital. "Definitely yes."

The silence on the other end was profound.

"Charles?" Her voice was sharp. "Are you still there?"

"I'm still here." She almost felt sorry for him, he sounded so shell-shocked. Almost but not quite. "When's it due?"

"March first, give or take."

Another silence. She wanted to ram her fist into that silence.

"You're healthy?"

She exhaled loudly. "As a horse. My doctor expects no complications."

"Great," he said in a falsely hearty voice. "That's great."

The third silence of the ninety-second conversation. *Three strikes and you're out.* "I must go," she said without preamble. "I simply wanted to let you know of the results."

"Yeah," said Charlie. "Thanks."

She hung up the receiver, stung by his sudden indifference. It couldn't have disturbed her more if he'd ended the conversation with, "Have a nice life." What in hell had happened to his talk of marriage, his dissertation on the importance of family, his easy acceptance of responsibility?

Gone, that's what. He'd had a chance to think, to evaluate, to consider his options, and he'd done a great job of it. Besides, everything she'd told him last night at the restaurant was true. This wasn't the dark ages where an illegitimate birth could blight a woman's life forever and ever. This wasn't the era of *Ozzie and Harriet* and *Leave It To Beaver* where families were arranged with the precision of a Japanese centerpiece. The perfect lockstep arrangement of mommy, daddy and child was as much dream as reality these days, a joy if you were lucky enough to have it but certainly not necessary for happiness.

And, oh, how much Caroline wanted to believe that was true as she climbed into her low-slung sports car and headed toward home.

BILL O'ROURKE gave Charlie the night off and he didn't ask questions. You didn't find many men like that these days. Bill was one of a kind. "I owe you one," said Charlie as he headed out the door.

"Damn straight," said Bill with a bemused grin. "And I'll make sure you pay up one of these days."

Charlie had no idea where he was going; he only knew he had to get the hell out of Rocky Hill as fast as he could. The walls were closing in on him. There was only one cure for the way he was feeling and that was to jump into his car and drive as far and as fast as he could.

It didn't work. He got as far as Reisterstown, Maryland. "Better get yourself together," said the highway patrolman who decided to let him go with only a warning. "Keep breaking speed limits and you'll end up on a slab some place."

The notion wasn't one Charlie felt like dwelling upon. In the past the idea of dying didn't unnerve him any more than it did the average man. Now that he was about to become a father, the thought of dying before his time held a poignancy that nearly buckled his knees. He didn't want to care this much but there didn't seem as if there was anything he could do about it.

You can run from your values but you can't hide forever. Even two hundred miles away from Rocky Hill he could see the fear in Caroline's eyes and the loneliness, and that fear and loneliness spoke to him in a way few things in his lifetime ever had.

"IT DOESN'T HAVE to be forever," he said to her later that night as they sat in a diner in Belle Mead and talked. "After the kid's born we can dissolve the marriage, but at least we'll have done things right."

Caroline was silent. Her sandwich and glass of milk were both untouched. "That seems so calculated," she said after a few minutes had gone by. "Does it make any sense to marry with divorce in mind?"

"I think it does."

"We could have your name on the birth certificate without marrying, Charles."

"Take it or leave it," he said, his dark eyes fierce with determination. "The world may have changed but it still matters to a kid that his parents cared enough about him to try to give him the best shot in life they could."

She wanted to argue with him that his thesis had enough flaws in it to drive an eighteen-wheeler through, but she also knew that at the core of his argument was a truth so basic, so visceral, as to be unshakable. Why make their child go through his or her life carrying their excess baggage? How much easier it would be to say "My parents split up," than to explain about an evening that never should have happened. About a pregnancy that no one had planned for or wanted.

"You're right," she said with a sigh. "Our child deserves more."

"We'll get married?"

She nodded. "We'll get married."

They stared at each other across the remains of Charlie's cheeseburger and her untouched sandwich.

"I guess we should set a date," said Charlie.

"The sooner the better," said Caroline. "I'll be showing before you know it."

"Saturday?"

"Saturdays are pretty busy at the store." She ran through her appointments in her mind. "How about Sunday afternoon?"

It was Charlie's turn to hesitate. "I had tickets for the Yankees against Boston at the stadium."

"After the game?"

He nodded. "Sounds great. Say around seven-thirty?"

"Seven-thirty."

"Where?"

"I don't know." She took a sip of milk. "Sam and Murphy's house?"

"I guess that's as good a place as any."

"I—" She cleared her throat. "I think we should keep it small . . . for obvious reasons."

He looked as relieved as she felt. "Just Sam and Murph and Patty."

"And Bill."

Charlie grinned. "And Scotty?"

The thought of her pal the professor made her smile in return. "And Scotty, of course."

No family. No limousines and fancy photographers. No bridal shower or bachelor party or three-tiered cake with a bride and groom balanced on the top.

"A business arrangement," said Charlie, extending his right hand.

"A business arrangement," said Caroline, clasping it.

"No entanglements."

"Absolutely not," she said. "And no false expectations."

"Once the baby's born, it's over."

"Guaranteed."

The future Mr. and Mrs. Charles Donohue shook on it. Eight months tops and their marriage would be nothing but a memory.

iii

"You look beautiful," said Sam early Sunday evening. "Radiant."

Caroline leaned forward to look into the mirror, then grimaced. "I look bilious."

"You're glowing."

"I'm retaining water," said Caroline. "Two months along and my feet are turning into paperweights."

Sam surveyed Caroline from her head to her feet, taking in the severely chic Grace Kelly chignon, the oyster-white silk suit, the pale hose and kid shoes. She nodded with approval. "Charlie is going to be knocked off his feet, kiddo."

"Only if the governor calls with a reprieve at the last minute."

Sam glared at her. "I don't think gallows humor is exactly the thing for your wedding day, do you?"

Caroline glared right back and wiped an imaginary smudge of lipstick from the corner of her mouth. "This isn't your run-of-the-mill wedding day, or haven't you noticed?"

"All I've noticed is that two of my favorite people in the world are getting married."

Caroline turned around in her chair and took her friend's hands in her own. Sam's hands were sweaty. Caroline's were dry and cool. "We don't love each other, Samantha. We never have and we never will. This is strictly a marriage of convenience. We intend to dissolve it soon after the baby is born."

"That's a long time from now," Sam pointed out. "Anything could happen between now and then."

"Right," said Caroline, adjusting the peplum of her suit jacket. "Like we might kill each other."

She and Charlie had been at each other's throats these past few days. He had the notion in his head that they should actually *live* together, and there was nothing she could do to dissuade him. He suggested she move into his ramshackle cottage in Rocky Hill but she pointed out that pregnant women rarely fared well in unheated bedrooms once the cold weather came along.

Charlie had conceded her point and she'd thought she was halfway home when he said, "Looks like we'll be living in your place then." She'd almost swooned at the idea of this big, swaggering hunk of male superiority filling up her elegant garden apartment condo on the outskirts of Princeton proper.

"Aren't you taking this a bit far?" she had asked, striving for the right note of amusement in her voice. "I mean, no one will care if we live together or not. It's no one's business."

Charlie paid no attention to anything she had to say. He steamrollered each of her objections in turn, pointing out that she'd need someone around to do the heavy stuff as her pregnancy advanced.

"I have money," she said. "I'll hire someone."

"Hire me," said Charlie. "I work cheap and some of the benefits are pretty damn good."

How it was she hadn't killed him right then on the spot was beyond her. He was insufferable, opinionated, self-righteous and easily the most irritating male it had been her misfortune to know.

And in less than fifteen minutes he would be her husband.

CHARLIE HAD PLANNED on showing up at Murphy's house in pressed jeans and a cotton sweater, but his boss had set him straight. "Do it for your future loved ones," he said, while Charlie searched for a decent suit to wear to his wedding. "Don't want any ugly pictures passed down from generation to generation."

Charlie stopped in his tracks. "What made you say that?"

Bill grinned. "That disgusting fleabag sweater you're wearing, that's what. You could break a camera with that thing."

Charlie ignored the gibe. "I'm talking about the pictures. What makes you think I'm gonna have anybody to pass things down to?"

"It's the thing to do, isn't it? Sooner or later most of us get around to adding to the planet. Why should you be any different?"

So that's what this was all about. "You know about the baby?"

"I didn't think it was a secret."

"It's not. I'm just surprised."

"Sam told me."

Charlie nodded. "I suppose she thinks her matchmaking finally hit pay dirt."

"She *is* looking pretty pleased with herself these days."

He wanted to say that Sam should enjoy herself while she could because the marriage was a temporary deal but he held his tongue. No matter what the situation, this was their wedding day. He might as well do his best to enjoy it.

Of course, that was easier said than done.

As soon as he pulled up in front of Murphy and Sam's house and saw the white banner draped across the front door, he wanted to gun the engine and bolt for the state line. *Play it out,* he warned himself. *This isn't going to last forever.*

Sam greeted him at the door with a bear hug that felt more like the Heimlich maneuver. "I'm so happy for the both of you," she said, acting as if this were the culmination of the love affair of the century.

"Yeah," said Charlie, feeling the yoke of domesticity, however temporary, tightening around his shoulders. "Thanks."

Patty, her red hair bobbing around her narrow shoulders, raced up to him. She wore a very grown-up looking pink dress and she carried a basket of flowers. "We're tossing these instead of rice," she said in that matter-of-fact tone of hers that used to unnerve him. "Rice isn't healthy for the birds."

Patty was a genius. If she started explaining environmental issues as they pertained to avians, he'd be up the creek without a paddle. "Great, Patty," he said instead. "I bet Caroline's going to love that."

Patty's freckled face grew more serious. "Actually, Aunt Caroline says it isn't necessary to resort to tradition and toss anything at her." Her cheeks reddened slightly. "After all, fertility rites aren't necessary."

Charlie choked on his own spit.

"Are you okay?" asked Patty. "I learned how to administer CPR in health class."

"I'm fine. You—" He narrowed his eyes at the child, wondering if just maybe she was a midget in disguise. "You know about the baby?"

She stood up straight and tall. "Of course I do. My mom doesn't believe in hiding the facts of life."

"Yeah, well, it isn't your mom who's having the baby."

For once the brilliant Patty O'Rourke was without an answer. He took that as his chance to make a getaway.

He didn't get far. Bill and his second wife were waiting for him near the archway to the living room.

"Getting nervous?" asked Bill, clapping Charlie on the back.

"Not much," Charlie lied. He glanced into the living room and saw baskets of flowers, flickering candles and a harpist. A sense of doom settled over him like a winter coat. "Where's Caroline?"

Sam appeared at his side. "Don't worry, Charlie. She'll be back any moment."

Charlie's stomach did a back flip. "What do you mean, she'll be back? Where did she go?"

Sam gave him a reassuring pat on his forearm. "Nothing serious. She left her earrings at home."

Earrings? Was everyone crazy or just him? What the hell kind of crazy stunt was that, bolting from the ceremony to get some damn fool pair of earrings?

"I hear her car," said Sam, cocking her head to the side. Her smile was triumphant. "I told you she'd be back on time." Sam clapped her hands together and called for attention. "Places, everybody. The wedding is about to begin."

Charlie watched in shock as a score of people streamed into the house through the French doors at the far end of the living room. Scotty and his lady friend. Bill's bowling pals. Two of Patty's schoolmates. Most of Murphy and Sam's neighbors. A man in a dark blue suit who looked as if he could be the judge Caroline had arranged to perform the ceremony. They took their places on either side of the length of white carpet bisecting the floor from archway to exit. They turned and faced him. The expressions on their faces could best be described as expectant.

He wondered what they would do if he ran the 440 through that living room and sailed through the French doors without saying goodbye. For a good five seconds he was tempted to give it a shot, but the harpist took her chair and began to play, and he realized he couldn't vault the instrument without doing major bodily harm to himself.

Show time.

"I'M GOING TO BE SICK." Caroline forced a deep breath into her lungs. "I need some air."

"You're fine," said Sam, smoothing the back of Caroline's hair. "You're just nervous."

"I am not," Caroline protested. "There's nothing to be nervous about." This was strictly a business matter. Nothing more, nothing less. She and Charlie were doing the right thing for their baby and, once the baby was born, they would undo it as fast as they possibly could. "What on earth is wrong with this place? It's freezing in here."

"We have central air-conditioning," said Sam with a laugh. "What *you* have is known as cold feet."

Caroline started to argue the point but decided against it. Her teeth were chattering too much for her to say a thing. She followed her friend down the hallway, aware of the sound their shoes made as they scraped softly against the polished wood flooring. And then she became aware of another sound.

"A harp?" She stopped dead in her tracks, halfway to the living room. "You hired a musician!"

Sam shrugged and refused to meet Caroline's eyes. "Mrs. Duryea needed the practice."

"Frances Duryea is with the New Jersey Symphony Orchestra."

Sam's gaze guiltily slid right past her best friend. "So I thought we needed a little music for the occasion. Is it a crime?"

"I told you we wanted to keep this as simple as possible, Sam. Didn't you hear anything I had to say?"

"It's your first marriage, Caroline. That means something."

"Maybe under normal circumstances it does, but this is different."

This time Sam's dark blue eyes met Caroline's head on. "Either way you're going to remember this for the rest of your life. Why not have something nice to look back on?"

Caroline had no answer for that. She knew there was something specious about her friend's argument but she was hard-pressed to articulate exactly what that was. The harpist segued into an incredibly slow, rococo version of "Here Comes the Bride" as Caroline glided into the archway to the living room. The music was so sweet it set her teeth on edge, but as it turned out, the harp music was the least of it. Sam had invited everyone on Worthington Street to the ceremony, in addition to Scotty and the rest of the crew from O'Rourke's Bar and Grill. What had happened to keeping this as simple and low-key as possible?

"Thanks a lot," she hissed at Sam who was a few feet ahead of her. "Why didn't you put an ad in the local paper while you were at it?"

Sam just smiled and continued making her way toward where Donohue and the judge awaited them.

At last Caroline took her place next to Donohue. She'd been so upset by the music and the crowd that it hadn't dawned on her that he wasn't clad in his usual jeans and T-shirt. Instead he was resplendent in dark pants, immaculate white shirt, dark tie and jacket. His hair was combed neatly; his expression was somber. If it hadn't been for the worn Reeboks on his feet she wouldn't have recognized him.

"I had nothing to do with this," she whispered as the judge paged through his book in search of the wedding ceremony. "It was all Sam's idea."

Donohue looked skeptical, and she couldn't blame him. She considered asking for an intermission so she could wring Sam's neck. The judge, however, found his place, cleared his throat, then cast his gaze upon the crowd. "If there is anyone among you who can show good reason why these two people should not be joined together, speak now or forever hold your peace."

This is insane! screamed Caroline. *Somebody stop us because we don't know what we're doing.*

What the hell am I doing here? Charlie wondered. *Nobody put a shotgun to my head.*

But the moment passed and neither one uttered a sound. The judge continued, each word taking Caroline and Charlie closer and closer to wedded bliss.

"I, Charles, take you, Caroline..."

"...to be my wedded husband...to have and to hold..."

"By the power vested in me by the State of New Jersey, it is my pleasure to pronounce you man and wife."

The harpist launched into a lusty "Lohengrin." The wedding guests burst into spontaneous cheers. Caroline and Charlie stared at each other with something approaching terror.

The judge gave Charlie a hearty pat on the back. "Go on, young man. It's now legal to kiss your beautiful bride."

The beautiful bride wanted to stick a sock in the judge's mouth. Why didn't people just leave newlyweds alone?

"Go ahead," she said through her frozen smile. "They already have too much to talk about as it is."

"We could always shake hands," said Charlie.

Caroline couldn't help it. She burst out laughing. Charlie's vivid green eyes crinkled with mirth. Their first seconds as Mr. and Mrs. Donohue had passed without a hitch. Maybe there was hope for the next seven and a half months.

But there was still the matter of the kiss to be disposed of.

Charlie spanned her waist with his hands.

Caroline rested her hands on his shoulders.

He bent forward.

She lifted her head.

His mouth was as warm and sensual as she'd remembered.

She tasted as sweet as she had that night in the store.

And it occurred to both of them that this arrangement might be more complicated than they had figured.

iv

The newlyweds took separate cars to Caroline's place because Charlie's truck was packed with his belongings. Admittedly it had looked a trifle odd when the wedding guests split up into two divisions, each armed with rose petals to toss at the departing bride and groom as they ran to their respective vehicles, but why should this be any different? From the very first, nothing about Caroline and Charlie's alliance had been anything approaching normal.

Caroline took the back roads from Rocky Hill to the outer edge of Princeton where her condo was located. The country lanes wove in and out of neighborhoods too new to have lawns or trees or lamp posts, and Caroline experienced a brief stab of regret that the open expanses of wild and free land she'd known as a child would be long gone by the time her own child was old enough to enjoy them. She drove slowly, glancing into her rearview mirror from time to time to make certain Charlie was still behind her. It would be easy to lose him on one of these winding roads that she had followed on her great earring hunt earlier in the evening. She hadn't lost her earrings; she'd lost her nerve.

The thought also occurred to her that she could keep driving all night and eliminate the awkwardness she knew lay ahead of them but she turned right into Princeton Park and Gardens. Each apartment owner was assigned two parking spaces. She took her usual spot and motioned for Charlie to park next to her. How strange it was to see his truck angled beside her sports car.

Good Lord, she thought as she swung her legs out of her car, *if you're having trouble adjusting to sharing your parking spaces, what on earth are you going to do with your bed?*

Now that was a topic that didn't bear close scrutiny. At least not at that particular moment with Donohue, her new husband, standing next to her.

"The end unit's mine," she said. "Number fifteen. Make sure you put that number on all your mail."

"Won't need to," said Donohue. "I'll get my mail at my place."

She nodded, oddly stung. *Get a grip on yourself, Bradley. Why would he sell his house over a temporary arrangement?* "I can help you unload the truck if you like."

"Just open the front door. I'll take care of the rest."

She did as he said, kicking off her shoes in the foyer. It was wonderful to be back home on familiar ground. For a while tonight she'd felt as if she were Alice disappearing through the rabbit hole. Here, surrounded by her Wedgwood and Lalique and English country garden furnishings, she felt anchored. Grounded in reality. Her place. Her things. *Her husband?*

"Where do I put my gear?"

She jumped at the sound of Donohue's voice in the doorway. "What do you have there?"

He looked down at the tangle in his arms. "Clothes mostly. CDs. Tapes. That type of thing."

"Leave the tapes and CDs on the hall table. I'll show you where you can put your clothes."

The closet in the guest bedroom had been turned into an elaborate storage area for gowns, palazzo pants and one-of-a-kind items she absolutely adored. In fact, the entire room functioned strictly as a dressing area for Caroline, a fact that made her feel enormously uncomfortable as Donohue took in his surroundings.

Why on earth hadn't it occurred to her to order a bed for him?

She turned on her heel and hurried down the hallway to the master bedroom. The closet situation in there wasn't much better. Yves St. Laurent mingled with Chanel. Galanos and Donna Karan were on intimate terms. Not to mention the vintage Balenciaga, 1947 Dior and the wonderful Courreges minidress from the age of Aquarius.

She gasped in horror as Donohue's huge paw of a hand reached into her closet and shoved her treasures to one side.

"I don't need a hell of a lot of space," he said, blissfully unaware of the havoc he was causing. "Just room enough for my jeans, a few shirts and my fishing pole."

The thought of his Levi's 501s sharing closet space with her Chanels made her feel light-headed and she sank down onto her watered silk bedspread.

He was next to her in a flash. "You okay?" he asked, crouching down in front of her.

She lowered her head between her knees in the position that was quickly becoming second nature to her and waited for the dizziness to pass. It didn't. Each time she opened her eyes and saw the flash of gold on the ring finger of her left hand, her stomach turned inside out and her life seemed to pass before her eyes.

It took him a few seconds but Charlie finally caught on. Caroline was having an anxiety attack and it was a beaut. As close as he could tell, the anxiety had something to do with her clothes closet. The random daydreams he'd entertained about a *real* wedding night vanished. He'd be lucky if he ended up sleeping in the same town with his new wife.

He yanked the offending garments out of the sanctuary of her closet and tossed them over his arm. There had to be a coat closet some place in this museum she called home, he thought as he stormed through the place. A broom closet, maybe, where his stuff could hang without endangering world peace.

"This isn't exactly a walk in the park for me, either," he mumbled as he shoved his clothes into a closet off the kitchen that held cleaning supplies, a vacuum cleaner and a ten-year supply of Ultra Slim-Fast. It would have been a hell of a lot easier if he'd done what some other guy might have done, what Caroline herself had suggested he do. He could've paid lip service to the pregnancy, tossed a few dollars her way, then bailed out until the kid was all pink and cute and wrapped in a pastel blanket. Kids were flexible. They learned how to roll with the punches. Charlie'd had more than his share of stepfathers in his day, and he hadn't turned out too bad.

But the young Charlie Donohue was still there, lurking behind the scenes, ready to strike. The young Charlie remembered how it felt to be on the outside looking in, wanting the one thing he couldn't have: a father who belonged to him alone. Maybe this idea of his to marry Caroline was a stupid one; maybe it wouldn't save the kid one damn bit of pain in the long run. Maybe the kid wouldn't even remember that his parents had been married at all.

But Charlie would, and that made all the difference....

"Charles! Did I hear you in the music room? You know you're not supposed to touch anything in there."

Yeah, and so what else is new? You can't touch anything in this stupid house.

Charlie Donohue, ten years old and growing, ducked behind the comforting bulk of the grand piano and waited. He'd been out playing stickball miles away from home and he'd clean forgotten he was wearing his new clothes. Who had time to think about things like keeping your knees clean when you'd finally convinced the guys you weren't a snotty rich kid and you really and truly could play ball with the best of them? Not Charlie! He hadn't been about to let this chance pass him by, not even if it meant incurring his mother's wrath later on.

Now he wasn't so sure he'd made the right choice.

His mother's footsteps clicked across the polished parquet floor then sank into the carpeting. Closer...closer...he could see the expensive suede shoes right there in front of his nose. He pulled deeper into the shadow cast by the piano and held his breath. A sneeze began working its way up from the soles of his feet and his eyes watered as he struggled to fight it down. If his mother saw what had happened to his new pants and shirt—well, he didn't want to think about it.

Muttering something about children being a trial of the soul, his mom left the room and with her went Charlie's urge to sneeze. Wouldn't that be funny? he thought, crawling out from his hiding spot. Allergic to his own mother! And it could happen, too. He just knew it. He'd bet his electric train set that his latest stepfather was as allergic to Charlie as Charlie was to him. Franklin's lean and ruddy face wrinkled into a network of creases each time he saw Charlie and his voice sounded all puffed up and scratchy the way a grown-up's voice always sounded when he had a real bad stuffy nose.

Uncle Franklin was Charlie's second stepfather. Uncle Tony before him hadn't been too bad. At least Uncle Tony had understood that kids liked to get dirty. There'd been a few others in between, men his mom had come real close to marrying, but once they met Charlie those men had vanished into the woodwork.

Sometimes Charlie thought about his real father but he never could quite bring the picture to life inside his head. His mom never talked about him; all Charlie knew about his dad was what he'd overheard his grandma Donohue whispering about in the kitchen one Christmas. "Such a handsome boy," Grandma had said, *"but so selfish. Ran off, he did, at the first sign of trouble . . . no surprise that he came to a bad end."*

Charlie knew what *"trouble"* meant: a baby. Him. *There was something about kids that made grown-up men run faster than the Road Runner when that coyote was on his tail.*

A steak of mud followed him out from under the piano. The reddish-brown color of clay, the streak striped the ivory carpet in a pattern of dark and light that Charlie knew would get him the whipping of his young life. The way the house looked was everything to his mother, from the perfectly hung silk drapes at the windows to the fancy upholstery on the furniture to the floors that really and truly did look like somebody could eat off them.

Now that was a funny thought. Charlie tried to imagine his mom and his latest dad sitting down on the spanking-clean kitchen floor while they ate whatever fancy food with the impossible-to-pronounce names they were eating this week. Charlie hated food with fancy names. Once they'd given him something called *"pat-tay"* and he'd thrown up on his sneakers. They said he'd learn to like it when he grew up but Charlie knew he was never going to like anything with liver in it. Not ever. When he grew up, he was going to make sure he ate steak and French fries and hamburgers and corn on the cob every day of his life.

He glanced around at all the shiny glass and silver in the music room. Everything had an invisible *don't touch* sign on it, as if the entire room had been designed with making kids miserable in mind. He'd never live in a house like this when he grew up. His house would be big and sloppy, crammed with dogs and cats and roller skates and baseballs.

And he would never, ever forget how it felt to be a kid. Or how it felt to want a father of his own who really cared

about him and not just some man who happened to be
married to his mother....

CAROLINE SAT on the edge of her bed and listened as her
husband shoved baseball mitts and worn-out jeans into her
linen closet. Why hadn't they decided to be civilized about
this arrangement and keep separate addresses? There was
something terribly outdated about Donohue's insistence
upon actually living together. Being married should have
been more than enough to satisfy him, but no. Not Donohue. Only moving into her beautiful home lock, stock and
fishing pole was enough for him.

Gently she cupped her still-flat stomach and sighed.
"Seven months and one week left," she said into the perfumed air of her boudoir. "I can do it."

She heard Donohue's footsteps retreating toward the
front room. Rising from the bed, she quickly unbuttoned
her suit jacket and slipped out of her skirt. A narrow ridge
of red flesh remained where the waistband of her skirt had
been, and she stared at it in the mirror. Apparently there
was more truth to the statement she'd made to Sam days
ago than even Caroline had imagined: her days in civilian
clothes were numbered.

She draped the jacket and skirt over the chaise longue by
the French doors then retrieved a jade green kimono from
the right side of her walk-in closet. Her panty hose felt like
a tourniquet. Reaching under her half-slip, she began easing them down inch by inch until a noise in the doorway
brought her up short.

"Don't stop on my account."

Donohue, still in his wedding finery, was leaning against
the jamb, watching.

"How long have you been there?" she asked, sliding the
hose off her feet and reaching for the kimono tossed across
the bed.

"Not long."

She tied the belt and reached for the panty hose. "Will you excuse me?" The last thing she needed was for him to hang around while she put her lingerie in the clothes hamper.

Donohue, however, was not a subtle sort of man. He followed her into the master bath at the near end of the bedroom.

"Decadence is alive and well," he said, whistling low. "Is that a tub or a swimming pool?"

"Garden variety bathtub." She lifted the lid on the built-in clothes hamper and deposited her panty hose. Everything else would have to wait. "Don't tell me," she said, casting him a look over her shoulder. "You have a shower stall and cold water only at your house."

His grin was a wicked blend of self-mocking and brazen. "You're half right. I get plenty of hot water in the summer."

She started to ask him why he lived in such Spartan quarters but common sense told her you didn't make a fortune working as a short-order cook in a neighborhood bar. Property was expensive in central New Jersey and he had probably bought exactly what he could afford.

He was fiddling with the swan's neck faucet at the sink, making appreciative male noises about the plumbing fixtures in general, and there was something about his proprietary interest that set off warning signals in Caroline's brain. "Before you get too attached to that swan, let me show you your bathroom."

"Should've known this was too good to be true." He gave the swan a fond farewell glance. "What do you have for me, Bradley—a slop jar and basin?"

She couldn't help chuckling at the image. "Afraid you'll have to make do with something a little bit more upscale than that." She led him down the hallway, then opened the second door on her right and flicked on the light. "Will this do?"

Charlie made a show of checking out the sleek, ultra-modern fixtures, the elaborately papered walls, the elegantly recessed lighting that flattered everything and everybody in the room. "It's either this or the gas station down the road."

"I take it you're satisfied?"

He nodded. "Do I sleep in here, too?"

She thought of the big bed in her room and for an instant she imagined she saw Donohue, bare-chested and glorious, sitting in it waiting for her with a can of beer in his hand. Fortunately for her sanity, the image receded quickly. "Why—why don't you take my room for tonight and I'll see about fixing up something in the guest room tomorrow?" She'd take one of the overstuffed sofas in the living room or the leather recliner in the den. Anything rather than face the inevitable showdown across the sheets.

"Let me guess: you'll be some place else."

"You're a smart man, Charles." She told him of her alternatives.

"I'll take the couch," he said. "Just point me toward the pillows."

"You're certain you don't want the bedroom?"

The look he gave her erased all doubts. She'd forgotten what it was like to deal with the more macho type of man. "I'm taking the couch."

Strange, but she'd expected him to kick up more of a fuss. "You're not angry with the arrangement?"

"I may not be one of those preppies you usually hang out with, but I have some rules. The first one is, I don't take beds away from pregnant women."

She swallowed hard. "I—I apologize for being thoughtless. I should have made some arrangements for you." She waved her hand in the general direction of the guest room. "I promise things will be in order tomorrow."

"Yeah, well, I forced the issue on living together, didn't I? I'm probably lucky I'm not sleeping on the patio."

Her first smile in hours flickered to life. "That could still be arranged."

He smiled back. "Hell, no. I'll take the couch."

They stood there in the bathroom, Charlie near the toilet, Caroline near the tub.

"I suppose I'll say good-night." Caroline hesitated. Did they shake hands? Kiss cheeks? What on earth was the protocol for a situation like this? "There's work tomorrow and all...."

Charlie shifted position. "Would you mind if I put the TV on?"

"No, not at all. Enjoy yourself."

He started to say something, some double entendre reference to a honeymoon for one probably, but instead he only smiled. "Good night, Caroline."

"Good night, Charles."

And so the newlywed Mr. and Mrs. Charles Donohue retired for the night—to their separate beds.

v

Charlie couldn't sleep. He'd considered hot milk (disgusting), counting sheep (ridiculous), doing push-ups in the middle of her living room (pointless). Nothing worked. He wasn't used to hitting the hay this early. Normally he worked until two a.m., then shot a little pool or went to an all-night gym to unwind.

Tired or not, there was no way in hell he could sleep surrounded by all these fancy little knickknacks and things scattered all around the room. Turn over in his sleep and he'd wipe out half the Wedgwood in captivity. He'd never seen so many damn little *things* in one room in his life—or, at least, not since he was a kid.

What possessed a fairly normal, rational woman to surround herself with so many useless objects? Did she buy them just to give the cleaning lady something to do or did she actually like these idiotic things? Damn. If he had an answer to that, he'd be able to put most shrinks out of business. Everywhere he looked he saw tiny crystal bud vases, silver candlesticks, green plants in china pots, and other unidentifiable pieces of junk. Not that the stuff didn't look good, because it did. Everything about the apartment looked as if it had been picked out by a decorator from *House Beautiful*. It was just that the room was so overwhelmingly *female* that Charlie felt like a bull let loose in a roomful of Steuben glass.

Sneeze once and it was all over.

He thought about sleeping out on the deck but decided against it. Knowing Caroline, she'd probably be scandalized if her neighbors saw him out there with his pillow and his Walkman.

He punched the pillow, scrunched it under his head, then squeezed his eyes tightly closed. His head was butted up against the unyielding arm of the sofa while his legs dangled off the other end. Sleeping on a bed of nails would be more comfortable than this modern nightmare.

He had a lot to look forward to.

CAROLINE wasn't faring much better.

Lying in her big brass bed, she felt alone for the first time in many years. Her home was different with Donohue in it. She couldn't explain how or why, but it seemed to Caroline that his presence was everywhere. Was he asleep, she wondered, or roaming around the apartment, feeling uncomfortable and out of place? Maybe he was hungry. She hadn't even bothered to show him the kitchen. She had sandwich fixings in the refrigerator and, thanks to Sam and Murphy, a few six-packs of Coors tucked away. Beer wasn't one of her favorite things. She hoped he didn't make a hobby of drinking the stuff or—dear God, what a thought!—collecting the beer cans.

She could just imagine her elegant dining room walls with a mosaic of Coors, Bud Lite and Heineken framing the doorway.

That did it. She reached for the telephone and dialed Sam's number as she had been doing during times of trouble for the past twenty years....

The first day of school was always the hardest.

Carly Bradley stood in the doorway of her second grade classroom and felt that old familiar pain in her stomach. She hated school almost as much as she hated her step- father. Both made her feel small and insignificant, as if the slightest breeze would scatter her in a million different directions. Her stepfather did his best to pretend she didn't exist. He hated it that her mom had been married before he came along, and he especially hated Carly, the living, breathing proof that there had been someone else. Tom Gretchner was a foul-tempered sort, the kind who scratched his belly and belched and did all sorts of disgusting things, but at least he did it in the house he shared with Carly's mom and twin baby brothers. Carly's shame was as pri- vate as her hopes and dreams.

But school was different. In school they tried to push and pull at you until you had no secrets left at all. Why, even the clothes you wore could tell a story. A story that you might not want anyone to hear.

Annie Riley was wearing a brand-new plaid skirt and matching vest that Carly had seen in the window of Ep- stein's department store last week. The Rileys didn't have a whole lot of money, but Mrs. Riley always saved up her nickels and dimes so she could outfit her daughters in the finest clothes come September, even if it meant she went without. Connie Venturo's mom had knitted her a beauti- ful sweater in hunter green. It wasn't easy for Mrs. Ven- turo, with a job and everything. Carly just knew there was love in every stitch. Even Sandy Adamson, the most stuck- up girl in school, had someone who loved her. The pleats on her charcoal gray skirt were knife-sharp, and her shim- mery white blouse with poet sleeves and a portrait collar was ironed to within an inch of its life.

Carly glanced down at her mended cardigan and thrift- shop jumper and bit back tears of embarrassment. Why, even the boys looked prettier than she did.

"Now don't you be worrying what people think of you, miss," her mother had said that morning as she tugged a comb through Carly's tangled blond hair. *"You've got clean clothes on your back and that's more than you deserve."*

"Is she bellyaching again?" Tom had lumbered into the room, his face bristly with stubble. *"That's what you get for sending her to that fancy school."*

Her mother tugged harder with the comb and Carly cried out. *"Stand still!"* Letty barked. *"The school bus will be here any minute."*

"School bus," muttered Tom. *"Damn stupid crap. Why can't she walk to the town school like everybody else? Who do you think she is, anyway? Princess of the world?"*

Carly waited, breath caught in her throat, for her mother to say that Carly wasn't like everybody else, that's why, but those words never came. She wanted her mother to say her daughter was special, too good for the run-down grade school at the bottom of the hill. But, of course, Letty didn't say anything like that. Carly's mom had a lot of faults, but she wasn't a liar. She'd sent her daughter to the school in Rocky Hill because it sounded better and for no other reason. Carly had seen the pleased look on her mother's face when customers on her checkout line at the A & P heard that Letty's kid was in a real nice school on the right side of the tracks.

Everything Letty did, she did for Letty and no one else. That was a fact of life, same as the fact that the first day of school set the tone for the rest of the year.

Inside the classroom the kids laughed and pushed each other and told stories about their summer vacations. Carly clutched her schoolbag and pencil box closer to her chest and tried to shrink even smaller. If only she looked like them, all crisp and neat and new, things would be different. She wouldn't be standing in the doorway, agonizing over which seat to take. If she marched right into the room *and took a place next to—oh, right next to Billy Walker, the whole class would buzz about it. "Who does she think she is?" they'd say. "Billy's the richest boy in school."*

If she sat up front it would look like she was begging for attention. If she slunk to the back, the kids would snicker and say that's where she belonged. Her stepfather had himself one terrible reputation in Rocky Hill and the surrounding towns, and Carly could only thank her lucky stars that he and Letty had been too lazy to see that he formally adopted Carly and changed her name from Bradley to Gretchner.

"Hi, Caroline!"

She turned in the direction of the friendly voice next to her. Samantha Dean, her inky black hair neatly braided and tied at the ends with red grosgrain ribbons, smiled at her with a mouth full of silver braces. Sam's family didn't have money, Carly knew, but even the Deans managed to do what was right for their daughter.

Carly looked down at her feet, feeling suddenly tongue-tied and shy. "Hi," she mumbled. Samantha was one of the most popular kids in the whole school. There wasn't a kid around who didn't like Sam.

"I like your locket," Sam said, peering at the gold charm hanging from a thin chain around Carly's neck. "It's pretty."

"It was my grandma's. She's dead."

Sam nodded. "My grandma Dean is dead, too." She stuck her head into the classroom. "We better get in there fast or we'll end up sitting right under Mrs. Sullivan's nose."

Carly froze in place. There were five empty seats. Did she follow Sam inside? Did she lead the way? She knew she would die of embarrassment when Sam chose to sit far away from her. The choices seemed endless and every single one of them could only lead to pointing out just how Carly didn't fit in with the rest of them.

"There are two seats by the window. Let's take them be-fore Mrs. Sullivan gets here."

Carly still didn't move. What was the matter with Sam, anyway? Didn't she know that Carly wasn't like the rest of them, that she just didn't fit in? All Sam had to do was look at Carly's mended clothes and choppy haircut to see she wasn't like the others.

But Sam didn't seem to care. She slipped her arm through Carly's. *"Well, come on, will you?"* she said, pulling Carly toward the door. *"You don't want to sit on opposite sides of the room, do you?"*

Carly choked back the great big fat lump that had popped up in her throat. *"N-no, I don't,"* she managed. *"I wouldn't like that at all."*

"Good," said Sam with a great big silvery smile, *"be-cause I think we're going to be best friends."*

A GREAT DEAL had changed in the twenty-plus years since that fateful day, but one thing had not: Caroline and Samantha were still the best of friends.

"Talk to him," said Samantha after she'd reassured Caroline that Donohue didn't collect beer cans or hang fish faces on the walls of his den. "He's a good man, honey. You'd like him if you'd give him a chance."

Caroline couldn't help but laugh. "Strange statement considering the circumstances, wouldn't you say?" She was pregnant with his child and married to him, to boot.

Sam, however, didn't see the humor in the situation. "Trust me on this one. Charlie Donohue is one of the good guys. Give the situation a chance, Caroline. You might be surprised."

You're wrong about that, Sam, she thought as she put the receiver in its cradle and lay down, looking at the ceiling. She doubted if there was much left in life that could sur-prise her more than the predicament she'd gotten herself into.

Pregnant, newly married and alone in a bed built for two. Dear Abby would have a field day with it.

CHARLIE FINALLY dozed off to sleep around three o'clock, only to be awakened a few hours later by the blare of an alarm somewhere in the distance.

"What the—" He reached for his bedside lamp, only to knock a vase of roses onto the pale carpeting. Where was his lamp? Why was his bed pushed up against the wall? What in hell was going on?

Swearing, he got up and stumbled around in the dark, trying to get his bearings. "This is *her* place," he muttered, stubbing his toe against the leg of an end table. Caroline's booby-trap-filled apartment. He was sure she had a kitchen but where it was hidden was anybody's guess. He uncovered two walk-in closets, both filled with clothing and shoes, a small office, then finally a large but Spartan kitchen that would be right at home in an operating room. He hadn't seen so much white in one place since the last *National Geographic* special about Antarctica in winter.

"Paper towels...paper towels..." He hunted around for the ubiquitous paper towel rack that hung in 99.9% of the kitchens in America. "What's the matter with you?" he mumbled. "Don't you ever spill anything?" Finally, on a built-in shelf beneath the sink, he found a roll and made his way to the living room. The water from the flowers had darkened the carpet in a spot the shape of North Dakota. He did his best to sop up as much liquid as he possibly could and was relatively satisfied with reducing the spot to a small version of Rhode Island when a sound caught his attention.

A moan? A strangled yelp?

He dropped the soggy paper towels on the floor and made his way through the narrow hallway that led to the rear of the apartment. A light was on in her bedroom. "You okay?" he called from the doorway.

No answer.

He stepped into the room. The covers on her extremely comfortable-looking bed were folded back neatly. Except for the robe draped across her pillow, he wouldn't have known a real live woman had actually spent the night between the covers. By contrast, the living room sofa looked as if it had been visited by a plague of locusts with a yen for upholstery.

Again that strangled sound issued from somewhere close by. "Bradley? Say something if you're in here."

Her voice, weak but clear, floated out from the master bath. "Go away, Donohue."

"Are you okay in there?"

No answer, only the sound of someone in agony.

He moved farther into the room. "Hey, if something's wrong I can help you. That's why I'm here, isn't it?"

The bathroom door swung open and Caroline, hair hanging into her eyes and her nightgown drifting off one shoulder, staggered into the room, heading straight for her bed. "Say one word, Donohue, and so help me I'll..." Her last words were muffled by the pillow as she fell across the mattress.

The light finally dawned. "Morning sickness?"

She looked up from the pillow. "Give the man a cigar."

"Is it always this bad?"

"No," she said. "Sometimes it's worse." She took a sip of water from the glass on her nightstand. "They say it means it's a good pregnancy. Has to be some light at the end of the Tunnel of Nausea."

He chuckled. "Tunnel of Nausea. I like that."

"It isn't an E-ride ticket at Disney World, Charles."

He was losing his grip on the conversation with every second that passed. "Why don't I make you a cup of tea or something? Toast? Some eggs?"

"Eggs . . . Oh, God." She leaped from the bed and made a beeline for the bathroom. Donohue turned and bolted for the safety of the kitchen.

Sure, he'd heard all about morning sickness. Stand-up comedians joked about it. Women complained about it. Movies and TV made it sound like an almost-romantic part of the pregnancy.

Well, hearing about it and observing it firsthand were two entirely different things. He'd always imagined a gentle queasy stomach that a woman could wipe out with a few soda crackers. This gut-wrenching vomiting was something else entirely. How did she cope with this, morning after morning, then get all dolled up and go off to work as if she hadn't a care in the world?

He couldn't even manage shaving on a regular schedule.

CAROLINE FELT too dreadful to even worry about how she looked. If Donohue was going to be around for the duration, he might as well see her in all her technicolor glory right off the bat. Theirs wasn't a storybook romance or marriage. There was no reason to expect a storybook pregnancy.

No illusions. No surprises. That way nobody would be hurt when it came time to say goodbye.

She stepped into the kitchen, wincing at the sharp sting of the overhead light. "Herbal tea," she said with a sigh, as she accepted a mug from Donohue. "I appreciate it."

"Glad I was awake," he said. "I'm usually sacked out until eleven or so."

She nodded. "I'm long gone by that time." Usually she left for work by seven-thirty in the morning and didn't return home until nearly nine at night. "I guess we won't be seeing much of each other."

"Probably not."

She watched as he poured himself a cup of coffee.

"So you figured out the coffee pot," she said. "Most people are stymied by it."

"Tell you the truth, I had you pegged as the freshly ground beans type." He grinned and pointed toward the store-brand coffee can on the counter. "Could've fooled me."

"Nothing wrong with that coffee, is there?" Amazing how the tiniest details could trip you up.

"You don't have to get defensive, Caroline. You just surprised me."

She put her mug down on the table with a thud. "You're not going to analyze everything in my refrigerator, are you?"

"You mean, like those two Tupperware bowls filled with mystery meat in the back?" he countered.

"I know everything that's in that refrigerator."

He opened the door and removed two covered plastic dishes. "I'd take the lids off them, but I don't think your stomach is up to it."

Caroline frowned in the general direction of the containers. "I know exactly what's in those bowls," she lied.

"You'd need a psychic to figure out what's in those bowls."

A smile tried to force itself on Caroline but she fought against it. "A past-life regression might help."

His vivid green eyes met hers. Damn him. He looked as if he was enjoying himself. "Why don't I chuck them?"

"I'd be forever in your debt."

He opened the trash can with his foot and tossed the containers inside. "A hell of a wedding night, wasn't it?"

She picked up her mug and took another sip. "Memorable."

"Having second thoughts?"

She looked at him over the rim. "Are you?"

"I'll say."

"This was your idea," she pointed out, smiling at last.

He laughed. "You should've tried to talk me out of it."

"Well, I'm glad I'm not the only one with doubts."

A wicked gleam appeared in his eyes. "Sam convince you I'm not a beer-guzzling ax murderer?"

Caroline froze, mug halfway to her mouth. "You eavesdropped?"

"Didn't mean to. I went into the guest room looking for another pillow." He shrugged his broad shoulders. "You were talking kind of loud."

"How much did you hear?"

"Enough to know I'm going to be sleeping alone for a long time."

"Oh, God." She buried her face in her hands. She almost wished for a wave of nausea. Any excuse to escape the intimacy of the kitchen and Donohue's penetrating gaze. "I—I don't know what to say." *Say you're sorry. Say you didn't mean it. Tell him he misunderstood. Don't leave the guy standing there with his ego on his sleeve.*

"Forget it," said Donohue, beating her to the punch. "It's not like we'll be seeing that much of each other anyway. We'll be lucky if we cross paths on the weekends."

CHARLIE'S PROPHECY turned out to be accurate.

By the time she was dressed and ready to leave for work that first morning, Donohue was asleep on the couch. She stood in the living room for a long moment, watching him. To her surprise, he slept quietly. She would've bet last week's profits from the store that he was a snorer. Instead, he lay across her couch, long legs hanging over the arm, his body half-covered by one of her flowery peach sheets, and the only sound was his deep and even breathing. The sight should have been humorous; after all, he was too tall for his makeshift bed and the frankly female bed linens were at odds with his decidedly male form.

Caroline, however, neither smiled nor laughed. It occurred to her that she knew his body more intimately, in some ways, than she knew her own. She knew the feel of every inch of muscle and sinew. She knew the faintly soapy smell of his skin, the delicious feel of his mustache against her cheek, the sound of his passion. But his thoughts and dreams and hopes for the future were still uncharted territory and destined to remain so.

My husband, she thought, her gaze traveling his body from head to foot. Less than twenty-four hours ago they had said the words that made them husband and wife. Caroline Bradley was no more; she was now Caroline Donohue.

"Caroline Donohue," she whispered. Donohue had done something her stepfather had never thought enough of Caroline to do: given her his name. Somewhere inside that macho exterior was a man she wanted to understand. He could be very likable. God knew, everyone at O'Rourke's thought the sun rose and set on their favorite short-order cook. She wanted to like him, too, but every time he opened his mouth Caroline found herself annoyed beyond measure.

You know why, she thought, breath catching as he turned onto his side on the narrow couch with the light shining on his tanned and muscular torso. He was from a place she no longer recognized, a place she no longer wanted to go. She could feel in her bones that his past was too close to her own for comfort. If she let her guard down for even a second, he would know her for the fraud she was and she wasn't about to let that happen.

He lifted his head from the bunched-up pillow and gave her a sleepy, unfocused look. "Going or coming home?" he mumbled.

"Going," she managed, voice softer than she would have liked. His silky black hair was appealingly tousled and she yearned to push it from his forehead with a gentle hand. She cleared her throat. "Get some sleep, Charles. It's still early."

He said something that sounded like, "Drive carefully," and was asleep before she could say another word.

Maybe they weren't off to such a bad start after all.

ONE HOUR LATER she wasn't so sure about that.

"Married!" squealed Rhonda as she hugged her boss. "You got married and didn't tell us!"

"You know we hate surprises like that," said Denise. "Why didn't you let us know? We would've made a shower for you."

Caroline, embarrassed to the roots of her hair, tried to disengage herself from this unexpected show of affection. "It was somewhat of a surprise to me, too." Little did her employees know they'd soon have another opportunity to plan a shower for her.

Of course, both Rhonda and Denise went out of their way to make the day special for Caroline. Balloon bouquets appeared in the showroom. Roses popped up in her private office. Champagne showed up on her desk next to her container of yogurt.

"No champagne," she said with a rueful laugh. "That's how I got into this situation in the first place."

Neither of her employees understood the reference, but that was okay.

Mondays were usually one of the busiest days at Twice Over Lightly and this one was no exception. A slew of customers, all returning splendid gowns, traipsed through the store, and each and every one of them had to tender her congratulations to Caroline personally.

"What! No diamond?" Lena DiSalvo, one of her steadies, made a face at the plain gold band on Caroline's left hand. "Who is this man anyway? An untenured professor? A struggling novelist?"

"A short-order cook," said Caroline, trying to ignore the sharp pinch of embarrassment that disclosure gave her.

"Play coy," said Lena with an amused laugh. "I'll find out soon enough." Lena was still laughing when she exited the store.

"Whatever made you tell Mrs. DiSalvo that your new husband was a short-order cook?" asked Rhonda as the door closed.

"Because he is a short-order cook." Caroline busied herself with a stack of Adrienne Vittadini sweaters.

"You're joking."

Caroline looked up. "Do I look like I'm joking?"

Rhonda hesitated. "Well, no. Actually, you don't."

"Charles works at O'Rourke's Bar and Grill in Rocky Hill."

"Oh."

"That's it?" she asked. "Just oh?"

"I don't know what else to say."

"I take it you're surprised."

Rhonda nodded.

"You probably expected me to wind up with a millionaire, didn't you?"

Rhonda nodded again. "The thought had crossed my mind."

"Well, I didn't end up with a millionaire." She picked up the stack of sweaters and held them against her chest. "It seems I've ended up with Charles."

She met Rhonda's eyes, almost daring the younger woman to question her choice. Rhonda, however, was wiser than that and she kept silent.

CHARLIE GOT TO THE BAR a little after noon.

"Hail the conquering hero!" cried Scotty, leading the cheer. "One of our own has married the beauteous Caroline."

A gaggle of gray-haired patrons gathered around Charlie, congratulating him and clapping him on the back. He bore up under their teasing with good grace but the reality of his wedding night was definitely a sore point. Not that he'd really expected anything different; he'd gone into this arrangement with his eyes wide open. However, there'd been a certain percentage of supremely male optimism at work that had kept him hoping that maybe, just *maybe*, the nuptials might have worked a little magic over the two of them.

Well, the nuptials had changed her name but they hadn't changed her mind, and Charlie had become intimately acquainted with her living-room sofa. The thought had occurred to him that living together was pretty damn stupid, under the circumstances, but he was stubborn enough to hate admitting to being wrong about anything. Especially anything pertaining to their relationship. He'd made up his mind to stop by his house and grab his mattress to use in her guest room.

He tied his apron around his waist and headed for the kitchen. "Burgers on the house!" cried Bill O'Rourke with a wink for Charlie. "Gotta keep our newlywed's strength up, don't we?" Charlie shot his boss a look and kept on walking. When it came to romance, his sixty-something boss had probably had a better night than Charlie.

"What is so terrible about marrying a short-order cook?" Caroline fumed to Sam a few hours later over lunch at the O'Rourkes' house. "Why is everyone making such a big fuss over what Charlie does for a living?"

Sam's dark eyes traveled over Caroline's expensive clothes, flawless manicure and perfect makeup. "Do you really want an answer to that one?"

"No." Caroline sighed and reached for her lemonade. "I suppose I should have chosen the father of my child with my wardrobe in mind, shouldn't I?"

Sam just smiled. "Was your first night that bad?"

"It wasn't much of anything," said Caroline. "I slept in the master bedroom. He slept on the sofa in the living room." She leaned over and retrieved her purse. "That reminds me. I have to call Macy's and order a bed for the guest room."

"Isn't that like locking the barn door after the horse has escaped?"

"Charming analogy," Caroline snapped. "I appreciate it."

Sam leaned over and patted her best friend's hand. "You're married now. There's nothing so terrible about living as if you're husband and wife."

"I thought you understood the situation, Sam. This isn't a real marriage. It's for the baby."

"I don't think so."

"Don't try to analyze the situation," Caroline warned. "You, of all people, should understand."

"Sorry," said Sam. "I'm the one who went down that road alone. Remember?"

Caroline felt her cheeks flame. "I didn't mean it like that."

"I know you didn't, but there's an enormous hole in your logic. Don't tell me you can't see it."

"Charles has very strong feelings and he convinced me he was right. He believes a baby deserves a mother and father who are married to each other."

"An admirable position, but you two intend to divorce right after the delivery. I don't see how that benefits the child."

"Think back, Sam. Think about those early years when Patty kept asking you about her daddy. Wouldn't it have been easier if you'd been able to say it didn't work out and you divorced?" Harsh words but Caroline wanted Sam to feel the same sting Caroline had felt.

"Just don't kid yourself," Sam went on, unhurt by Caroline's barb. "You didn't marry Charlie only for the baby. Maybe you should take a good look at what's really going on before you order that bed for the guest room."

"IN THERE," said Caroline early that evening. "Put it in the guest room, second door on your right."

The two burly deliverymen hefted the queen-size mattress and box spring and disappeared down the hallway.

Sam's words had hit home, though not quite in the way her best friend had intended. Like it or not, Donohue was her husband now and living under her roof. She couldn't expect him to sleep on the sofa for the next seven months. And he certainly wasn't expecting an invitation into the master bedroom, although that would seem the next logical step. So that left the guest room. It killed her to move her delicate ball gowns and cocktail dresses from their specially made closet and scrunch everything together in her bedroom but she owed Donohue more than a pantry where he could hang his jeans and T-shirts.

"Excuse me," she said, stepping into the guest room where the delivery men were assembling the bed frame. "I'd like your opinions on something."

The two men, muscled to within an inch of their lives, looked up at her. "Yeah?" said the bigger one. "If you're tellin' me you want a different mattress, we're not takin' this one out. It's not our job."

She summoned up her best smile. "Oh, no, it's nothing like that. I'd like to know what you think of this room."

"What?" asked the smaller of the two. "Y'mean, like how it's decorated?"

"Exactly." She beamed. "Do you like it?"

He shrugged. "The missus would."

"But you don't?"

"Too much frilly stuff," said the bigger one, scowling. "Makes me nervous."

"Can you be more specific?"

"Ruffles and bows, for starters," said the man with "Frank" embroidered on the pocket of his shirt. "Wouldn't catch me dead in a room with ruffles and bows in it."

"Unless you got the right woman," said the other man. "You got yourself the right woman and it don't matter how the room looks."

The two exchanged guffaws while Caroline backed gracefully from the room. Ruffles and bows were out. Footballs and beer cans were in. Her entire life had been turned inside out and now her beautiful extra room was about to become an extension of O'Rourke's Bar and Grill.

It's either that or your bedroom, whispered a little voice. *It's up to you, Caroline.*

Plaid curtains instead of Laura Ashley chintz. Stark white walls instead of palest shell pink. Copies of *Sports Illustrated* stacked up as far as the eye could see.

Considering the alternative, she was probably getting off easy.

AND SO THE FIRST few weeks of the marriage of Caroline and Charlie passed without incident. She saw to it that the once frilly guest room was transformed into a more masculine lair, and he abandoned the sofa in favor of the new bed. He did his best to steer clear of the living room with the alarming array of expensive—and breakable—junk. He'd seen the look of horror on Caroline's face the day he'd stretched and almost decapitated a Lladro figurine. Caroline, in turn, was struggling to ignore the appalling litter of laundry that seemed to accompany her new husband. Dirty socks were everywhere. If she didn't know better, she'd swear they were multiplying like rabbits in the laundry basket.

Charlie, in the meantime, was doing his damnedest to understand why women found it necessary to have three open bottles of ketchup, two jars of mustard and five different types of pickles in the refrigerator at the same time, but no milk or bread or orange juice or beer.

He was asleep when she got up in the morning. She was deep in dreams when he came in at night.

"A marriage made in heaven," said Sam with a sardonic smile. "You never see each other."

Caroline and Charlie both had their own lives to live, and for the next few weeks they did a good job of pretending nothing out of the ordinary had happened. No sparks. No fireworks. Not even a glimmer of the unexpected attraction that had brought them together that night in her shop.

The baby was a fact of life but not one they spoke about. Nor did they speak about their marriage. The truth was, they didn't see each other often enough to speak about anything at all. Scribbled messages on yellow Post-it notes stuck to the refrigerator was all the communication they had.

Plumber due at 11 a.m., wrote Caroline. *Please let him in.*

Sam called, wrote Charlie. *She'll be up until nine.*

One night in the third week of their marriage, Caroline came home late. She'd spent a grueling day in Manhattan, haggling over some magnificent Dior originals with Mrs. Hotshot Poindexter from Park Avenue, and she was beyond exhausted. Once upon a time she'd thrived on these jaunts into the city, drawing energy and enthusiasm from the bustling pace and frenetic activity packed into that small urban island.

Today it had only left her yawning and thinking about twelve hours of sleep. All afternoon she thought about her home and her bed, about a warm cup of milk and a quiet evening all to herself. She pushed open the door to her apartment, expecting to feel the usual rush of pleasure at being home again.

Funny thing was, she felt nothing.

Kicking off her shoes, she padded down the hallway to her bedroom then changed into nightgown and knee socks. What on earth was the matter? This was her haven. Her oasis. She had planned each and every detail of her condo apartment with her happiness in mind. Color, form, texture—all were absolutely what she'd always dreamed of. Why did it feel so strange, so barren now?

"Don't be ridiculous," she chided herself out loud as she made her way to the kitchen to heat up some milk. Caroline had spent most of her adult life alone and had rarely, if ever, felt loneliness. She'd taken deep satisfaction from making her own way in the world, from lifting herself up from her background and becoming a success. Solitude was something to be savored.

Now, however, as she heated her cup of milk, she was strangely aware of the deep silence in her apartment. All day she'd longed for the sanctity of her apartment and now she felt desolate. If only Charlie were home.

It took a second for the thought to register.

"My God," she whispered, taking a seat at the kitchen table. "That's ridiculous." She and Charlie might be married but they were two ships who passed in the night, occupying the same space but never at the same time. How on earth could she miss someone who wasn't really part of her life? The notion that Charlie Donohue was becoming important to her sent a ripple of unease through her body.

He might be the father of her baby but he could never be more than that to her. He certainly couldn't be her husband in the deepest sense of the word. She'd created herself from whole cloth, from dreams and imagination and willpower, and she couldn't risk exposing the secret part of her heart where the little girl she once was still lived.

They said pregnancy changed everything, and perhaps it was true. Maybe she could blame her rocketing hormones for the odd way she felt. The first trimester was the hardest, Sam had said. It took awhile for the mind to adjust to the body's changes. Her emotions were scrambled pieces from a jigsaw puzzle with no picture to guide her in putting them together again. In a month or two her clothes would no longer fit, but her old routines would. All she had to do was be patient and wait.

IT DIDN'T TAKE a genius to figure out that Charlie and Caroline's marriage wasn't your garden-variety union. In fact, the guys at the bar picked up on that fact long before Charlie had completed his first full week of wedded bliss— or what passed for it in the Bradley-Donohue household.

The congratulations petered out. The jokes about his wedding night suddenly stopped. The question, "When's our Caroline coming in to see her hubby?" was asked once and never again.

Charlie had the feeling Bill O'Rourke had finally realized the way things were and had quietly gotten the word out to the regulars. Scotty had looked at him with a mixture of curiosity and disappointment, and at that moment Charlie wished he were fending off more misguided advice on how to keep a wife happy.

He supposed he should be grateful that he didn't have to pretend to be the lusty and satisfied bridegroom but somehow he found he missed the good-natured banter. Who would've figured it?

He'd counted on Caroline's presence in her fancy apartment to help keep the strangeness of their situation at bay. He'd sure as hell never counted on the silence that had accompanied their marriage. Before they'd married, they'd enjoyed an adversarial relationship second to none. She was the one woman who could toss back one-liners as fast as he could dish out the setups. While he hadn't exactly liked her, he'd liked the way his adrenaline started humming whenever she showed up at the bar in one of her ridiculous beaded dresses and flirted her way from table to table.

Funny thing, though. Looking back he realized she'd made a point of flirting with men eligible for social security. Anyone born after 1950 was treated to an icy glare that quite clearly said, "Don't come near me." Interesting. He'd dismissed her as a world-class flirt but had never paid that much attention to exactly who was reaping the benefit of her flirting. Sure, he'd noticed the way she doted on Scotty and his pals, but he'd assumed the golden agers at O'Rourke's were only a warm-up for the real thing.

Well, it seemed as if there *was* no real thing. At least, not if her silent telephone was any indication. He'd been prepared to break the news of their marriage to at least a score of Caroline's admirers and, truth to tell, he would've enjoyed doing so. However, in the past four weeks only one man had called, and he had accepted the news with both surprise and good grace.

Her social life was the stuff of legend. He'd heard Sam and Murphy laughing about Caroline's endless round of society parties, country club dances and intimate soirees for three hundred. Was it possible that she'd kept her dates at a distance, the way she did Charlie now that they were married?

"Leaving early?" asked Bill as Charlie tossed his apron on the counter.

"Thought I'd try seeing my wife before she falls asleep," said Charlie. "Okay with you?"

Bill shrugged. "Far be it from me to deny a man his conjugal rights."

Charlie glared at his boss and headed for the door. Dangerous territory, that remark. He wasn't about to touch it with a ten-foot pole.

The roads were empty. He honked at Sam's cousin Teddy, a local cop, at a traffic light, and Teddy waved back. Charlie liked being part of a neighborhood. Especially a neighborhood of real people. He wondered how Caroline could stand the homogenized blandness of her condo community.

Her car was in the parking lot and he swung into the spot next to hers. There was something nice about seeing her sports car tucked away each night. It wasn't that he worried about her actively, but a part of him relaxed when he pulled in at night and saw that she was safely home. He glanced at the clock on his dashboard. Only a little after eleven. The lights were on in the living room.

With a little luck she'd be awake and maybe in the mood to talk. Making love was too much to hope for. Conversation, however, seemed a definite possibility.

"Caroline!" he called out as he opened the front door. "I told Bill I was cutting out early. I thought maybe we could—"

He stopped cold. There, curled up in the big chair in the far corner of the living room, was his wife, a small bundle of silk-clad woman with golden hair. Quietly he crossed the room, hearing the soft sound of her breathing. Dark circles enshadowed her eyes and those circles touched his heart in a way few things did. He placed a hand on her shoulder, expecting her to spring awake immediately, but she merely shifted position and drifted more deeply into slumber.

"My wife." He tried out the words. They sounded strange to him, almost foreign. He'd never imagined himself with a wife—or a child on the way, for that matter. It wasn't that he'd been against either prospect but somehow life had taken him along a different road, one that ran counter to domesticity.

Not that this was domestic bliss, exactly. There were times he wondered why he'd been so adamant about living together. For all they saw of each other they might as well have been living on separate continents.

He reached out and fingered a lock of pale blond hair, mesmerized by the way it drifted between his fingers like spun gold. She was easily the most beautiful woman he'd ever known and she was his wife, the mother of his child, and he didn't know a damn thing about her. Grinning, he took note of the red-and-white striped socks on her slender legs. Like why in hell she was wearing those, for starters.

She shifted position, a small frown furrowing the space between her brows. How comfortable could she be, curled up in that chair? She was pregnant. She needed her sleep. The least he could do was see her safely to her room.

He hesitated only a moment, then carefully scooped her into his arms and carried her to the master bedroom where he laid her on her bed. Gently he eased her robe off her slender frame and an ache grew in his belly at the sight of her breasts, round and full and tempting, barely confined by the delicate top of her nightgown. Even those stupid, incongruous candy-cane striped knee socks did something to him. She was so small, so finely made, that his breath caught as he tried to imagine her further into the pregnancy. It almost hurt to think of that slight frame grown huge with their child, and a feeling not unlike tenderness flooded him.

It was an odd combination, tenderness and desire, and that combination was the toughest thing Charlie Donohue ever had to fight. All her carefully structured defenses were down. Asleep she was helpless, at his mercy. If he wanted to, and he did, he could lean forward and cup her breasts in his hands, savor their weight and taste with his tongue. He could strip off his clothes and, easing the nightgown up over her hips, take pleasure from her body.

She was his wife. He had the right to share her bed.

But, damn it, if and when they ever again made love, it had to be because they both wanted it. Anything less was wrong, no matter how you looked at it—and no matter how much it hurt to turn away.

CAROLINE'S FIRST official prenatal visit to her doctor was finally upon her. There was absolutely no reason to be nervous about it—the visit was as routine as it could be—but still she found herself dressing with a ridiculous amount of care.

Dress? Suit? Summer slacks and top? Her closets bulged with beautiful outfits, but not a one satisfied. Truth was, she was counting the hours until she was back in her apartment, curled up in her bed asleep. All she thought of these days was sleep. She craved it the way an addict craved his narcotic of choice. She napped in her office. She napped over *fajitas* at Martita's Cantina. She had even napped during Mel Gibson's latest movie, something Sam had previously claimed was biologically impossible for any normal red-blooded American woman.

Dressed only in bra and panties, she stood in the middle of her bedroom with a pile of discarded clothes around her feet and started to laugh. "You're losing it," she told her reflection in the mirror. The one thing she'd always been able to do was dress herself with style. Now she was having trouble choosing a basic outfit. Another few months and she'd be reduced to a shadow of her former self, wandering the streets in polyester stretch pants and an old shirt.

She took another, closer look at her reflection. A shadow? Not very likely. Unless her eyesight was failing her, there was a decided roundness to her belly, a roundness that hadn't been visible just a few short days ago. Her flesh seemed more generous, straining the lace-trimmed elastic of her bikini panties. She frankly stared at her torso, amazed by the sight. She'd grown accustomed to her swollen breasts, but this was something entirely different. This was the real thing.

Gently she ran her fingers across her navel, laying her palms flat against her flesh, as if to cup the baby forming within. Loneliness, deep and aching, stole her breath away. If only she felt something other than fear and bewilderment. Where were the deep maternal feelings that had flooded Sam from the very first moment she'd known she was carrying both Patty and James? Caroline felt like an alien adrift in a hostile world, as if all the things that had made her unique had been stripped away from her that night in the fur vault, turning her into a stranger even to herself. She'd conjured Caroline Bradley up from whole cloth: style and personality and ambition had all been crafted to create the perfect life.

A life that had never once included a husband or a baby.

She jumped at the sound of the front door slamming shut, then the boom of a deep voice calling her name. She grabbed for her silky robe and slipped it on just in time, for she turned to find Donohue standing in the doorway.

"What are you doing here?" she asked by way of greeting. "It's only six o'clock." *You don't usually get in until ten minutes after two in the morning.* Not that she'd paid much attention to his comings and goings, mind you....

CHARLIE WAS about to say something flip and funny when it dawned on him that his wife wasn't wearing many clothes—and what few clothes she *was* wearing didn't cover all her assets. His words died in his throat as he caught tantalizing glimpses of rounded woman peeking out from the unbelted blue robe. This was a lot different from a sleeping Caroline in dishabille. This was infinitely more dangerous.

"I—uh, I had the day off. I thought I'd stop by and—" He grinned, tearing his gaze from the swell of her breasts. "Hell. I saw your car in the parking lot and I thought maybe we could go out to dinner tonight." There. That wasn't so hard, was it?

"You're kidding."

"Do I look like I'm kidding?"

A smile flickered at the corners of her luscious mouth. "You always look like you're kidding, Charles. That's why they love you so much at the bar."

He took a deep breath. Might as well go for broke. "I was driving around down by the shore and I realized we haven't had a meal together since our wedding night."

"I know," said Caroline, tugging at the sides of her robe. "I realized that the other day."

"Damn stupid, wouldn't you say?"

She hesitated. "Well, it seems to me we've both been quite good at maintaining our agreement."

"What agreement?" asked Charlie, running his hand through his hair. "We got married. We didn't sign an agreement."

"The point of our marriage was to give our child a name and a foundation. We never talked about having a relationship."

Charlie squared his shoulders. Why did he feel as if he was facing off against a flank of opposing linebackers instead of one beautiful, pregnant woman? "Maybe we were wrong."

She said nothing, just watched him, her big blue eyes wide and calm.

"Let's go to dinner, Caroline, and try to sort this whole thing out. I think we owe it to each other."

"Thanks, but I can't."

He'd been doing so well at keeping his cool, but that calm indifference of hers was getting to him. "Why can't you?"

"I have another engagement."

"Break it."

That elusive smile of hers was back, twitching at the corners of her mouth. It infuriated him. "Not this one."

"Who is he?" *You're giving away the farm, Donohue. You sound jealous.*

"His name is Stephen. Stephen Burkheit."

"Do I know him?"

She started to laugh. "Oh, somehow I doubt it."

"Give me his phone number. I'll call and tell him you have a date with your husband." Dating. They'd talked about everything but dating. Wouldn't you think she'd have known married women don't date?

"Charles," she said, placing a hand on his forearm, "Stephen Burkheit is my doctor."

A couple of months ago, Caroline would have enjoyed having the last word on Charlie Donohue.

A couple of months ago, she would have delighted in putting him in his place as neatly as she had moments ago.

Why, then, wasn't she enjoying her victory? Instead of throwing back her head and laughing in triumph, she felt like crying.

"Your doctor?" asked Charlie.

"My doctor," said Caroline. "Obstetrician, actually. Now if you'll get out of here and let me get dressed . . ."

He left the room as a wave of melancholy swooped in out of nowhere and enveloped her in a moody gray fog.

She stared at the skirts and slacks and tops scattered on every available surface in the room. *I can't do it,* she thought, bursting into irrational tears. Choosing one outfit over another was beyond her capabilities. Putting one foot before the other was taxing her intellect to its limits. Why hadn't someone told her pregnancy was dangerous to the brain cells?

Donohue tapped on the door. "You okay in there? I don't hear anything."

She sniffled. "I'm fine."

"You don't sound fine."

"Oh, go away, Charles. Let me fall apart in peace."

The door swung open and Donohue strode into the room. This time she was too tired to bother with her robe. Let him look at her in her underwear. Everyone in Dr. Burkheit's office might end up doing the same thing.

CHARLIE HAD never seen a more pathetic sight in his life. Sure, he couldn't help but notice she was half-naked—and looking damn good at that—but the tears streaming down her beautiful cheeks reached a part of him that wasn't governed by his glands.

She sank onto the edge of her satin-covered bed and buried her face in her hands. Huge sobs racked her slender body. From the look and sound of her, you'd think somebody had died.

"Come on," he said, stroking her hair with his hand. "You don't want to be late for your appointment."

"I don't care." She sniffled all the louder. "I don't care if I never leave this house again."

"Yeah, well, you've got a doctor's appointment."

"I'll cancel it."

"The hell you will."

Her head snapped up and the look she skewered him with was pure Ms. Bradley. *Good,* he thought, knowing better than to grin. There was still some fight left in her.

"Don't think that marriage license gives you the right to tell me what to do, Charles." Amazing how quickly a woman could stop sniffling if you gave her a good reason.

"I don't give a damn if you never see a doctor," he retorted, "but I damn well do care about that baby you're carrying."

She looked semichastened but still unbowed. "I'll go next week."

"You'll go tonight."

"You're trying my patience."

"Don't throw around any of that upper-class b.s., lady, because it doesn't work on me." He picked up a pair of pale blue pants and a silky green T-shirt and tossed them into her lap. "Put them on."

She looked at the items and wrinkled her nose. "Good Lord, Charles, they clash."

"Put them on or I carry you out in your underwear."

"You have no right to treat me like this. I won't allow it."

"I don't give a damn what you'll allow. That kid is as much mine as it is yours and if you don't want to do what's right for him, I'll make damn sure you do it anyway."

Her voice shook with outrage. "Marriage doesn't give you the right to treat me like this."

"Yeah?" He met her outrage with some healthy outrage of his own. "You're the expert. Tell me what rights marriage *does* give me. Far as I can tell, they're few and far between."

Unfair, a little voice inside him said. *You knew the bargain when you married her.*

And then the most amazing thing happened. Right before his eyes, the perfect Caroline Bradley lost her cool.

"You think this has been a bed of roses for me?" she hollered, her soft, cultured voice rising like a fishwife's. "If I see one more dirty sock behind the sofa cushions, I swear I'll—" She spun, eyes darting around the room.

"Don't even think about it," he warned. "I don't go for those *War of the Roses* scenes."

"You infuriate me, Donohue."

"Feeling's mutual, Bradley."

They glared at each other across the room, Caroline in her fancy underwear, Charlie in a pair of cutoffs and a T-shirt.

"Get dressed," he growled, heading for the door. "I'll meet you out front."

"Why? To wave goodbye?"

"No," he said. "To take you to the doctor."

I DON'T BELONG HERE, thought Caroline as she glanced around Dr. Burkheit's waiting room a half hour later. The chairs and sofas were filled with women in advanced stages of pregnancy ranging from any day to any minute. Pictures of Madonnas cradling infants in their arms covered the walls. The reading material ran the gamut from *American Baby* to *You're Nursing* to *Bringing Baby Back Home*.

Next to her Charlie shook his head. "Why is it I feel like I don't belong?"

She met his eyes. "I was thinking the same thing."

He started to laugh. "I thought you're the one who *does* belong here."

"Tell that to my nerves."

"You're jumpy?"

She swallowed hard. "Very."

Charlie started to say that he thought all women took to the experience the way a duck took to water but he wisely kept that observation to himself. Lately it seemed that everything he'd believed about women had been turned upside down and inside out. Either he'd been unbelievably wrong all these years or his new wife was unlike any other woman he'd ever known.

A pregnant wife and husband came out of the inner sanctum of offices, both of them glowing radiantly.

"I guess you belong here, too," Caroline observed. A lump formed in her throat as she looked at the obvious love and pride on the husband's face.

It was Charlie's turn to swallow hard as another of his misconceptions bit the dust. He hadn't paid a hell of a lot of attention to things when Sam and Murphy O'Rourke were expecting their kid, but looking back, it seemed as if Murphy had been almost as involved in things as his wife. "Another one of those Lamaze classes tonight," Murphy's dad had remarked once over a beer. "In my day, you sat in the waiting room and smoked a cigar while the wife did all the work."

In my day, too. Or so he'd thought. Charlie zeroed in on a woman who looked ready to pop. Panic swamped him as he thought of his tiny, delicate wife racked with pain and—

"Put your head between your knees," Caroline whispered. "It really does help."

"I'm not dizzy."

"You look dizzy."

"I'm fine."

Her blue eyes twinkled. "You don't look fine."

She knew exactly what he was feeling. Somehow he kind of liked that. "Is it too late to change our minds?"

"Afraid so," said his wife. "It's all up to the baby now."

The baby.

Geez.

DR. BURKHEIT was a youngish man in his midforties whose manner was naturally ebullient and prone to inspire confidence in the most nervous of patients.

Unfortunately, Dr. Burkheit's bedside manner, fine though it was for expectant mothers, hadn't done much to alleviate Charlie's galloping sense of panic. By the time the doctor finished the pelvic examination on Caroline then invited Charlie into his office to join them for a chat, Charlie was beside himself.

"Something wrong?" he asked the second he sat down on one of those plastic horrors that passed for chairs in doctors' offices. "Is Caroline okay?" He'd made the mistake of reading one of those pastel-pretty magazines scattered around the waiting room. Toxemia. High blood pressure. Edema. Placenta previa. Why hadn't someone told him that having a baby was like tap dancing through a mine field?

"Your wife is doing splendidly, Mr. Donohue. I'm pleased with her progress."

Caroline, who was as nervous as Charlie but better at dissembling, beamed. "I've gained three and one half pounds so far."

Charlie looked from Caroline to the doctor. "Is that good?" One of the magazines had said a twenty-five-pound weight gain was optimal for Caroline's size, but the article hadn't specified exactly when you were supposed to gain the weight. He'd probably wake up one morning and her belly would be out to there. . . .

"It's good," said Burkheit with a chuckle. "So far we have a textbook pregnancy here."

Relief coursed through Charlie like the tidal waves he'd heard about while in the Navy. He hadn't realized how much this all mattered to him until that very moment. "My—my wife is . . . she's kind of small-boned. Will that . . . ?"

"Not at all," said the doctor. "We want to keep her weight gain under control, of course, so as not to put too great a strain on her, but we have no reason to expect anything but a perfectly normal vaginal delivery with only the usual episiotomy."

Charlie blanched. "Episiotomy?" Even the word sounded painful.

Caroline explained the procedure of precautionary incision and subsequent stitches.

That did it. Charlie put his head between his knees, visions of gore dancing before his eyes.

"I MADE AN ASS out of myself back at the doctor's office, didn't I?" he asked an hour later as they took their seats at the Rusty Scupper.

Caroline unfolded her napkin and placed it on her lap, wondering how much longer she would have a lap. "I wouldn't say that."

"He had to put a bag over my head to get me breathing again," Charlie muttered. "I've seen guys handle combat better."

Caroline smiled as a busboy deposited two glasses of iced water at their table and hustled away. "You hyperventilated. It happens all the time."

"Not to me it doesn't."

"There's always a first time."

He was the picture of male despair. "Makes you wonder what the hell I'll do in the delivery room, doesn't it?"

Caroline missed her mouth and spilled cold water on her chin. "The delivery room?"

It was Charlie's turn to look surprised. "Standard operating procedure these days, isn't it?"

"Maybe for some people, but I really never imagined that you . . . I mean, we aren't exactly the norm, are we?"

"What is the norm these days?" Charles countered. "To most people we probably seem like Ozzie and Harriet."

Single women with their mothers as Lamaze coaches. Whole families in attendance for home births. In Russia, babies had even been born under water and thrived swimmingly. By comparison, Caroline and Charlie's situation seemed downright average.

"Know what you want, folks?" The waitress popped up next to them. "The red snapper is great today."

Caroline blanched at the thought. "Broiled chicken and rice for me. Tossed salad." She folded her menu and handed it to the waitress. "Oh, and a large glass of milk."

The waitress grinned. "Expecting?"

Caroline nodded.

"When are you due?"

"March first or thereabouts."

"A Pisces baby," said the waitress with a knowing smile. "Got myself two of them. Real sweethearts." She scribbled something on her pad then turned to Charlie. "And you, Daddy?"

Charlie could have cheerfully strangled the waitress but he exhibited admirable restraint and ordered himself some swordfish.

The contrast between this dinner and the last one they'd shared was obvious to both of them but neither knew how to broach the subject.

"Great salad bar, isn't it?" asked Charlie.

"Try the broccoli," said Caroline. "It's wonderful."

"This is ridiculous," said Charlie after a few minutes of concentrated grazing. "What the hell are we doing?"

Caroline put down her fork. "I was thinking the same thing."

"Those pictures Burkheit showed us." Charlie leaned forward. "It doesn't seem possible, does it?"

Caroline thought of the amazing photographs taken of a fetus in utero. The size of a peach it was, so small yet so perfect. "It's beginning to seem real to me," she said softly. "I was afraid it never would."

"The hands...the tiny feet..." Charlie shook his head. "I guess it *is* a miracle, isn't it?"

No, she thought. *The miracle is that we're sitting here together talking like this.* Who would have imagined it? "How would you feel about attending Lamaze classes with me?"

"I'd probably embarrass the living hell out of you."

She met his eyes. "I'm willing to risk it if you are."

He was quiet just long enough for Caroline to wish she could pull her words back and make them disappear.

"I figured you'd ask Sam."

In for a penny, in for a pound. She might as well make a total fool of herself. "Sam's my friend, Charles. She's not my husband."

His expression changed so many times in the next few seconds that she almost laughed.

"You want me with you?" he asked.

"Yes," she said. "I do."

A slow smile spread across his face. "I was there for the conception, I guess I should be there for the birth."

"A reasonable philosophy."

"You won't hold it against me if I pass out cold on you?"

"Not if you don't hold it against me if I scream down the hospital."

His hand inched forward along the tabletop, stopping just shy of her fingertips. "Scared?"

Casually she adjusted her position until her fingertips brushed against his hand. "Terrified. I'm not very brave when it comes to pain."

"Maybe we can help each other."

"I'd like that, Charles."

The waitress approached the table with their food. Reluctantly they drew apart and leaned back in their chairs. The moment had passed but, to their mutual delight, the mood lingered. They chatted amiably during dinner, touching on subjects from *glasnost* to the leaky faucet in Caroline's kitchen.

I'd forgotten how much fun he can be, Caroline thought during the entrée. *He makes me feel less alone.*

I like her laugh, thought Charlie. *Why didn't I remember that?*

The sky was dark when they left the restaurant, a clear summer night sky spangled with stars. Caroline leaned against the fender of his four-wheel drive and looked up toward the Big Dipper.

"I missed the Perseid showers this year," she said, thinking of the annual meteor displays. "First year since I was a child."

"Nothing spectacular this time around," said Charlie, leaning next to her. "Too hazy."

"You know about the Perseid showers?"

"I'm not as dumb as I look, Caroline."

She touched his forearm. "I didn't mean it that way."

"You sure about that? You sounded pretty surprised."

"Remember I don't know all that much about you, Charles. Your choice of toothpaste might surprise me."

"Colgate."

She smiled. "Tartar control?"

"Regular," he said. "I don't go for frills."

"Now that doesn't surprise me."

"You probably like all that fancy stuff with the pump-top containers."

"Actually, no." She hesitated. "I use a natural peppermint toothpaste from a little apothecary in Princeton."

Charlie's groan could have been heard all the way in Manhattan. Caroline gave him a good-natured poke in the ribs.

"None of that," she said. "We're all entitled to our idiosyncrasies."

He grinned; she could see the flash of his white teeth in the gathering darkness.

"Like those knee socks of yours?"

"I don't know what you're talking about, Charles."

"Those knee socks you wear to bed. White with red stripes." His chuckle sounded low and particularly male. "Who'd've figured the glamorous Caroline in red-and-white striped knee socks?"

One month ago she would have been humiliated to have Charlie know about her candy-cane knee socks. Tonight she felt strangely warmed by his teasing, almost the way a wife might.

"And how do you know about my footwear?" she asked.

"You were wearing them the night I carried you to bed."

"You never carried me to bed."

Again that laugh. "The hell I didn't. I came home one night and found you sacked out in the big chair in a frilly nightgown and knee socks. I didn't want to wake you up so I carried you into your room."

"Thank you," she said, suddenly prim. "I appreciate it." *Good grief,* she thought. *What on earth was I wearing besides those blasted knee socks?*

"I liked that shorty nightgown," he said, as if he'd read her mind. "You should get one in black."

"I should get one in extra large," she said, shaking her head. "My shorty nightgown days are numbered." *Did you keep your hands to yourself, Donohue?* she wondered. *I only wish I could remember. . . .*

"You're a good-looking woman now," he said in a matter-of-fact tone of voice. "You'll be a good-looking woman when you're nine months along."

A compliment! The last thing on earth she'd ever expected from Charlie Donohue. "Thanks," she said, keeping her tone equally matter-of-fact. "I hope you're right."

They were quiet on the drive home. Charlie turned on the radio to a classical music station (another big surprise) and Caroline closed her eyes and let her mind drift. Why couldn't it always be like this, she wondered, so peaceful, so effortless? The evening had started out abysmally, what with her crying in her underwear and all, but to her amazement it had somehow evolved into something special.

Too soon Charlie turned into the parking lot and angled his truck into the spot next to her sports car. Caroline had been dozing beside him; her even breathing sounded sweeter to him than Brahms.

"Home already?" she mumbled, half asleep.

"Yep." He turned off the ignition and climbed out. Crossing behind the vehicle, he opened the passenger door. "Everybody out."

Caroline stifled a yawn. "I'm so comfortable," she said drowsily. "Why didn't anyone tell me how comfortable trucks are?"

"You wouldn't have believed it, princess. Now come on. Let's get you up to bed."

Later on he wasn't entirely sure why he did it but Charlie bent over and scooped her up into his arms, cradling her against his chest.

"You don't have to do this," she said. "I can walk."

"I know."

"This is silly." She snuggled closer.

"Right."

He carried her up the stairs and into the foyer.

"You can put me down now," said Caroline.

"Not yet I can't."

She looked at him.

He looked at her.

"Charles," she whispered, her hand against his chest. "We don't need complications."

"Quiet," said Charlie, his voice gruff. Lowering his head he kissed her full on the mouth as he'd wanted to do for hours. Her lips were softer than he'd remembered, more sensual. She tasted sweeter, though maybe that was because he wanted her more than he had realized.

He felt as if he could stand there in the middle of that foyer for the rest of his life, as long as she was in his arms. What the hell was happening to him that he was reduced to hanging all his hopes on one kiss?

They broke apart for an instant and he heard her deeply female sigh of—what? Bewilderment? Pleasure?

Resignation?

That sigh acted upon Charlie like a bucket of ice water. All the insecurities and doubts that had plagued him the past few weeks flooded over him. *You don't have any rights over her.... This isn't about love, it's about the kid.... Just because it happened once, doesn't mean it was right.... You're not her type and you damn well never will be....*

With regrets, he put her down.

"I'd better hit the sack," he said, dragging a hand through his hair. "Gotta get to the bar early tomorrow."

Caroline nodded. Her cheeks were flushed as if with fever and her eyes looked teary. "I have an early day, as well." She hesitated then raised up on tiptoe. "Good night, Charles. Thank you for going to the doctor with me."

He nodded. *Kiss her, you moron. Don't you know an invitation when you see one?* "Sleep well."

"You, too."

They hesitated, each praying the other would take that one important step, but the moment flared once then faded away. Caroline went to her room and Charlie went to his, but it was a long time before either one of them slept.

The Second Trimester

i

From that night on everything was different between Charlie and Caroline Donohue. The tension that had existed between them was still there but it was no longer the tension caused by two very different people forced together under the same roof.

No, this tension was something else entirely, and it had sprung to life, taut and dangerous, with that kiss in the hallway. Oh, they tried to pretend things were still the same, but with that kiss had come the knowledge that there was more between them than the baby.

Caroline awoke the next morning sleepy, disoriented and still aching for his kiss. She'd spent the whole night tossing and turning; every time she closed her eyes she saw Charlie's face swimming before her. His vivid green eyes. His powerful jaw. That marvelous, sexy, unattainable mouth. One moment she was eminently thankful that he hadn't seen fit to kiss her, while the next moment she was swept with bitter regret.

She stumbled into the kitchen, dressed in her bathrobe, and started in surprise at the sight of her husband sitting at the kitchen table nursing a cup of coffee.

"Charlie!" She fumbled with the belt of her robe and wished she'd taken time to curl her hair before venturing into the front of the apartment. "What are you doing up?"

"I go in early today, remember?" His smile was easy, but the look in his eyes was sharp and all-encompassing. She could feel his gaze as it trailed up the length of her legs and lingered at her breasts.

She cleared her throat. "Regular or decaf?"

"This is regular," he said, "but decaf's on the stove."

Gratefully she turned toward the stove. Her hand trembled as she lifted the coffeepot and poured the liquid into her favorite cup. He wasn't wearing a shirt. Charlie Donohue was sitting there at her finely made kitchen table in nothing but a pair of cutoffs and a smile. His muscles rippled in the morning sunlight that streamed through the front window. His stomach was flat as a washboard, and she'd already managed to memorize the line of curly black hair that furred his belly and angled down past his waistband.

"You okay?" he asked, pushing back his chair and walking over to the stove.

"I'm—I'm fine." She added a generous splash of milk to her cup.

"You sound like you're having trouble breathing."

"Allergies," she said smoothly. "I have allergies."

It wasn't exactly a lie. Temptation made it very hard for her to breathe.

THE LAST FEW days of August were hot and steamy. Caroline was short-tempered and irritable; she spent most of her time in air-conditioned rooms, sipping decaffeinated iced tea and dreaming of winter. She went out of her way to steer clear of her husband. The sheer power of his sexuality unnerved the daylights out of her, and she decided retreat was the smartest course of action she could take.

Charlie pulled double shifts at the bar, holding down the fort as cook and bartender while Bill O'Rourke and his wife vacationed in the Poconos. Three times in three days he'd seen Caroline in dishabille and his willpower was running out.

Charlie and Caroline saw little of each other and both felt the tug of loneliness inside their hearts. It looked as if they would continue along their solitary paths until Caroline reached her due date, both so careful to avoid temptation, but Sam unknowingly stepped into the breach with a Labor Day barbecue invitation, offering them the perfect opportunity to reconnect.

Caroline was at work on the Saturday before Labor Day. Both Rhonda and Denise were on vacation and Caroline was alone, save for a soft-spoken young woman looking for the perfect dress to wear to a wedding that very afternoon.

"I wish you had come in yesterday," Caroline said. "We had a lovely garden party taffeta you would have adored. It's not due back for another three days."

"I'll take anything," said the woman. "Sack cloth and ashes if that's all you have."

"We can do better than that," said Caroline with a chuckle. "Why don't you go in the back and take off your clothes and I'll bring you a selection of outfits."

The woman disappeared down the hallway and Caroline yawned. She'd been stifling that yawn for the past five minutes and it was an enormous relief to give in at last.

"Not sleeping well these days?"

She started at the sound of her husband's voice in the doorway.

"Charles! I didn't hear you come in."

"I've been meaning to talk to you about that," he said, closing the door behind him. "Don't you think you should hang some bells on this door or something? An army could march through this place and you'd never know it."

"Princeton isn't exactly a high-crime area," she pointed out gently. "I think I'm safe."

"I'll come by tomorrow before work and rig something up," he said, ignoring her protests. "You can't be too careful."

Oh, Donohue, she thought as he helped himself to a cup of coffee from the display on the sideboard. *Don't you know that you're what's truly dangerous?* That army Charlie talked about could storm her shop and not cause her half the trouble that he could simply by showing up on her doorstep and reminding her that she had needs that money and success could never fulfill.

"So what brings you here?" she asked, smiling at the sight of his large, masculine hand surrounding the fragile china teacup. "I'm certain you're not doing a spot check on my safety."

He looked vaguely uncomfortable, appealingly vulnerable. Her heart did an odd little leap inside her chest and she took a deep breath to steady herself. A clear vision of how he'd looked at her kitchen table, shirtless and unbearably sexy, flooded her memory. *Ridiculous! The man is your husband.*

"Sam and Murphy are having their annual Labor Day bash. I thought we might like to go together."

A smile played at the corners of her mouth. "Are you asking me for a date, Charles?"

"Weird, isn't it?" He pushed his silky dark hair off his forehead and grinned. "Asking your own wife to a barbecue."

"I'd love to go with you." *This isn't a high school prom, Caroline. You don't have to be so blasted happy about it.*

The look of uneasiness vanished and his old cocky expression took its place. "Sam wants us to bring potato salad and a dessert. I'll take care of it."

Caroline sighed in mock relief, struggling to maintain her cool composure. "The other guests will be forever in your debt."

"You're not off the hook entirely."

She arched a brow. "Oh, really?"

"It won't be easy, you know, acting like a real married couple."

"I'd thought of that." She hesitated. Was he flirting with her? "I think we can handle it."

"Yeah?"

"Yeah," said Caroline, imitating his inflection. "I do."

He reached over to brush a strand of hair away from her face. His hand lingered near her mouth. She found herself yearning for the touch of his lips on hers. Her breath caught in her throat. He stepped forward. She swayed toward him. The question was in his eyes and the answer in her smile. He lowered his head and moved closer, closer—

"I knew it!" said a female voice from the hallway. "I waited too long and there isn't a thing in the world for me to wear this afternoon, is there?"

Caroline and Charlie leaped apart like two guilty children.

"A customer," said Caroline, regaining her equilibrium. "I forgot all about her." She raised her voice and called out, "Stay right where you are, Ms. Walker. I'll bring your selections to you in a second."

Charlie had a triumphant look in his vivid green eyes and Caroline looked away, both embarrassed and pleased.

"I don't want to get you in trouble with your customers," he said. "I'll shove off for now."

"Tell Sam we said yes." She draped a Donna Karan and a Calvin Klein over her arm and searched for the Arnold Scaasi she knew was in there somewhere. "Oh, and ask her to make sure she has decaf iced tea on hand by the gallon."

"I'm going to fix up an entrance bell for this door," he said.

"You don't have to."

"I know," he said. "I want to."

"Drive carefully."

"Better watch out, Caroline," he said. "You're starting to sound like a wife."

She stood in the doorway and watched him walk down the sidewalk toward his truck. The battered pickup looked out of place parked among the BMWs and Jaguars, same as Charlie had looked in her frilly, fussy dress shop. "You didn't have to drop by, Charles," she murmured as he disappeared down the street. "You're starting to act like a husband."

THE O'ROURKES' barbecue was rained out but Sam threw open the doors to her house anyway. "So we cook indoors," Sam said with a snap of her fingers. "We'll have a great time."

Sam was as good as her word. The crowd from the bar poured in, as did Murphy's newspaper buddies and Sam's employees at her catering firm. Even young Patty's pals showed up, undeterred by inclement weather. The house was jammed to the rafters, noisy and growing messier by the second. By comparison, Caroline's immaculate town house seemed like a mausoleum. She tried to imagine it in a few years, when her baby was a rowdy preschooler, but she came up empty. Somehow her perfect house no longer seemed like a home. Not compared to this joyful madness.

Of course, there would be plenty of time to think about things like that after the baby arrived and she and Charlie were once more living their separate lives. It was just that on a day like this, surrounded by friends, their uncertain future was the last thing she wanted to ponder.

Caroline and Charlie shared a chair in the overcrowded living room. Perched on his lap, Caroline felt both out of place and extremely comfortable. It was an odd feeling, to be treated as part of a couple, and to her surprise she enjoyed playing the part of a happy newlywed for the day.

Sam and Murphy nudged each other in the kitchen and exchanged I-told-you-so smiles. Bill O'Rourke and his wife whispered in the hallway and favored the Donohues with their best why-marriage-is-wonderful stories.

Even Caroline's goddaughter, Patty, got into the act.

"He's cu-u-ute," Patty said, perched on the edge of her mother's bed as she watched Caroline comb her hair. "Margaret says his eyes are so green they must be contact lenses."

"Margaret is a terrible twelve-year-old cynic," said Caroline, smoothing her bangs, "and you, my dear Patricia, are to tell her that Charles's eyes are indeed green." She paused, tapping the comb against the palm of her hand. Were they? Truth was, he could have a different pair of green contacts for every day of the week and Caroline would never know it. Married almost six weeks and she didn't know the most basic of facts about her very own husband.

She marched into the living room and called Charlie out onto the porch.

"Do you wear contact lenses?" she asked without preamble.

Leave it to Charlie to not bat an eye. "Nope."

"Your eyes are really green?"

"Last I looked."

"I thought so." She marched into the kitchen where Patty and Margaret were cadging cookies from the platter Sam had arranged the night before. "His eyes are a natural shade of emerald, girls, and I'll thank you very much to forget about contact lenses."

"You told her what I said!" Margaret's face turned as red as Patty's ponytail. "How could you, Patty?"

"It was a valid question," said Patty, looking at Caroline with undisguised curiosity. "I wear contact lenses myself now."

You're overreacting, Caroline thought. She was getting defensive, and for what? Charlie's honor was scarcely at stake. Contact lenses or no, the two girls hadn't impugned his character, for heaven's sake. She was acting like a woman in love with her husband and that was patently ridiculous.

Hormones, she thought, rejoining Charles in the living room. *Nothing more than hormones.*

THERE WAS A TIME when Caroline would have jumped at the chance to be center of attention, but when Scotty asked her to accompany him in a rendition of "Danny Boy," she said, "Not this time, Scotty. I think pregnancy has ruined my vocal cords."

"Nonsense," said the elderly professor. "You sound as splendid as ever. You just want to be coaxed."

The gang from O'Rourke's clapped and cheered their encouragement.

"You don't have to sing if you don't want to," Charlie said to his wife. "Just tell 'em you're too tired."

"It's my own fault," she said. "A bit late to claim shyness, wouldn't you say?"

He watched as she made her way to the piano in the far corner of the room and sat on the bench next to the old professor. Jealousy nipped at Charlie's gut. Jealous of old Scotty? What a crock. Scotty was eighty if he was a day. It was no secret that Scotty adored Caroline—and it was also no secret that Caroline adored him right back. But if ever there was a relationship to define the word "platonic," this was the one.

You're in trouble, man, thought Charlie. *Next thing you know you'll be jealous of Sam's baby boy.*

Caroline seemed tentative at the start; her clear soprano wavered on the first bar and it was obvious her heart wasn't in it. Charlie leaned forward in his chair. *Come on, princess,* he thought. *You can do it.* She met his eyes and he smiled encouragement. She visibly relaxed as her voice gathered power. The old Caroline took over and before his eyes she turned into the world-class flirt he remembered from his first visit to O'Rourke's Bar and Grill. Only this time it was different. This time he knew there was someone else lurking behind that glamorous facade. Someone he kind of liked—and might like even more if he ever really got to know her.

Don't go getting sentimental, Charlie. You knew what this was all about when you started the whole thing. This marriage was for the kid and nothing else. The moment that baby was born, he'd be booted out the door of her fancy apartment quicker than he could say goodbye. Being at each other's throats for the next six months didn't make any sense, but expecting anything else from the relationship was asking for trouble.

So they'd had a nice day together. Big deal. No point to reading anything into it. Pretending their relationship was anything but what it was, was asking for trouble.

"DANNY BOY" had always made Caroline feel melancholy, but tonight it made her downright ornery. The last time she'd sung that song had been at Sam's Labor Day party the year before. Caroline had come with an account executive from a Princeton investment firm, and she'd relished being the belle of the ball. Life had been good that year. She was young and healthy, and so was her business. One by one she had achieved each of the goals she had set for herself as a little girl, and she experienced a deep sense of pride that she'd been able to accomplish so much with so little to start with.

This year found her married to a man she barely knew and pregnant with a baby she hadn't planned on. Her life was out of control and as she sang the plaintive words to the old song, she knew in her deepest soul that nothing would ever be the same again. She could never go back to being the woman she'd been just a few short months ago. So confident, so in control. That part of her life was lost to her now as surely as if she'd never lived it at all. This time next year she would be a mother. An infant would be looking to her for love and guidance—for his or her very existence. For the rest of her life she would be somebody's mother.

Unlike her marriage. This time next year she would be the ex-Mrs. Donohue. But, the thought occurred to her, would she be able to put the experience away with her maternity clothes and forget it had happened?

She could divorce Charlie after the baby arrived but she couldn't divorce him from their lives. He would always be part and parcel of her existence, connected to her by the child they had created on that warm June night.

By the time Sam's Labor Day bash was over, Caroline was exhausted and queasy. Charlie was queasy, too, from battling feelings he'd sworn he would never feel for anyone, much less the former Caroline Bradley.

They rode home in silence. Caroline kept taking deep breaths, struggling to calm her jittery stomach, while Charlie concentrated on the dark and winding road. "Why the hell don't they spring for some streetlights?" he muttered, straining to see ten feet ahead of him. "We pay enough damn taxes...." A flash of something white caught his eye near the side of the road then darted closer.

This time of year the woods were filled with white-tailed deer, just waiting to play chicken with unsuspecting drivers. He slammed on the brakes just in time as a doe and fawn scampered past his headlights.

Caroline's sharp intake of breath echoed in the quiet truck.

"For God's sake, Charles. Can't you be more careful?"

"I saw a deer," he said. "Two of 'em. If you don't mind killing Bambi and his mother—"

"Oh, do be quiet," she snapped. "I only asked you to be more careful. I didn't ask you to lay a guilt trip on me."

"If you put your seat belt on, you wouldn't have a problem."

"My seat belt *is* on. It's your driving that's the problem."

He stopped dead in the middle of the deserted road as something inside him snapped. He didn't know if it was the stress of playing the happily married couple or the stress of being married in the first place, but suddenly he couldn't manage to be civil or polite or considerate. What he wanted was to bail out. "You wanna drive?"

She lifted her chin defiantly. "I'm sure I would do a more competent job."

"Fine." He shifted into neutral, put on the emergency brake, then flung open the door. "You got it, lady."

"You're being ridiculous, Charles."

"Ridiculous?" He crossed around the front of the truck until he was looking straight at her through the open window of the truck. "What's ridiculous is this marriage of ours?"

"And whose bright idea was this marriage anyway? It certainly wasn't mine."

"Yeah, well, don't think I haven't lived to regret it, Bradley. Living with you isn't exactly fun."

He yelped as the passenger door swung open and clipped him in the flank. "Why the hell don't you watch what you're doing?"

She leaped to the ground, a small and volatile bundle of rage unleashed. "I did watch what I was doing, and you should be extremely glad my aim wasn't any better."

"Go ahead," he said, flinging his arms wide. "Take your best shot."

"Don't tempt me."

He moved closer, all male dominance and anger. "What's the matter, Bradley? Losing your nerve?"

"The name's Donohue," she said between clenched teeth. "Or have you forgotten?"

"How could I?" he countered. "That's the whole problem."

That did it. She was on him with all the power at her command. She pummeled his chest, swung wildly for his jaw, then was about to knee him in the groin when he grabbed her under the arms and swept her off her feet and onto the fender of the truck.

"One shot," she hissed. "You promised me one clear shot."

"You had three of them. One more and I fight back."

"Just like you, Donohue. What kind of man would hit a pregnant woman?"

"Who said I'd hit you?"

"I doubt if you intended to dazzle me with your wit."

The fight went out of him and he backed away, palms up. "You fight dirty, lady. I'm out of here." Turning, he headed off down the road.

CAROLINE SAT very still atop the fender of the truck and watched as Donohue disappeared into the darkness.

"Charlie!" Her voice broke the stillness of the late summer night. "Please don't go."

No answer. She hadn't expected one. If ever a man had made the perfect exit, it was Charlie. Why on earth hadn't she bitten back those words? For years she'd prided herself on being able to keep her temper under control in situations that would have sorely tested a diplomat. Unfortunately it had only taken Charlie Donohue a little over six weeks to undo more than thirty years of discipline.

She slipped from the fender and climbed into the driver's seat of the truck. At least he'd been thoughtful enough to leave the engine running. She released the emergency brake and shifted into first. He couldn't have gone far. Adjusting the beams to high, she eased the truck down the road, craning for a glimpse of him.

"Come on, Charlie," she muttered. "Enough's enough."

Her husband, however, had chosen to avoid the road entirely, and a few minutes later Caroline found herself on the main thoroughfare that led to her apartment. She doubted if there were bears in the woods of central New Jersey but still the thought of Charlie alone in the darkness made her feel absolutely terrible.

But no more terrible than the fact that she'd hurt him.

ii

Charlie didn't come home that night or the next. Caroline knew he was still alive because the truck had miraculously disappeared from its parking lot in front of her apartment along with two pairs of jeans while she was at work the day after the blowup, but Charlie was nowhere to be seen.

Tuesday turned into Wednesday and Wednesday became Thursday and still no Charlie.

She was distracted, ill-tempered and generally worthless at the store, and to make matters worse, she missed her appointment with Dr. Burkheit and had to make a new one for the following Monday. Her hair suddenly developed a mind of its own, sticking out in all manner of weird angles that neither gel nor mousse could tame. She couldn't button the waistbands of any of her fitted suits and was reduced to fastening her skirts with safety pins and elastic bands.

"You look awful," said Sam, who had dropped by the store to rent a dress for a UPI function where Murphy was being honored. "Are you having a tough time of it?"

Caroline sighed and looked at the gigantic run in her stocking. "Tougher than you could ever imagine."

"I don't think I've ever seen you quite so..." Sam stopped, apparently searching for the right word.

"Sloppy? Unkempt?" She laughed hollowly. "Stop me when I get close."

Sam leaned forward, moving the baby from one arm to the other as she grabbed for the diaper bag. "You're not very happy, are you?"

Caroline chucked her godson under his chubby chin. "I didn't know that being happy was part of the bargain."

"He's at the bar today," said Sam, laying James down on a thick stack of bath towels so she could change him.

Caroline said nothing.

"You could always drop by casually to say hello to Scotty."

Caroline shook her head. "I don't think that's a terribly good idea."

Sam deftly unfastened the old diaper and replaced it with a new one. Caroline burst into tears.

"I'm a reasonably intelligent woman," she said. "I can balance a checkbook and understand the principle behind deficit spending. Why does changing a baby's diaper look so darned hard?"

"It's no harder than talking to your husband."

"Spoken by a married woman of two years," said Caroline with a sniff. "I love you, Sam, but you're not the authority on marriage."

"I know when someone is being too stubborn for her own good."

"You don't understand," said Caroline, wiping her eyes with a tissue. "I was terrible."

"You're pregnant," said Sam. "That comes with the territory."

She met her friend's eyes. "I punched him."

Sam's mouth dropped open like a cartoon character's. "You did what?"

"I punched him. We had a fight. He told me to take my best shot and so I punched him."

"Oh, my God."

"Don't look at me like that, Sam. He deserved it."

"I can't believe you actually punched that poor man."

"Poor man? He was insufferable." She recounted the argument over the deer that had precipitated the whole thing. "The least you can do is stop laughing."

"It's that or cry. Maybe you were right in the first place and you two never should have gotten together."

Funny how her friend's words found their target in the center of Caroline's heart. Maybe this really was the end to their attempt at marriage. What she'd done to Charlie was unthinkable. In her wildest imagination she never would have considered hitting another human being. They were a lethal combination, truly oil and water, and he was right to stay away.

CAROLINE USUALLY worked late on Thursday nights to accommodate customers who had big plans for the weekend. The weekend after Labor Day was normally a slow one, but if the crowd that stormed her shop that night was any indication, life in Princeton was zipping along just fine without her.

"Join us for a drink," said Mary Ann Freitag, an attorney with offices in Palmer Square. "Some of the old crowd from Drew are getting together at The Place. I know they'd love to see you."

Caroline hesitated. "I'm exhausted," she said with an apologetic laugh. "Maybe another time."

"Who knows if there will *be* another time," said Mary Ann. "We're all in town, we're all free, let's do it tonight."

Caroline glanced at the clock. It was almost closing time and she knew Rhonda wouldn't mind doing the honors. The apartment had seemed so empty these past few nights that, exhausted or not, she welcomed the opportunity to escape her thoughts for an hour or two. "Who am I to argue with the legal mind?'' she said at last. ''Lead me to the crowd.''

MARY ANN HAD a brand-new showroom-fresh Jaguar, and she insisted on driving Caroline to The Place near Forrestal Village. ''Don't worry about getting back,'' she said, signaling a left turn into the pub's parking lot. ''I'll deliver you myself.''

You should only know what a straight line that is, thought Caroline as she climbed from the low-slung car and adjusted her linen skirt. Had there ever been a better opportunity for telling an old friend you were pregnant? Unfortunately, Mary Ann was off and running on another topic and the chance slipped away.

Maybe it was for the best. Wouldn't it be wonderful to spend a comfortable evening with old friends who knew absolutely nothing about the hash her life had become? For a few hours she could be Caroline Bradley, rising entrepreneur and well-known flirt, a woman who could make a party come to life simply by walking through the door.

''Look who's here!'' cried a red-haired woman in tennis whites who was seated near the door. ''It's been ages, Caroline.''

Caroline hugged Lucy Fitzpatrick, noting the familiar scent of liniment and sunshine that clung to the woman. ''Too long,'' she said.

Lucy put an arm around Caroline and tapped her beer mug for attention. ''Everybody! The long-lost Caroline has reappeared.''

Mary Ann hadn't been kidding when she said most of the old crowd from college was there. Girls—*women* now—she hadn't seen in ten years waved hello while men she remembered all too well as goofy frat brats pressed kisses to her cheek. She knew the punch lines of every joke and the dollar value of each and every stock option these ambitious old friends had ever been gifted with.

And she knew she'd made a mistake before her fanny hit the chair.

Red suspenders, she thought, staring at the bright young men standing around the bar. Had she ever really believed red suspenders belonged on anyone save Santa Claus? All this talk about money and position depressed her. Charlie never talked about things like that. With Charlie, conversation could touch on anything from football to music to politics. Of course, the fact that Charlie *had* no money probably had something to do with it, but maybe he'd caught on long before Caroline to how boring a topic personal finance really was.

"And then I told my banker..." What was Stu Bergman now anyway? Rumor had it he owned five pieces of prime Princeton real estate and half of Bucks County, Pennsylvania.

And Margie Lipari—wasn't she the girl who was always five dollars in debt to everybody? Margie now wore designer clothes—clothes that weren't rented—and had enough money to buy and sell the teachers who'd told her she wouldn't amount to anything.

They said they were happy. They laughed and joked as if they had life by the tail. Who was Caroline to judge? Maybe they really did. Only why did their laughter and jokes suddenly make her so sad—and so eager to get home?

"Margaritas all around," said Mary Ann, motioning for a waitress. "Let's get this party moving."

"Not for me," said Caroline evenly. "Make it club soda with a twist."

"Come on," said Mary Ann. "You introduced us to margaritas."

"Well, now I've been introduced to club soda."

"Just one," Mary Ann urged. "A toast to the future."

"It's the future I'm thinking about," said Caroline, looking around the table at the familiar faces. "I'm pregnant."

The uproar was deafening. Mary Ann leaped to her feet and ran to the other side of the table to hug Caroline. The other women kissed her cheek and patted her on the back while the men sat there, bemused and more than a little bit disappointed.

Caroline sat in the eye of the storm, amazed that nobody, not one single person, asked her about the father of the baby. You would have thought that someone would have at least mentioned the fact that hers hadn't been an immaculate conception.

"When?" they asked. "Do you know if it's a boy or a girl? Lamaze? Breast-feeding?"

"I'm married," she blurted.

Utter silence descended upon the group.

"You're joking." Margie Lipari stared at her as if she'd said the Dow was down fifty points.

"Actually I've never been more serious." She took a sip of water from the glass before her. "Charles and I were married in early July."

Stu thought for a moment. "Charles Banyon from Sci-Tech on Route 1?"

She lifted her chin. "Charlie Donohue from O'Rourke's."

"Call him," said Lucy. "Have him drop in to meet us."

"He—he works late on Thursdays," said Caroline truthfully. "He simply couldn't."

"Burning the midnight oil, huh?" asked Stu. "On his way to his first million."

"Is O'Rourke's a brokerage firm?" asked Mary Ann, eager for a new contact.

Fasten your seat belt, Mary Ann. "It's a bar and grill."

"Keeping a new venture under wraps?" asked Stu. "Clever girl."

"O'Rourke's Bar and Grill," said Caroline, louder this time. "The best joint in Rocky Hill. Charles is the cook."

"You're joking," said Mary Ann. "Aren't you?"

"I've never been more serious."

Nobody knew what to say. They didn't make jokes or congratulate her. They didn't even talk about the baby. Mary Ann turned to Lucy Fitzpatrick and engaged the red-haired woman in a spirited discussion on state taxes. In the blink of an eye everyone was involved in the debate.

Everyone, that was, except Caroline. She might as well have been invisible. She sat there, sipping her club soda, wondering why on earth she'd ever thought coming to The Place had sounded like a good idea. Once upon a time, she'd been the center of attention at gatherings like this, captivating everyone with her beauty and her wit. Funny thing, though. She'd wanted to go home then, too, only she hadn't the guts to admit it. Their conversations had been just as boring; their outlooks every bit as self-centered; the stink of expensive after-shaves just as overpowering.

Only Caroline had been different, more interested in promoting her business than in promoting herself. She had so much to prove, both to herself and to others, that she never allowed discomfort to get in the way. Not one of these old friends had ever come close to learning anything about who Caroline Bradley really was. The candy-striped socks Charlie liked to tease her about were a deep dark secret and Caroline doubted if anyone seated at this table would understand the joke. But then, not even Charlie knew just how funny it really was....

"I hate Christmas parties," Carly said as she and Samantha walked to school. "They're stupid."

"I think they're great," said Sam. "You get to wear holly-berry pins and plaid satin ribbons."

Carly clutched her book bag closer to her chest, feeling small and mean to even think such thoughts. "I think I'm getting the flu," she said, stopping in her tracks. "Feel my head. Isn't it hot?"

Sam pulled off her mitten with her teeth and pressed her bare palm against Carly's forehead. "Cool as a cucumber," she said. "You're just fine."

"My stomach hurts," said Carly. "Maybe it's appendicitis."

"There's nothing wrong with you, Carly Bradley," said Sam in exasperation, "except these fibs you're telling."

"I don't want to go to school," Carly whispered. "I can't."

Suddenly Sam's dark blue eyes softened with understanding. "You don't have a present for the grab bag, do you?"

Carly shook her head and whispered, "No."

"And you don't have anything Christmassy to wear?"

Carly shook her head again. "Mom said there's no extra money and that everyone will have to understand." There was truth to her mother's words but Carly at eleven was too young to hear it. Besides, eleven-year-old children weren't known for their compassion. She would be the laughingstock of the school, like one of those poor kids the nuns forced to take home baskets of food for their families. Imagine taking charity from nuns who'd been sworn to vows of poverty! She would rather be dead.

"I have an idea," said Sam after a minute. "Let's go back to my house."

"We can't! We'll be late for school."

"It's your choice, Carly. You can either be late for school or go without candy-cane knee socks."

Carly's eyes widened. "You mean like the ones in the window of Bantam's?"

"Exactly."

They'd be just the thing to perk up her dark green wool skirt and white blouse. She'd look so Christmassy, like one of the crowd.

"Come on," she said, grabbing Sam's hand and starting to run. *"If we hurry we can get to your house and back
to school before they take attendance."*

CAROLINE WANTED nothing more than to go home, put on
a pair of those candy-cane knee socks and a comfortable
nightgown and watch television. It would be wonderful if
Charlie happened to be there, as well, but she'd never been
one to wish for the impossible.

"I'm afraid late nights are too much for me these days,"
she said at a few minutes after ten. "I think I'll call a cab
and head home."

Mary Ann did the expected and offered to drive her, but
Caroline shook her head. "Stay and enjoy yourself," she
said. "I'll be fine."

"I'm out of here, too," said Stu, rising to his feet. "I'll
drop you off."

Caroline started to protest but Stu was adamant. He lived
in Princeton, and her store was only a stone's throw away.
Besides, a wave of bone-numbing exhaustion was moving
its way through her body, making it almost impossible for
her to keep her eyes open. "Thanks, Stu," she said, stifling a yawn. "That would be wonderful."

Stu was an amiable sort, not quite as bombastic as the
other red-suspendered fellows who were part of the old
Drew University crowd. He chatted pleasantly enough as he
took her to the store, touching on football and the latest
Broadway sensation. All Caroline had to do was nod and
smile at the appropriate times.

"Here we are." He whipped into a parking spot in front
of Twice Over Lightly and shut off the engine. "Which
car's yours?"

She pointed toward the red sports car.

He whistled. "Feel like giving me a ride around the
block?"

"Not tonight, Stu. Why don't I give you a rain check?"

He tilted his head to one side and studied her. "You know, I may not be a psychologist but I know an unhappy woman when I see one. Anything wrong? That new husband of yours treating you right?"

She bit her lip against a flood of emotion. "Nothing that a good night's sleep won't cure."

"I take it that's my cue to say good-night."

"You always were perceptive." She leaned over and kissed him on his cheek. "Thanks for the ride."

He saluted. "Anytime."

Stu waited until she was safely in her car and pointed toward home, then with a beep-beep of his horn, they parted company at the corner of Nassau Street and Route 206. The roads were empty and so was the local Super Fresh where she stopped for a quart of milk and some whole wheat bread. She wasn't hungry but that really didn't make any difference. The baby needed food, even if she didn't care if she never ate again.

She had no business being surprised when she reached her apartment and didn't see Charlie's truck. There was no reason to think Charlie'd be coming back to her apartment any time soon. Not after the way she'd treated him.

She stumbled through the foyer, wishing for the thousandth time that she'd invested in timers. Anything to avoid coming home to a dark and lonely place. Maybe she should get a dog, too. Someone who'd be happy to see her when she came home at night. Kids loved dogs. Caroline had spent hours in front of the television set watching *Lassie*, wishing she had a dog of her own.

"I'm thirty-one years old," she grumbled as she made her way toward the living room light switch. "I should have a dog of my own."

The male voice seemed to come from nowhere. "How about a St. Bernard?"

She screamed and punched at the switch. Light flooded the living room. "What the hell are you doing here?" she demanded.

Charlie was sprawled across her immaculate sofa, his big ugly running shoes perched against the arm. "Nice to see you, Mrs. Donohue," he drawled. "I was wondering when you'd show up."

iii

Caroline struggled to regain her composure. "I thought you were at the bar."

"Yeah," he said. "Evidently."

She didn't like the sound of his voice. "What do you mean 'evidently'?"

He got to his feet, looking impossibly large and male against the feminine backdrop of her living room. "I saw you with your friend," he said without preamble. "What the hell was going on?"

She was at a loss for a moment then she realized what he was talking about "Not that I owe you any explanations, but Stu was kind enough to drop me back at the shop."

"'Stu was kind enough,'" he mimicked. "A real prince of a guy."

"There's no reason to get nasty," she said, heart racing. "I was out with a group of old friends and Stuart gave me a lift." *Are you jealous, Charlie? Could you possibly be acting like a jealous husband?* "How on earth did you see me with Stuart?"

"My truck's in the garage. I had the mechanic drop me off at your shop. I saw your car was still there and I got wor—I hung around awhile to wait. You and your pal pulled up just after I called for a cab."

"You were spying on me."

"That's nothing compared to what you were doing."

She glared at him but her pique had absolutely no effect on him.

"Where'd you go?"

"The Place." She moved toward the kitchen with her grocery bag.

"That dive on Route 1?" He was hard on her heels.

"It's not a dive." She flung open the refrigerator and put the bread inside. "The Place caters to an impressive clientele."

"Red suspenders," said Charlie with a snort of derision. "I should've known you'd find another guy with red suspenders."

"I hate red suspenders," she shot back. "And for your information I couldn't wait to get the hell out of there and get home."

"Yeah?" He looked both suspicious and hopeful and her damnable heart twisted with emotion. "What were you doing there in the first place?"

She took a glass from the cupboard then poured herself some milk. "That, Mr. Donohue, is none of your business."

He grabbed her wrist, spilling milk on the countertop. "The hell it isn't."

She looked pointedly at his hand. "Let me go."

"First tell me what you were doing at The Place."

Somehow this didn't seem the right time to assert her independence. Quickly she told him about Mary Ann's visit to the shop and her impulsive decision to meet up with her old university crowd.

"I suppose you had yourself a swell time with all your frat brat pals."

"Frankly, no." She hesitated then decided to opt for the truth. "I was bored out of my mind."

"Probably all that talk about stock options and inheritances bored you stiff."

"That's right," she retorted. "I almost fell asleep with my face in my club soda."

His grip on her wrist changed subtly. "I'd pay a lot to see that, princess."

"I'll just bet you would."

"Why is it I get the feeling there's a hell of a lot I don't know about you?"

"Because you're a smart man, Donohue. You know a lost cause when you see one."

He stroked the inside of her wrist with his thumb, lazy, circular motions that made her pulse quicken. Damn the man. "Still, though, I bet I know a few things about you that you don't even realize."

"I wouldn't bet on that." Oh, God, the touch of his hand was making it hard to think.

"I would."

"Sure of yourself, aren't you?"

"When it comes to this, I am."

One instant they were standing separate and apart; the next instant she was in his arms, his mouth on hers, seeking, demanding, questioning.

"This doesn't prove anything, Charles," she managed. "This doesn't mean a thing."

"Shut up," said Charlie, claiming her mouth again and again until she was breathless with desire and leaning against him for support.

"We don't need this," she whispered as he swept her into his arms. "The one thing we don't need is complications."

"This *is* complicated," said her husband, striding toward the bedroom at the rear of the apartment. "It's time we stopped pretending it isn't."

"Making love won't solve our problems."

"Pretending we don't want each other won't, either."

"Sex isn't everything."

His laughter was deep and earthy. "Say no before we walk through that bedroom door and this won't happen again, but once we cross that threshhold, all bets are off."

"You're a tough man, Donohue." She pressed a kiss to the base of his throat, his collarbone beneath his work shirt. He smelled wonderful, like soap and fresh air.

He stopped in front of the bedroom door.

"It's up to you, Caroline." His face was inches from hers, and the expression in his green eyes matched the heat gathering inside her chest.

"Oh, Donohue," she said, "did anyone ever tell you that you talk too much?"

The first time they had come together out of desire, pure and simple. This time desire ran high but there was much more to their union than sexual need. Neither one was willing to admit to that, however, at least not with words. But Caroline's heart resonated with unfamiliar emotions and Charlie felt as if he were reaching for a taste of paradise.

She stood in the center of her bedroom, trembling, as he reached for the zipper at the back of her dress. The rasp echoed in the throbbing silence, followed by the slither of silk as the garment dropped to the floor at her feet. He hooked his thumbs in the waistband of her lace-edged half slip and eased the garment over her hips and thighs until it, too, puddled around her ankles.

Gently his hands cupped the fullness of her breasts, weighing their softness in his palms. "Beautiful," he murmured, brushing his lips against that softness.

"I have cleavage at last," she said, trying desperately to retain the last remnants of sanity. "I've always wanted to be voluptuous."

His head dipped lower, his lips trailing fire across her midriff and coming to rest against her belly.

"Donohue," she whispered. "Please, don't . . ."

But he didn't listen. She didn't want him to listen. She wanted him to continue what he was doing, moving his hot and restless mouth with the silky mustache across her rounded belly, stroking her hips and thighs with knowing hands, murmuring words she couldn't quite hear but understood intimately.

She rested her hand atop his head, letting the strands of jet black hair slip through her fingers like raw silk. It felt so right to be in that room together, to feel her body against his, to know that before too much longer they would be tangled together on her bed, giving and receiving the same dark pleasures they had found on that night in June when it all began.

Of course, it hadn't begun in June. Not really. She sighed as he lowered her to the mattress, his warm and eager body covering hers with fierce gentleness, controlled abandon. This had been ordained from the first moment they met, from the first look they'd exchanged, the first words they'd spoken.

But there were no words between them now. Words were unnecessary against the spectacular burst of fireworks that exploded as he found her with his hand. She shuddered with pleasure, shifting restlessly, urgently, on the soft bed while he took his sweet time with her pleasure.

SHE WAS HOT to the touch, moist with desire. He wanted to bury himself in her again and again, seeking the source of all things wondrous and holy. There was nothing about his wife that wasn't beautiful. She was perfectly made, on a scale so delicately feminine that he almost hesitated to possess her as completely as he wanted to. And there was the baby to consider.

"Can we...?" His words were muffled as he pressed his lips to her navel.

"The baby won't mind." Her voice reached him as if through a cloud of dreams.

"We won't hurt him . . . or you?"

She shook her head. "I promise. You couldn't possibly hurt either one of us."

He stretched full length atop her, supporting his weight on his arms while he drank his fill of her beautiful face.

"Donohue," she whispered. "Don't hesitate. . . ."

That was the one thing he could no longer do. His control snapped and, with an urgent groan, he took her for the first time as his wife. He moved slowly within her, conscious of a hundred different emotions cascading through his body and his soul.

"I've never made love to a married woman before."

She laughed softly, her breath soft and sweet against his lips. "I've never been with a married man."

"Do you like it?"

Her sigh was like silver bells. "I like you."

He reached between them and caressed her belly, trying to imagine the baby floating in its primal sea. She placed her hand between them as well and he caught her fingers with his and placed them against her navel. Gently he rolled them onto their sides, initiating a slow and sensual rhythm that she quickly caught and made her own. It was a communion of the souls, a sacrament, every good and wonderful thing he had ever imagined or dreamed of imagining.

Her climax was bottomless, shattering. Her body pulsed around him, drawing him deeper inside. He held on for as long as he could, wanting to postpone the inevitable, but he caught the flame, same as she had caught his rhythm. His release was primitive, intense and not even close to being enough.

THE FIRST TIME they had been together, morning had found them embarrassed, self-conscious and eager to get as far away from each other as modern transportation would allow.

How times had changed.

Six o'clock found Caroline and Charlie still wrapped in each other's arms, blissfully unaware of the rain beating against the bedroom windows and the lightning that streaked across the sky.

"We probably should get some sleep," said Caroline, curling closer to his side. "We'll regret this in the morning."

"Too late," said Charlie. "It's already morning."

She leaned up on one elbow, craning for a glimpse of her alarm clock. "It can't be. Why, we've only been in here for—"

"Hours," said Charlie, pulling her down next to him. "A lot of hours."

"You're an amazing man, Charles." She pressed a kiss to his stomach.

"Keep doing that and I'll be even more amazing."

She laughed and kissed her way up to his mouth. "We need our rest."

"What we need is some food."

"I don't know, Charles. I haven't been able to eat in the morning for three months now."

He glanced at her. "Are you feeling sick?"

"No." A big smile spread across her face. "Actually, I'm feeling simply wonderful." She had begun her second trimester the day before yesterday, happy to see that her how-to books were right when they promised morning sickness would soon fade into memory, along with that mind-numbing need for endless hours of sleep. The possibility of a miscarriage also had been drastically reduced now that the first three months were over, and Caroline felt ready to settle into a pleasurable routine of expectancy.

"Why don't I fix us some breakfast?" Charlie kissed her on the mouth then swung his legs over the side of the bed. "Stay put. I'll bring it here."

"Be careful, Charles," she said, easing the covers up over her chest as she looked at him. "You might find yourself making breakfast every day."

"Sam told me about your cooking, Caroline. This is definitely the better part of valor."

She lay there in bed, luxuriating in the warm afterglow of their lovemaking. Her body felt rich and lush, but more than that her heart was at ease. For the first time in months she was at peace with herself. Being with Charlie had felt *right* in the deepest sense of the word. The tension between them, the walking-on-eggshell nerves, had vanished with the first kiss. So had the loneliness.

She glanced at the stack of books piled atop her night-stand. *What To Expect When You're Expecting. Your Baby and You. Healthy Babies, Healthy Choices.* Every how-to book on the subject of childbirth had found its way into her house, but not one word of their collective advice had found its way into her brain. She'd been holding this pregnancy at arm's length away from her heart. It was real only when she buttoned her waistband or slipped into a larger sized bra. Morning sickness was real. So was the way the needle on her bathroom scale inched its way upward. That much she could handle. But she had done her best to skim over the fact that a child, one with needs and desires and an entire life pattern already imprinted in its genetic code, was growing beneath her heart. Her child and Charlie Dono-hue's.

She wasn't in this alone. She wasn't just renting him a room in her condominium apartment. He was her hus-band and the father of her child and now, at last, the final barrier between them had fallen and they were ready to share the experience ahead. It may not be a forever kind of marriage, but it was real and they were no longer afraid to admit it was exactly what they wanted—if only for right now.

Tossing aside the bed covers, she reached for her bathrobe and slipped it on. She needed Charlie beside her, his warmth and protection, as she grew bigger with their baby. Once the baby was born, she would be her old self again, independent and strong. But right now, as each day carried her further away from the woman she used to be, she needed someone to lean on and, for better or worse, her husband, Charlie, was that someone.

CHARLIE COOKED fast and he cooked good, but he didn't cook neat. By the time he finished, the kitchen looked as if it had been attacked by a horde of trash-tossing locusts. Bread wrappers littered the countertop. Crumpled-up paper towels sat on top of the bread wrappers. Eggshells, coffee grounds and an accumulation of other debris covered every other available surface.

But he'd turned out one hell of a breakfast. Cheese omelet, crisp bacon, toast with strawberry jam—if she didn't like this, there was no pleasing the woman. Despite her burgeoning belly, Caroline looked too damn thin to him. He wanted to see those hollows in her cheeks fill out a little.

"Get a grip on it," he muttered as he headed toward the bedroom. One great night together and he was acting like her keeper. But, damn it, it *had* been a great night and he didn't want it to end—not one second before it had to. "Sit up!" he bellowed as he approached the door. "Breakfast!"

He stepped into the room. The bed was empty. He put the tray on her dresser and tapped on the bathroom door. "You in there, Caroline?"

No answer. He stood in the middle of her room, glowering into the mirror. Some great night. She'd abandoned ship and she hadn't even left him a note. "You really have a way with women, Donohue," he muttered. "Drive them out of their minds then out of their apartments." He rubbed his bristly chin with his hand. Maybe he should have shaved before making breakfast....

"Out of the way, Charles!" Caroline's voice, remarkably cheery for so early in the morning, reverberated through the hallway between the guest room and hers. "It's moving day."

He spun around in time to see his pregnant wife, arms loaded with jeans and sweatshirts and copies of *Sports Illustrated,* march into the bedroom.

"What the—"

She smiled at him and deposited the bundle on the foot of her bed. "I don't know where you want these things, but I thought they should at least be closer at hand."

He looked from his clothes to his wife then back again. "You want me to move into your bedroom?"

"You're clever, Charles," she said, pressing a kiss to the base of his throat. "I like that in a man."

"I'm a slob," he said, drawing her into his arms. "You sure you want me infiltrating your territory?"

"I'm a reformer," said Caroline, snuggling closer. "I'd enjoy the challenge." She paused a moment. "How *big* a slob?"

"Garden variety. Socks all over the place. Crumbs on the carpet." He shot her a glance. "An empty beer can or two."

She raised her hand in protest. "I draw the line at the empty beer cans." A grin spread across her face. "Actually, I draw the line at dirty socks and crumbs on the carpet, but I'm willing to overlook those minor transgressions."

"Generous," he drawled. "You're all heart, lady."

"I know," she said. "But then the compensations are worth it."

It was his turn to grin. "Sex?"

"There's that," she admitted slowly, then stopped.

"But?" he prodded.

She flushed an adorable shade of strawberry. "I want your company."

"You're kidding!"

"Is it that hard to believe, Charles?"

"Coming from you, yeah. I didn't think my company was the attraction."

"It's nice to be able to share things with someone who cares as much as I do about the baby." Her eyes filled with sudden tears and he instantly regretted his words. Her emotions were right on the surface these days. He'd have to remember that.

"Come on," he said, kissing the top of her head. "I didn't mean it that way. You took me by surprise, is all."

"I thought—I mean, after last night it seems that perhaps..." Her voice trailed off and she looked away.

This was a Caroline he'd never seen before. A softer, more approachable woman with uncertainties and insecurities that he'd never have imagined existed.

"You sure about this?" he asked.

She nodded, wisps of pale blond hair dancing around her face. "I'm sure."

"I hog the covers."

"I noticed."

"Sometimes I snore."

"If you do I'll make certain to wake you up."

"If you do that, I might want to make love to you again."

"I was hoping you'd say exactly that, Charles."

They were on familiar territory again, snappy, saucy one-liners batted between them at lightning speed. She made him laugh with her remarks about his *Sports Illustrated* collection while he set up the tray in the center of the bed.

"It's getting cold," he said, patting the spot next to him. "Come on and eat."

"Temperamental chef, are you, Charles?" She arranged herself with the pillows fluffed between her back and the headboard.

"Things should be eaten the way they should be eaten," he said. "Otherwise why bother to cook?"

"My view exactly."

They ate together in companionable silence, broken only by the crunch of toast and the splash of more decaf being poured. It was their first really married morning, and neither Caroline nor Charlie found it difficult to imagine an endless string of mornings just like that one, stretching out into their future.

But, of course, neither one said anything like that. How could they? They were still too new to each other, too convinced that their marriage was simply one of convenience, too fearful of being hurt. The end of their marriage had been preordained from the very beginning and both Caroline and Charlie were wary enough to keep that fact in mind.

Once the baby was born they would return to their separate lives, as planned. Oh, they'd see each other from time to time but never again would it be like this. Like a real marriage.

Like a real family.

That morning both Charlie and Caroline vowed to enjoy it while they could, because the memories they made would have to last a lifetime.

The Third Trimester

i

It happened for the first time in the middle of October.

Caroline was fitting a slinky, sexy Halson showstopper to one of the damnably slender mannequins in her shop when she felt it. At first she thought she'd imagined the delicate flutter and continued pinning the bodice, but then it happened a second time and she knew.

"Mind the store," she said to Denise, who was typing figures into the computer. "I'll be back in a little while."

Grabbing her coat, Caroline hurried to her sports car and, gunning the engine, raced for O'Rourke's Bar and Grill.

"Where's Charles?" she asked as she burst through the door. "I must find him!"

Her old pal Scotty was sitting at the bar, nursing a Scotch and soda. "Caroline, my dear!" He rose to his feet and executed a courtly, if shaky, bow. "It's been too long."

"Flatterer," she said, kissing his weathered cheek. "I had you over last week for tea."

"Seven days without seeing your lovely face is an eternity to me."

"Where's Charles? I have the most wonderful news!"

"In the basement checking stock," Bill O'Rourke called out from across the room. "Is everything okay?"

"Everything is splendid," she called back. "Absolutely splendid."

"You'll share a few minutes with me before you leave?" Scotty asked as she raced for the basement door.

"I promise!" she tossed over her shoulder, then disappeared down the steps.

Charlie was up to his eyebrows in beer kegs, cartons of Scotch and vodka, and more cases of peanuts and pretzels than even the gang on *Cheers* could imagine. He looked up at the sound of her high heels clicking across the cement floor and grinned. "Don't tell me—you can't live without one of my cheeseburgers."

She stopped a few feet away from him, heart pounding crazily inside her chest. "Come here."

"Even better," said Charlie as he tossed down his ledger and came toward her. "You're gonna get physical."

"How right you are." She drew in a deep breath and reached for his hand, placing it across her belly. She waited for it to happen again, and when it did she threw back her head and laughed joyously. "Did you feel that? The baby moved!"

Charlie's dark brows drew together in a frown. "I didn't feel anything."

"Oh, Charles... there! It happened again. Did you feel it this time?"

"I don't know...I think—" His eyes widened and color appeared on his cheeks. He pressed his hand more closely against her belly. "I can't believe this."

"Neither can I," said Caroline. "Isn't it miraculous?"

The baby seemed to somersault within her womb, a gently rolling motion that made Caroline giggle and Charlie stare in amazement.

"How does it feel?" he asked.

"Wonderful... like a tiny creature tumbling around on a water bed."

"Apt description."

"It is, isn't it?" She threw her arms around him and planted a kiss right beneath his mustache. "It happened for the first time not twenty minutes ago and I raced right over here."

A warmth that had nothing to do with sexual desire grew inside Charlie's heart. He wanted to say things to her that he'd never said to any woman before, to utter words that would change his life even more than it had already been changed. If things were different between them, if this was a *real* marriage, he would have said, "I love you." But things weren't different between them and it wasn't a real marriage and so he just hugged her close and wondered why the best part of life always seemed to come with strings attached.

THE NEXT TWO MONTHS passed in a happy blur for Caroline. Bursts of great activity were followed by bursts of equally great serenity. Both the morning sickness and the numbing fatigue had disappeared, replaced by a sense of such well-being that she pitied women who would never know the joys of pregnancy. She ate with gusto, worked with inspiration and slept the sleep of the well-satisfied woman. Charlie worked a bit of magic and somehow rearranged his hours at the bar for the duration so that he was home most evenings.

His wayward socks still made Caroline crazy while her love of closet space bordered on the obsessive to Charlie, but somehow they managed to mesh their differences in a way that worked for them—at least for now. There was something to be said for a short-term commitment. It made it easier to overlook petty annoyances and concentrate on what was wonderful about the relationship.

To Caroline's delight, there were *many* wonderful things about life with Charlie. His off-key singing each morning as he made breakfast. The soapy-clean smell of his skin after their shower. The solid feel of his body next to hers at night.

But not the least of it was the sheer pleasure to be found in sharing the day-to-day changes that pregnancy brought into their lives. Charlie's stacks of sports magazines were still prominent, but now stacks of baby books vied for space as well. The short-order cook par excellence had become the expert on prenatal care. He knew everything there was to know about the baby's development in utero and Caroline's progress. Words like pre-eclampsia no longer made him dizzy. Truth was, he was reveling in the experience, and his enthusiasm made Caroline happier than she'd been in her life.

Charlie cooked a gigantic twenty-eight pound turkey for Thanksgiving, and they took it to Sam and Murphy's house to share with their friends, thankful that they had been blessed with so much.

Oh, yes, life was good these days for all three of them, Caroline, Charlie, and the baby.

"LOOK AT YOU," said Sam in the O'Rourkes' kitchen two weeks before Christmas. "You look so beautiful it's disgusting."

Caroline groaned and placed her hands on her prominent belly. "Sixteen and one-half pounds and climbing." She rolled her eyes. "Give me another two months and I'll look like Roseanne Barr."

"You're radiant," said Sam, munching on a carrot stick. "I take it pregnancy agrees with you."

"It does," said Caroline, taking a sip of milk. "I feel as if I could tackle the world."

"From the looks of your store yesterday, I'd say the world was beating a path to your door."

"Wonderful, isn't it? Christmas is usually my best season, but this is unbelievable." Who would have imagined that the introduction of ultrachic maternity clothes would send her profits right through the roof? Pregnant women from as far away as Philadelphia were flocking to Twice Over Lightly for the most glamorous holiday gowns in the world. "I could kick myself for not catching on to this earlier."

Sam's smile was smug. "I believe I told you exactly that around Valentine's Day when I was desperate for something special to wear to Murphy's UPI dinner." She feigned deep concentration. "If I remember correctly, you told me you'd be wasting your time and money hunting down designer maternity clothes." Her smile widened. "Not a big enough market, I think you said."

Caroline shrugged broadly. "So I was wrong." She leaned across the kitchen table and grabbed a carrot stick for herself. "You must admit there seem to be more pregnant women than usual around here lately."

"Not so I've noticed."

"Really, Sam. You might not have noticed, but I have. They're everywhere. Princeton must be the most fertile town in the country!"

"You've just become aware of pregnant women," said the Voice of Experience. "Once you have the baby, you'll think there are more young mothers and new babies around than ever before. It's all a matter of perspective."

Caroline nodded but she wasn't buying it. There was a definite baby boom flourishing in central New Jersey, whether or not her best friend wanted to admit it.

Sam arranged the raw vegetables on a platter then went to work on mixing a dip of yogurt, chives and assorted spices. "How's the prospective daddy handling it?"

Caroline started to laugh. "As if he'd invented fatherhood. I swear the man knows more about fetal development than Dr. Burkheit."

"That's the way it always is. The reluctant types are the ones who fall hook, line and sinker."

Oh, Sam, she thought with an inward sigh. *You couldn't possibly know how right you are.* Once upon a time there had been no one more reluctant than Caroline.

Patty chose that moment to burst through the back door, her fiery red hair dancing around her face. Patty was bursting with excitement, something to do with a boy named Jeff, and Sam turned into Mommy right before Caroline's eyes. How did she do that, Caroline wondered, switch gears from being a civilian to being a mother without so much as batting an eye. It was as if a magician had waved a magic wand over Sam's head and the transformation was total and complete.

From the very beginning Samantha had been able to juggle all the different facets of her personality with little trouble. Caroline was good with dresses and sales figures, but would she be able to kiss away a child's tears or offer encouragement when a little girl was in the throes of first love?

She looked at her goddaughter, whose freckled face looked endearingly serious as she described her heartthrob. *I've never had any trouble getting along with Patty,* she thought as she listened. She'd always enjoyed spending time with Patty, offering advice, helping out with Halloween costumes and party dresses and the job of finding a husband for Sam.

Yes, but that's the fun stuff, a little voice inside her whispered. *Where were you for dirty diapers, chicken pox and monsters in the closet?*

"Oh, God," she moaned, burying her face in her hands. "Someone should offer classes in how to be a mother."

"They do!" said Patty, the resident genius. "My friend Amy's mother is a nurse and she said they have seminars at Princeton Medical Center on Tuesdays."

"Basic training or advanced infantry?"

"Basic training," said Patty. "Baths and diapers and all that kind of stuff." She wrinkled her nose. "Don't you know how to do that junk, Aunt Caroline?"

Caroline shook her head forlornly. "I was in the wrong line when they gave out maternal instinct. About all I *do* know is which end to diaper."

"Uncle Charlie knows more than that."

Both Caroline and Sam laughed out loud.

"I'm sorry, honey, but Charles is as backward on baby care as I am." So far Charlie's forte had been pregnancy. She prayed the baby came with instructions.

Patty, however, didn't budge. "He's giving Jimmy a bath."

"Good grief," said Sam, pushing her chair away from the table. "Where's Murphy?"

"He's coaching."

Caroline pulled herself to her feet. "Now this I have to see."

They tiptoed after Patty as she led them through the hallway toward the nursery. "Be real quiet," Patty cautioned, "and if you scrunch down near the doorway, they'll never see you."

Scrunching down was hard work for Caroline, but she managed. It was well worth the effort. Murphy was leaning against the window, looking exceedingly amused—and with good reason. The sight of Charlie, all muscle-bound and six feet three inches of him, struggling with a squirming five-month-old baby boy with deadly bladder aim, had Patty and Sam convulsed in silent laughter behind Caroline.

Even Caroline had to admit it was a comical sight. She'd seen Charlie heft hundred-pound beer kegs with greater ease than he was displaying with that bundle of little boy. However, there was no denying the sweetness of the moment or the effect it had on her heart.

Lucky baby, she thought, lacing her hands across her belly. *Your daddy already loves you.*

A thought, dangerous and impossible, came to life inside her soul, and she struggled to push it away but still it lingered, making her yearn for things she didn't want and could never have.

If only, she thought. *If only . . .*

CHARLIE WASN'T entirely certain he was ready to face a roomful of expectant parents, but when Caroline suggested they attend the Tuesday seminar at the hospital, he found it impossible to say no. What kind of man could look into the big blue eyes of his beautiful—and heavily pregnant—wife and say no to anything she asked?

Not Charlie, although when they walked through the door of the conference room he wished he'd managed it.

"This is worse than the doctor's office," he said as they claimed two seats near the front.

"I know what you mean," said Caroline. "I feel like someone should start boiling water."

"Why did we let the kid talk us into coming?"

"Patty didn't talk us into anything. She merely pointed out fifty separate reasons why it would be a good idea."

"Has she always been this way?"

Caroline nodded. "From her first word."

He shot her a look that made her laugh. "Sam's not a certifiable genius, too, is she?"

"Her IQ is high, but not stratospheric."

"How about Patty's father?"

"Ronald's no rocket scientist."

He took note of the edge in her voice. "So what you're saying is sometimes a kid is her own creation, nothing at all like the parents."

"It gives one hope, doesn't it?"

"I'm not so sure." He dragged a hand through his hair. "We might end up with a son who likes designer dresses."

"Or a daughter who prefers Old Spice to Chanel No. 5."

"I wouldn't mind if she looked like her mom." *Corny, Charlie. Real corny.*

She glanced down at her hands. "I wouldn't mind if he had his father's green eyes."

"I've been thinking a lot about a little girl."

Her eyes met his. "Most men have their hearts set on having a son to carry on the name."

He shrugged. "Plenty of other Donohues out there to carry on the name."

"A little girl," said Caroline softly.

"Only if she's exactly like you." *Okay, now you've gone too far, Charlie.* He wished he could reach out and snatch back his words, but it was too late.

"Why, Charles, I—"

The lecturer took the podium and Charlie breathed a sigh of relief that for the next two hours somebody else would be doing the talking. He'd already said more than enough.

"Charles, do be quiet. Why don't you go outside? Maybe the gardener will play ball with you."

Thirteen-year-old Charlie was all arms, legs and energy. He raced through his days full throttle, bounding up and down the curving staircase of the Donohue house like a race car at the drop of the flag. His mother had no idea how to handle him, so she often passed him onto gardeners and cooks and butlers in her search for someone somewhere who could help her tame her wild child.

Not that he was bad. Far from it. Charles was a good child, enthusiastic and loyal and full of fun. Unfortunately he was exactly like his father, and that was the one thing Jean Donohue couldn't abide. What a disappointment William Donohue had been, pulling against the chains of respectability as if there was something illegal or immoral about playing by the rules. You would think that someone with William's fine upbringing would have tamed his rough edges, grown more comfortable living like a civilized gentleman, but William never had.

Jean sighed as she heard the front door slam, followed by the sound of her son's thudding footsteps as he tore through the front yard looking for the gardener. "Why couldn't you have managed to live, William?" she murmured into the perfumed air of her study. "I don't know how to handle your son."

Charles was his father incarnate, a living, breathing replica of William Donohue, faults and virtues both. With each day that passed Charles slipped farther and farther away from everything Jean held dear and important, and she didn't know what she could do to bring him back.

Of course, the truth was there was nothing his mom could do to hang on to him. A few years later, when Charlie joined the Navy, his mother told him how she'd felt on that summer afternoon when he was thirteen as she heard his footsteps running past her. Charlie listened impassively; his mind recorded the words but his heart remained untouched. Words that might have meant something when he was a kid carried little weight now that he was almost a man.

He'd spent nineteen years alone and turned out okay.

Now it was his mother's turn.

Maybe things would have been different if his dad had lived. Maybe if he'd had someone to play catch with or go fishing or whatever the hell it was sons and fathers did together, maybe then things between him and his mother would've been easier. But no use wishing for things you couldn't have.

Charlie was doing what he was meant to do, what he'd wanted to do from the day he was born: he was running as fast as he could. He needed to belong some place, a place where he could be himself: loud and brash and imperfect.

If he couldn't find that place sailing around the world with the U.S. Navy, then that place just didn't exist.

THE AUDITORIUM LIGHTS dimmed and a fifteen-minute film on basic infant care began. Next to Charlie, his wife sighed happily and snuggled closer, her hand tucked into his. He didn't know exactly why he'd been thinking so much about his childhood lately, except for the obvious reason. Looking at Caroline, he thought of his mother, left on her own with a rambunctious young son and no idea how to handle him. It couldn't have been easy on Jean. In a way he wished he'd known that years ago when it could have mattered.

He wouldn't make those mistakes—or put Caroline in the position his mother had found herself. He was going to be there for his kid, even after the marriage was only a memory. *A deal is a deal,* he thought. They would stay married until after the baby's christening and then part as friends.

Even if he could no longer remember why they had said they would part.

CAROLINE HAD ENJOYED the seminar but the lecturer had been extremely thorough in her descriptions of the myriad things that could go wrong in the last trimester. Placenta previa, epidurals, and C sections were among the more minor inconveniences discussed.

Was it any wonder she found it impossible to fall asleep that night?

She eased herself out of bed, careful not to awaken Charlie. The baby gave her a sharp kick beneath her rib cage and she smiled as she reached for her robe. *You, too?* she thought, making her way down the hallway toward the kitchen. *All that talk about due dates make you hungry?*

There was something very pleasant about bustling around in the kitchen in the dead of night. Bathed in the glow from a small wall lamp, the kitchen looked warm and cozy and inviting. Charlie had rearranged the table and chairs and put them near the window. ''That'll give you room for a high chair," he'd said, pointing to the perfect spot.

She thought abut Jud and Sarah Winslow, a mid-thirtyish couple with whom they'd shared coffee after the workshop. The Winslows had every accoutrement known to man and woman, all of which were designed to make caring for the baby as effortless as possible. In fact, keeping life effortless seemed to be their goal. Caroline had been impressed by Jud's solicitude of his wife, noting the way the businessman held doors open for Sarah and massaged her shoulders when she complained of the tiniest bit of stiffness.

"He'll be marvelous in the labor room," Caroline had remarked when she and the other woman retired to the ladies' room. "You're fortunate to have such a caring husband."

The look Sarah shot her in the mirror had been comical. "Oh, Judson is marvelous when it comes to the preliminaries, but he's already informed me he'll be at the club when I'm in delivery."

"I'm sure he's joking."

"Not Jud." Sarah ran a brush through her dark hair. "He's a wonderful husband, please understand, but when the going gets tough, my Jud is the first to get going."

Caroline had been overcome by a wave of emotion—as intense as it was unexpected—and she leaned against the sink.

"Do you need to sit down?" asked Sarah.

"No," Caroline said. "I'm fine." How lucky she was to have a man like Charlie by her side for the long haul. He may not have Judson Winslow's education or sophistication, but he had something Winslow would never have: he had a heart.

The baby kicked her again, sharp and demanding, and she laughed softly. "Okay, okay. Warm milk coming right up."

She swung open the refrigerator door and pulled out a half-gallon carton. Leave it to Charlie. These days her refrigerator was well-stocked with essentials. As organized as she was about most things, she'd never been able to muster up the wherewithal to keep on top of grocery shopping. Maybe it was the years of trekking to the market as a little girl while her friends were outside skipping rope and playing with dolls, but she would rather bring home a deli sandwich than go supermarket shopping.

"You okay?"

She turned, cup of milk in hand, to find Charlie, rumpled and half asleep, in the doorway. "Oh, Charles," she said, warming her hands around the cup, "did I wake you up?"

He yawned and dragged his hand through his thick, dark hair. "I turned over to hold you and you weren't there. I thought—"

She smiled ruefully. "That workshop got to you, too, didn't it?"

He stumbled into the room and reached for the milk carton that still rested on the counter. "This was worse than that first trip to Dr. Burkheit's office."

"No," said Caroline, grabbing the milk from her husband and pouring it into a glass for him. "I'm afraid there was something even worse than this seminar."

He looked at her then started to laugh. "Coffee with the Winslows?" His voice was a perfect parody of upper-crust elocution.

Caroline eased herself into a kitchen chair and rubbed her belly in gentle circles. "Aprica strollers, English nannies, worrying about getting Junior into the right preschool." She met Charlie's eyes. "Frankly I thought I was going to be sick."

Charlie claimed the chair next to her. "Makes you wonder what they were thinking about when they—"

Caroline's laugh cut him short. "Makes you wonder what *we* were thinking about, too, doesn't it?"

He leaned forward and ruffled her feathery bangs. "We were thinking about each other. Nothing else."

She sighed, wishing his touch didn't cause all manner of emotions to rush through her body. "Look where it got us, Donohue."

He reached for her hand and drew her from her chair and onto his lap. "Any regrets?"

The baby moved and she placed her hand atop her stomach. "No regrets."

He rested his hand near hers, his long fingers splayed across her belly, lightly caressing. "Me neither," he said softly. "Not a one."

Poor Sarah Winslow, thought Caroline as she closed her eyes. A husband with an MBA from Harvard Business School was fine for some people, but a husband with a heart—now that was something worth bragging about.

A FEW DAYS LATER, Caroline and Charlie were on their way home from Quakerbridge Mall. Caroline had long since outdistanced normal-size panty hose and a quick trip to a maternity boutique had been in order. Charlie didn't have to be at O'Rourke's until four o'clock and he'd elected to drive Caroline. The fact that it was getting harder and harder for her to fit behind the wheel of her sports car was tactfully left unspoken. Besides, it was a glorious midwinter day. The sky was a deep, throbbing blue laced by wisps of cloud cover, and the lemon yellow sun was bright enough to bring an unexpected warmth to anyone lucky to be outside.

"Back roads or highway?" Charlie asked after they'd hunted down the elusive maternity panty hose.

"The former," said Caroline, struggling with her seat belt. "I love those winding, country roads."

"I know," he said, raising a dark brow. "Remember our wedding night when you led me to your place? I thought you were trying to lose me."

She started to laugh. "The truth?"

"Go ahead. I can take it."

"I was scared to death, Charles. I couldn't believe we were actually married. It was the last thing on earth I was looking for."

His laughter joined hers. "Don't think I was walking around with a wedding ring in my hip pocket looking for Cinderella."

She glanced at her belly. "Life has a way of surprising us, doesn't it?"

"Always," said Charlie. "That's the one thing you can count on."

The rolling farmlands were lightly encrusted with snow, sparkling now as it began to melt in the bright sunshine. Charlie switched on the radio to a golden oldies station, and his beloved Motown music filled the truck. Caroline opened the window a crack and sniffed the crisp clean air. She was glad to be alive, to be in this truck on this afternoon with this very special man beside her. She was totally at peace with herself, content with her life, not searching for anything more to—

"Charles! Stop the truck!"

With one swift motion Charles braked, sliding gently into the shallow drainage ditch alongside the road. "You in pain?" He reached for the CB on the dashboard. "I'll call the doctor. We can get to the hospital—"

She started to laugh. "I'm fine." She pointed toward a sign a few feet ahead. "They're having an antique sale."

He blew out a long, unsteady breath. "And for that you nearly kill us?"

"A cradle," she said, enumerating one item listed on the sign. "I'd love a cradle for the baby."

"You know antique is another word for junk, don't you?"

"Oh, come on, Donohue. Let's just see what they have."

Charlie looked as if he'd rather spend a weekend in hell, but he maneuvered the truck up the lane where, behind a grove of trees, they found the most beautiful restored farmhouse either one of them had ever seen. It boasted bay windows, a sloping lawn that led down to a tiny stream and a wraparound front porch that begged for a glider and a pitcher of lemonade. A For Sale sign was posted in the front yard with a smaller Owner Anxious sign attached beneath it.

"This is like something out of a movie," Caroline breathed as the owner, a woman in her fifties, showed them around. "How can you bear to sell?"

The woman shrugged. "It's not mine. My mother has moved to Phoenix and she wants to unload the property."

"And you're not interested?" asked Charlie.

"Who needs it?" the woman answered. "I have a condo in Bridgewater. I'd just as soon never do yard work again as long as I live."

The woman's attitude was less than welcoming but the house—well, that was a different story. "Look at that stone hearth," Caroline rhapsodized as they stood in the doorway to the great room. "Can you imagine it on a snowy day in January?"

"And that workroom in the basement," Charlie pointed out. "That would make three of the one I have in my house."

The woman quickly sized them up then pounced. "You two in the market for a place? With a new baby and all, you probably need some more room."

Some of the magic disappeared from the day. "I'm afraid we're fine where we are," said Caroline. "We're just fantasizing."

"Yeah," said Charlie. "We're only daydreaming out loud."

The woman lost interest as quickly as she'd gained it. "Well, if there's nothing you want . . ."

"The cradle," Caroline said. "You had a cradle listed outside."

"It's nothing much," said the woman with another of her shrugs. "Been in the family for God knows how long. Hundred years probably." Her laugh was quick and brittle as she led them into a room piled high with the accumulation of a long life. "Looks like it anyway."

Even Charlie was taken by the lustrous pine cradle. Age had only added to its glow. Not even the nicks and chips along the runners could take away from its aura of family, of history.

"We'll take it," he said, running his hand along the angels carved at the head.

"I didn't say how much."

He pulled out his wallet. "Whatever's fair."

"Fifty dollars?"

He peeled off two twenties and a ten. "You've got yourself a deal."

The woman cracked a smile. "Too bad you folks *aren't* looking for a house. I got the feeling we could've had ourselves one sweet deal."

Charlie wrapped the cradle up in some old blankets he kept in the rear of his truck. "Don't want to get it all banged up," he explained to Caroline. "Not before I can get to work on it."

"You really know how to refinish furniture?"

"Did a lot of the stuff in my house."

There it was again, another reminder of just how separate their lives really were. Married five months and she'd never once seen his place. She didn't even know the address or the phone number or whether he had curtains at his windows.

"Quarter for your thoughts."

"Oh, nothing much," she said, suppressing a sigh. "Just daydreaming again."

She pressed her cheek against the window glass, wishing they were in the farmhouse again and that it belonged to them.

ii

Before they knew it, it was Christmas Day. As always, Sam and Murphy's house was Holiday Central; family and friends spilled from each and every room. They tripped over each other in the hallway and shouted to be heard over the din of laughter and Christmas carols. The house was decorated with two Christmas trees, shiny green holly with plump red berries, garland and tinsel and the soft glow of luminaria candles lining the curving driveway. Sam's daughter Patty was everywhere, dispensing eggnog and presents and advice on everything from the proper way to roast a turkey to why biweekly mortgages were the wave of the future.

Caroline and Charlie had been positively swamped with presents, all of which were for the baby. Tiny sleepers and stacks of T-shirts. Crib sheets and blankets and an assortment of playsuits so small that both expectant parents found it difficult to believe a real, live human being would ever wear the garments.

"Leave it to you to turn Christmas Day into a baby shower," Caroline said in the kitchen after dessert. She gave Sam a warm hug. "You're too much."

"Surprised you, didn't I?" Sam waved a dish towel overhead in triumph. "Murphy and I fought about this since Halloween. He's the superstitious type—didn't want me to even tell anyone I was pregnant until I was in transition.'' She stopped and stared at her friend. ''You're *not* superstitious, are you?''

''Absolutely not. Burkheit says the baby and I are textbook cases.''

Sam leaned against the counter. ''So when are you going to tell them?''

Caroline didn't bother to pretend she didn't know exactly what her best friend was talking about: Caroline's family. ''Not yet.''

Sam gestured toward the telephone on the far wall. ''No time like the present.''

''Mind your own business, Sam,'' Caroline said. ''I'll tell them when I tell them.''

''Knowing you, you'll wait until the kid is in college.''

''If that's what I want to do, I'll do it.''

''Grow up,'' said Sam gently. ''They're your family. They have a right to know you're pregnant.''

Caroline was silent. She'd cut emotional ties with her mother and stepfather many years ago, the summer when they picked up and moved to Ohio and left Caroline behind. ''It's just for now, honey,'' Letty had said. ''Samantha's folks have a room for you. Once we get settled, we'll send you a train ticket.''

Summer had turned into fall. Fall became winter. And before Caroline knew it, she was in senior year of high school, still living at the Deans' house, still waiting for the train ticket that never came.

Now and then she'd get a call or letter from one of her half brothers or sisters, filled with details on some crazy new business venture he or she was embarking on. ''It's not that I need anything, Carly, it's just that you're a smart businesswoman and I wanted to give you a chance to get in on the ground floor.''

So far she'd been in on the ground floor of six aborted business schemes, two failed franchises and three ''loans'' that she knew darned well would never be repaid. She knew she didn't owe her siblings anything beyond a Christmas card each year—why, she had never even *met* the three who'd been born after the move to Ohio. Still, she sent elaborate presents to her mother and tried not to analyze exactly why she bothered.

No one had ever thought to invite her out to visit. They were probably afraid she'd stay.

"What does Charlie have to say about it?" asked Sam.

Caroline fiddled with a knob on the stove.

Sam stared at Caroline, eyes wide. "Don't tell me he agrees with you."

"I don't know whether he agrees with me or not," said Caroline with a note of defiance. "We haven't discussed the subject."

"You're kidding."

"Do I look like I'm kidding?"

"He must have some opinion, Caroline. I mean, these are his in-laws we're talking about."

"You realize this is none of your business, don't you?"

"I'm your best friend in the world," Sam shot back, "and if it's not my business, then I don't know whose business it is." Her gaze narrowed. "You're not ashamed of your background, are you?"

Caroline hesitated a beat too long. "Of course not."

Sam, however, knew better. Caroline had never quite gotten past the insecurities of childhood or the feeling of not being loved.

"What about Charlie's family? How do they feel about the baby?"

"I—I don't know."

"Don't tell me Charlie's keeping secrets, too."

"Ask him," said Caroline. "What he says or doesn't say to his family is his business."

"This is ridiculous. I don't understand any of it."

"We don't talk about families," Caroline said after a moment. "We don't talk about the past and we don't talk about the future."

"Then what in blazes *do* you talk about?"

Caroline thought for a second. "The present...the baby." She laughed uneasily. "World affairs...the baby."

Sam looked as if someone had let the wind out of her sails. "You're still going to go through with it, aren't you?"

Caroline's gaze dropped. "End the marriage?"

Sam nodded.

"We made a deal," said Caroline, her voice catching on the words. "You just don't go back on a deal."

Sam made a ferocious face. "I could tell you what I think of your deal."

"But you won't, will you, Sam?"

Sam's dark blue eyes searched Caroline's face for a long moment then she shrugged in resignation. "No, I won't," Sam said, "but that doesn't mean I'll quit hoping for a miracle."

As FOR CHARLIE, he'd airmailed his mother a Christmas card signed "Charlie and Caroline" and let it go at that. If she wanted to know who Caroline was, she could phone him or drop him a line. Not that he expected she would do either; Jean Donohue Liguori Latham had more important things to do than catch up on family gossip. After two divorces in quick succession, Jean had abandoned the notion of marriage-as-sport and settled into London society as the resident American-héiress-of-a-certain-age.

When she was younger, Jean had relied upon her beauty. Now that she was in her early sixties, she relied on her pocketbook and her charm. Even with Charlie.

Money came with strings attached, even money that was part and parcel of your family structure. As far as he was concerned, his mother could spend every last dollar, pound and sou—and welcome to it. Money hadn't caused the problem between Charlie and Jean and money wouldn't solve it. Maybe someday they'd find common ground upon which to stand, but that ground wouldn't be paved in gold. Anything he needed, he could earn with his own two hands. He often wondered if that was why his father had left in the first place. Too bad William Donohue had died before Charlie had had a chance to find out.

Caroline never talked about her family and she never asked about his. Charlie had taken her cue gratefully. She probably came from a background a hell of a lot like his, one of money and position and such basic bone-deep loneliness that it still hurt to think about it. Who needed the memories?

The past was painful. The future was a murky blur. The only thing real and wonderful was the present and, by mutual consent, that was where Caroline and Charlie dwelled.

BY THE WEEK after New Year's, it was apparent that a baby would soon be living in Caroline's fancy apartment. Now that the guest room was no longer Charlie's retreat, Caroline and Charlie were hard at work turning that sunny space into a nursery.

Nursery! Even the word sent ripples of excitement up and down her spine. Walt Disney wallpaper with fairy-tale borders. Crisp dotted-Swiss priscillas in butter yellow. A crib and a bassinet and more adorable little toys than she'd ever known existed. Charlie was still working on getting the cradle into shape; he'd taken over her utility room with his sanders and buffers, and the whirr of power tools competed with his favorite Motown music. Everywhere she looked she saw changes, wonderful changes happening as they prepared for the baby.

She was nearing the middle of her eighth month, twenty-plus pounds away from where she'd been on that night in June. Her back ached, her ankles were swollen, and she'd long since forgotten how it felt to look down and see her feet. She'd abandoned her beloved high heels in favor of more sensible flats, but it gladdened her soul to discover that style didn't have to take a backseat to her monumental belly. She played tricks with scarves and brooches, overshirts and stirrup pants, and the other pregnant women of the Princeton area continued to flock to Twice Over Lightly for the most glamorous outfits in the area.

It wasn't all wonderful, however. Heartburn plagued her, and the stretched-taut skin on her abdomen itched maddeningly. Sleep, her bosom buddy during the early months of her pregnancy, was harder to come by these days, since finding a comfortable position was akin to the search for the Holy Grail.

What did manage to find her, however, were nightmares. And not just your garden variety things-that-go-bump-in-the-night kind of nightmares. Caroline's were vivid, medical nightmares complete with every disaster that could befall a pregnant woman and, more terrifyingly, her child.

The days seemed to last forever. The nights went on for an eternity. *Hurry, baby,* she thought. *I just need to see that you're all right.*

ONE MORNING in the second week of January, Caroline awoke tired and snappish. Charlie was in the kitchen brewing decaf and whistling something vaguely Motown, and both the smell of the coffee and the off-key melody instantly got under her skin.

"*Please,* Charles," she said, waddling past him and reaching for a glass of orange juice. "It's too early."

"It's eight-fifteen," said Charlie in the obnoxiously cheerful way of a morning person. "You're already ten minutes behind schedule."

"Then I'd better adjust my schedule." She sipped the juice, wrinkled her nose then poured the rest down the sink. "It takes me more than ten minutes to maneuver my way out of bed in the morning. It's easier to dock an aircraft carrier."

He made a show of looking over her figure. "You look pretty good to me."

"Oh, quit it," she snapped. "I look like Shamu the Killer Whale."

"You're pregnant," he reasoned, not a man to recognize danger when he saw it. "How are you supposed to look?"

She sighed in exasperation. "Don't you know you're supposed to tell me I'm slim and gorgeous, Charles?"

He reached over and rubbed her enormous belly. Leave it to a man to highlight the obvious. "What's the matter? Bad night?"

"The worst." She eased herself down onto one of the kitchen chairs, aware of every ounce of her bulk. Drawing a deep breath was a distant memory. "I just wish this whole thing was over and done with." She regretted the words as soon as they took shape. "I mean, I'm so tired of being pregnant."

Unfortunately those words were no better than the first group she'd uttered. Charlie's smile faded and a dark expression clouded his vivid green eyes.

She rose from the chair with difficulty and walked over to where he stood by the stove. "I didn't mean it like that."

"Yeah? How did you mean it?"

"Look at me, Charlie," she said, gesturing toward her immense belly. "I'm enormous. This is like having a beanbag chair strapped to your waist."

"Now you're going to tell me you can't see your feet."

"Feet?" She laughed despite her black mood. "I'm not sure I have feet anymore."

"It won't be much longer," he said, reaching out and drawing her to him. "Less than two months and you'll be back to your old self."

"I don't think I'll ever be my old self." It was hard to even remember who her old self was.

"You know, I kind of like you this way."

She arched a brow. "Barefoot and pregnant? Oh, really, Charles..."

He shushed her with a quick kiss. "Friendly."

"I'm always friendly," she said. "Being friendly is what I do best."

"Not with me it isn't. You always acted like you couldn't stand the sight of me."

She didn't deny it. "You always acted as if you couldn't get far enough away from me. Every time I came into the bar, you disappeared into the back and never so much as poked your head out."

"Why bother?" he countered. "You would've chopped my head off if I dared to say hello to you."

She sighed. "I was that big a snob?"

"Worse," he said. "Even after that night in your store, you still acted as if we'd never done more than nod to each other."

She rested her head against his shoulder, thankful for his warmth and solid male presence. "You must admit the circumstances were anything but ordinary. I could just imagine what you thought of me."

"That you were easy?"

"Exactly."

"I know more about you than you realize, Caroline."

Her heartbeat accelerated. "What does that mean?" Had she left a photo album around, or a letter from one of her brothers or sisters? Worse yet, had Sam spilled the beans about Caroline's less than elegant childhood?

Charlie sensed the fear in her instantly and hurried to put her at ease. "You're a flirt," he said, "but I know that's as far as it goes."

She relaxed against him, her skittering heartbeat returning to normal. "Flirtation is a lost art," she said airily. "More women should practice their feminine wiles."

He recognized a closed subject when he saw one and he let Caroline pull herself together. He might know more about her than she realized, but he was smart enough to know he hadn't begun to scratch the surface. There was a deep sadness inside the woman he called his wife, a core of loneliness so fundamental to her personality that there were times when he wished he could kiss away that uncertainty he saw lurking beneath her bright and breezy facade.

But of course she'd never admit to such a thing. Not Caroline. She was the darling of O'Rourke's, the belle of Princeton shopkeepers, the most glamorous pregnant lady in all of central New Jersey. The fact that every now and then a scared little girl peered out from her big blue eyes wasn't something she would acknowledge, much less talk about.

There weren't many things in his life that Charlie regretted, but that morning he regretted that his marriage would be over before he really got to know his wife.

SOMETHING CHANGED between Caroline and Charlie after that odd morning. Another barrier between them had fallen, bringing them closer than either had ever imagined possible.

Neither one said anything about the change, but by mutual consent they spent all their free time together. Things she had always done alone, like grocery shopping and picking up the dry cleaning, became almost fun with Charlie along. Funny how she had once been so happy with her tightly controlled world. Her serene apartment. Her meals for one. The absolute certainty that she would never marry or even want to.

This isn't forever, a voice warned her as they went off to the supermarket one evening. *Don't go getting used to keeping his favorite foods in the house.* Once the baby was born it would be back to her old life, her old ways. After all, it was what she wanted, wasn't it?

Charlie made grocery shopping an epic performance. Caroline didn't often go to the supermarket but when she did she was a methodical shopper, not given to impulse buying. She bought exactly what she wanted, price be damned, and got in and out of the store in record time.

Not Charlie.

Charlie was the perfect consumer. Shiny displays of candy bars drew him like a magnet. Popcorn. Cracker Jack.

"Oh, Charles," she groaned as he put a jar of Marshmallow Fluff in the shopping cart. "I haven't seen that glop since I was a little girl."

He grinned at her. "I'm surprised. I didn't figure you'd *ever* seen Marshmallow Fluff."

Careful, Caroline, she warned herself. *Dangerous territory.* She reached for a jar of hot chutney, one with a terribly British label.

"Chutney?" he asked. "Who the hell eats chutney?"

"Heathen," she said, putting the jar in her basket. "All enlightened diners enjoy chutney."

He cast a dubious glance at an entire row of various chutneys. "What is it?"

Caroline moved down the aisle. "You eat it with curry."

"I didn't ask what you eat it with. I asked what it's made of."

"Oh, this and that."

"You don't know." It was a statement, not a question.

"Of course I know." She didn't really. The only thing she was certain of where chutney was concerned was that it carried a certain upper-crust cachet.

He darted around to the front of the cart and stopped her in her tracks. "So tell me."

She giggled at the sight of her handsome, muscular husband playing traffic cop in the condiments aisle. "It's late, Charlie. We have shopping to do."

"I want to know what's in chutney."

Her gaze slid casually to the jar resting on its side in the basket of her cart. Most of the label was hidden but she was able to make out a word or two. "Sugar," she offered. "A little sugar."

He grabbed the jar and held it behind his back. "Okay. *Now* tell me what else is in the stuff."

"Snakes and snails and puppy dog tails. I have no idea. Are you satisfied now?"

"You eat it but you don't know what it is."

"You eat frankfurters from Dynamite Dogs and I'll bet you don't know what's in them."

His green eyes were twinkling with mischief and she felt the day's fatigue drop away from her. "Let's make a pact," he said, extending his right hand. "I don't introduce the kid to Dynamite Dogs and you don't introduce him to chutney."

"You drive a hard bargain, Charles." She extended her hand and they shook on it.

Charlie grabbed the cart from her and pushed it to the checkout line. Caroline walked behind him, enjoying the way his muscles bunched then relaxed as he maneuvered the cart through the crowd. *This is marriage, too,* she thought, glancing at the other couples stocking up for the weekend. Everyday things like shopping for food and doing laundry and even debating about chutney and Marshmallow Fluff. Sexual chemistry was wonderful, it was true, but it seemed to Caroline that it was the more mundane facts of life that provided the true foundation of a marriage.

"Any coupons?" asked the cashier.

Caroline shook her head. "Afraid not."

The cashier frowned. "Better start clipping 'em, honey. Once the baby comes you'll be glad you learned how to pinch a penny."

Charlie looked at Caroline and winked. "We'll start tomorrow," he told the cashier.

Caroline smiled and looked down at her jar of chutney nestled companionably next to Charlie's Marshmallow Fluff and for a few wonderful minutes she was able to pretend they were just another married couple out grocery shopping on a Friday night—and that there were an endless number of Friday nights stretching out into their future.

THE DAYS passed swiftly.

Caroline put in less time at Twice Over Lightly and Charlie put in more time at home. They faithfully attended Lamaze classes and Charlie proved to be a demanding but compassionate coach. Caroline felt closer to Charlie than she had ever felt to anyone in her life but there were still barriers between them, barriers that could never be toppled.

So much of who and what she was could never be shared with him without exposing her deepest insecurities. Carly Bradley was never far from the surface and there were times when Caroline almost felt that Charlie could see the girl beneath the woman. She tried to pull back, to be less willing to lean on him as her pregnancy advanced, but there was something so wonderful about his strong male presence that her attempts to distance herself failed miserably.

She told herself it wasn't weakness on her part, the way she turned to Charlie so often and in so many ways. She needed someone to lean on, for her sense of physical well-being was shaky at best. Going to work in the morning had become a feat of monumental proportions, and she was thrilled when a late January blizzard blew across central

New Jersey and snowed them in. Putting on makeup and panty hose was more than she could contemplate.

"Forget it," said Charlie, looking out the window at the foot of snow blanketing the landscape. "Nobody's going anywhere today."

Caroline breathed a sigh of relief. "Wonderful," she said, settling back amidst the sofa cushions. "I'm going to sit here all day and do nothing but read magazines and drink hot chocolate." She reached for her cup and winced. "Ouch! I must have pulled a muscle."

He turned away from the window and saw her massaging the base of her spine. "Your back?"

"Yes. No. Well, actually I'm not sure." She frowned and arched her back as far as her swollen belly would allow. "I feel a tingling sensation. Almost a tugging."

A thousand different thoughts, none of them pleasant, occurred to Charlie as he tried to stay calm. "You don't think you're in labor, do you?"

That, at least, brought a smile to her face. "Good heavens, no. We have another month to go."

"Yeah, well, babies don't always come with timetables." He hadn't forgotten that list of possible disasters he'd read about in the doctor's office months ago.

"I just slept funny," she said, taking a sip of cocoa. "That's all it is."

Charlie nodded but he wasn't convinced. She didn't look like herself. There were circles under her eyes and her complexion was paler than he'd ever seen it. She'd been restless these past few nights and twice he'd heard her moaning in her sleep.

"Don't look at me that way, Donohue. You're making me nervous."

"I'm concerned," he said, trying to downplay his anxiety. "Maybe we should call Burkheit."

"For what?" she asked. "Because I have a backache? Don't be silly. I'm sure I'll be fine in a few hours."

He nodded. No point in continuing the conversation. If he told her how he was really feeling, he'd scare the daylights out of her, and that wouldn't be good for either his wife or their baby.

So he went into the kitchen, picked up the telephone and called the doctor himself.

"I'm concerned but not alarmed," said Dr. Burkheit. "Has her water broken?"

"Not that I know of."

Burkheit laughed heartily. "Trust me, Charlie. You'd know about it." He grew more serious. "Any bleeding?"

"No." *Thank God.*

"This could be the real thing or it could be a dress rehearsal. We might even have miscalculated her due date." He went on to explain that Caroline might have conceived a month earlier than they'd believed; Charlie didn't bother to tell him that was impossible. "Call me in another two hours—sooner, if she starts bleeding."

Charlie hung up the telephone, only to find Caroline standing in the doorway.

"Who were you on the phone with?" she asked, in the tone of voice that he knew meant trouble.

"Burkheit." Why lie? It was too important.

"How dare you," she said, her voice thin and strained, "especially after I told you not to."

His hackles went up at her words but he reminded himself these were extraordinary circumstances and swallowed his annoyance. "Sorry you're mad," he said easily, "but I felt it was important."

Her expression wavered between anger, fear and curiosity. "Wh-what did he say?"

"He thinks everything's fine. He wants you to rest and for me to call him again in two hours."

She nodded, eyes closing for an instant. "I'm sorry I snapped at you. I'm overtired."

He crossed the room and draped an arm around her shoulder. "Go back to bed for awhile," he suggested. "Maybe you can get some sleep."

"Will you come to bed, too?"

He nodded. "Sure."

Once in bed she dozed fitfully, her breathing labored and shallow. Sleeping on her stomach had been impossible for months, and so now she was sleeping on her side. She lay flat on her back, with her hands folded across her belly, and his heart ached at the distended swelling of her breasts and stomach. Her delicate skin was stretched taut, the veins in her breasts highly visible, and it looked as if it hurt simply to draw a breath.

Despite the coolness of the bedroom, beads of sweat formed on her brow and in the valley between her breasts. Gently he placed a hand against her belly and moved it in circles. The baby was quiet inside her womb; normally it kicked hard against Charlie's hand at the slightest pressure against Caroline's abdomen. Knife blades of apprehension skidded along his spine.

Everything's okay, he thought as he watched the clock tick away the one hundred twenty minutes until he called Dr. Burkheit again. *In a little while, things will be back to normal.*

BY LATE AFTERNOON they both knew her days of being a textbook case were over. The pain had intensified from a subtle tugging to a deep ache at the midpoint of her back. Charlie spoke to Dr. Burkheit twice more and each time the obstetrician advised a cautious, watch-and-wait approach.

"It's worth your life out there," Burkheit said during their last conversation, referring to the vicious snowstorm that was buffeting the area. "I'd rather she stay put as long as she can. These are probably Braxton-Hicks contractions. I'm not worried, but call me again in an hour."

Charlie couldn't settle down and concentrate on anything. He paced the length of the living room like a caged tiger, trying to fight his fears with perpetual motion. Caroline spent most of the afternoon catnapping, awakening only to use the bathroom and force down some hot soup that Charlie prepared. She could no longer manage to keep up a brave front. Bravado had no place in the scheme of things any longer. Her face was pinched and drawn, her expression tense.

Around four o'clock she wandered into the kitchen where Charlie was beating holy hell out of some innocent eggs. "That's a full-fledged blizzard we're having out there, isn't it?" she asked.

Charlie glanced out the window as if he hadn't been cursing every inch of snow that fell. "Looks like it to me."

"What if—what will we do if the doctor needs to see me?"

Charlie muttered a curse as some egg yolk splashed onto the countertop. "Let Burkheit come here. He's not eight months pregnant."

"I don't think he makes house calls."

"Then this could be a first." He put down his whisk and took a good look at her. "Are you telling me things have gotten worse?" His insides quaked like the bare trees in the storm outside.

"I was only wondering," she said, her voice thin. "Just in case." Turning, she made to leave then grabbed the back of a chair for support. "Charles... something's happening." She looked down at her legs. "I'm wet all over."

Oh, God, he thought. *This is it.* "Your water's breaking." He struggled to remember what he'd heard about the occurrence. "Don't worry. I'll get some towels while you call the doctor." *It's happening. The baby's coming....*

He turned to leave the room when something caught his eye. "Caroline." This time it was his own voice that sounded shaky. "Sit down."

She looked at him blankly. He rushed to her side and helped her onto a kitchen chair.

"Sit tight," he ordered. "I'll be right back."

"The towels," she said, closing her eyes. "Get the towels."

He ran to the bedroom and picked up the phone.

"Doctor," he said the minute Burkheit answered. "My wife is bleeding."

iii

Charlie drove Caroline to the hospital. His truck had four-wheel drive and under normal conditions he loved driving in snow. This, however, was anything but normal.

He'd carried her into the bathroom before they left and helped her get cleaned up. She was bleeding heavily and a chill ran through him at the sight. He'd never seen so much blood before. *Don't let this happen,* he prayed as he bundled her up and put her in the truck. *God, if you can hear me, don't let me lose them.*

Nothing seemed real or familiar as he drove to the hospital. He knew these roads as he knew his own name or social security number, but with everything blanketed with a thick layer of snow, he felt as if he'd been abandoned in a strange town without a map.

"Hold on," he told Caroline as they neared the hospital. "Burkheit's waiting for us. You're going to be fine."

"The baby," she whispered. "They have to save the baby...."

Her tears glistened in the reflected light from the street lamps. He wanted to brush those tears away, kiss her and tell her nothing bad would happen but he couldn't. His hands gripped the wheel in a vise lock and he didn't dare risk a break in concentration. The roads were slick with snow and ice and the visibility was just about zero. He couldn't think about the baby now. If he thought about the baby he'd never be able to meet his wife's eyes and tell her everything would be just fine.

CAROLINE'S HEART beat wildly as Charlie stopped the truck and ran around to the passenger side to help her out. Two E.R. technicians skidded down a ramp with a stretcher and pushed Charlie out of the way.

"No!" Snowflakes fell into her eyes and mouth. "I want my husband."

"Be a good girl," said the female technician. "Hubby can follow right behind."

"I'm here," said Charlie, reaching for Caroline's hand. "Nobody's going to get rid of me."

She clung to his hand with all the strength in her. Snow swirled around her head as they carried the stretcher up the ramp and into the warmth of the hospital. All the planning and practicing. The Lamaze classes and the endless nights of dreaming.

"It's not supposed to be like this," she said to Charlie as the admissions clerk entered their health care numbers into her computer.

He knelt on the floor next to the stretcher. Snowflakes glittered in his jet black hair and she remembered the first time she'd seen him, so big and strong, behind the counter at O'Rourke's. "I'm with you," he said, pressing kisses against her forehead and nose and lips. "I'm not going anywhere until you and the baby can come with me."

Dr. Burkheit, already in his surgeon's scrubs, burst through the double doors. His smile was broad but the expression in his eyes was grave and concerned. "Couldn't resist a drive in the snow, could you, Caroline?"

She struggled to summon up a grin. "You know me, Dr. Burkheit. Always living dangerously." *Too close to the bone,* she thought as her words floated in the air. She didn't want to live dangerously at all. She wanted to be back, safe and sound, in her home with their baby growing bigger and stronger with each day that passed.

"We're going to take a look at you in the examining room," Burkheit said in his easy manner. "I know it's tough, but try to relax and we'll have some answers very shortly."

He motioned for the technicians to wheel the stretcher bearing Caroline into the first examining room beyond the double doors. Charlie made to help but Burkheit shook his head. "You wait out here, Charlie. I'll get back to you in a few minutes."

"The hell with that," said Charlie. "I go wherever she goes."

Burkheit said something low, too low for Caroline to hear.

"What was that?" she asked. "What did he say, Charles?"

Charlie bent down and brushed another kiss against her forehead. "You know hospital regulations. They're worried about their insurance policies."

"You'll stay here?" she asked, clutching his hand. "You won't go away."

"I promise."

Satisfied, she nodded and the technicians wheeled her through the double doors and into a cold and sterile examining room. A pleasant-faced nurse came in and introduced herself as Lisa. "It's freezing in here," she said. "Don't you wish we had a fireplace?"

Caroline forced a chuckle. "Maybe we could roast some marshmallows."

Burkheit entered the room and she heard the snaps as he rolled on his rubber gloves. "Okay now, let's take a look and see where we stand."

She shivered as the nurse gently removed her pants and draped her with a sheet.

"Bleeding's slowed down," the doctor said after a moment. "I see evidence of some clotting..." He pressed against her abdomen and she suppressed a moan. "That hurt?" She nodded, biting her lip. "And this?" She nodded again. He pressed a stethoscope to her abdomen.

"Can you hear the baby's heartbeat?" she asked.

"Yes," he said. Just yes. Nothing more.

Her own heartbeat accelerated dangerously. "What is it? What's wrong? Doctor, please—"

The doctor pushed back from the table and stripped off his rubber gloves. "We're going to do an ultrasound, Caroline." The jovial smile had been replaced by grim seriousness. "I think we're dealing with a case of placenta abruption."

"What does that mean? Is it dangerous? The baby—"

He rested a hand on her arm. "I'm not going to lie to you, Caroline. It's very dangerous, especially considering the blood you've already lost."

"I don't care about myself. Just tell me about the baby."

"I can't," he said. "Not yet."

Her mind raced like a runaway train as they took her to the room where they'd administer the ultrasound test. This wasn't really happening...not the pain or the blood...not the gel on her belly...or the quiet concern of the technicians administering the test. Things like this didn't happen to her...not in the perfectly ordered life she'd created for herself...not after she'd worked so hard to make a success of everything she touched.

Oh, God, Charlie, she thought. *What on earth are we going to do?*

CHARLIE HAD NEVER FELT so alone in his life. Caroline was somewhere beyond those swinging doors, maybe not more than fifty feet away from where he paced. She might as well have been on the moon, for all the good it did. He felt disconnected, rootless, terrified. As if everything he'd believed to be true in this world had suddenly been exposed as lies, lies and more lies.

"First child?" asked the receptionist.

He nodded, unsure of his voice.

"These things happen," she said, pouring herself a cup of coffee from the electric coffee maker on her desk. "Nature's way."

He wanted to fly across that desk and wrap the cord around her scrawny neck. Nature's way. This was his wife she was talking about, his child. Not some damn statistic found in a medical book. What the hell was taking them so long in there? Either she was in labor or she wasn't. He didn't know which to hope for.

The double doors swung open and Burkheit swept toward him.

"It's what I thought," the doctor said without preamble. "Placenta abruption."

Why the hell didn't doctors talk so you could understand them? "Meaning what?"

Burkheit explained that the placenta had separated from the uterus prior to the beginning of labor, thereby cutting the developing baby off from its oxygen and nourishment. "We don't know if it's a complete separation or not, but I have reason to believe it might be."

"Can you reattach it?"

He shook his head. "Caroline's losing too much blood."

And, of course, the unspoken words were that the baby was losing too much time.

"We could induce labor and let Caroline deliver vaginally, but I don't think that's in anyone's best interest."

"A cesarean?"

"I think it's our only alternative."

"And Caroline will be okay?"

"I'm positive.'

Part of Charlie relaxed. "And the baby—he'll be okay, too?"

Dr. Burkheit waited a beat too long. His silence told Charlie everything he didn't want to hear. "I don't know, Charlie," said the doctor. "I simply don't know."

"I'll tell her," said Charlie, squaring his shoulders. "I should be the one to break the news."

"I don't mind being the one," said Burkheit, looking at him closely. "Sometimes it's best if an outsider does it."

"No." Charlie was adamant. "It's the least I can do for my wife."

Burkheit sighed and rubbed his eyes. "Come on," he said, leading Charlie toward the swinging doors. "Time's wasting."

CAROLINE KNEW the moment she saw Charlie's expression.

"The baby," she whispered as he sat down on the edge of the bed. "Is the baby—"

He shook his head but she noted the way his Adam's apple worked as he swallowed hard. "So far, so good." He took her hands in his, rubbing them to bring back the circulation. "In fact it looks like we'll be meeting him sooner than we planned."

"I'm not in labor," she said slowly. Then, "A cesarean?"

Charlie nodded. "Inducing labor's too dicey. Burkheit wants to make it as easy on you and the baby as he possibly can." He explained what he understood about placenta abruption.

"It's bad, isn't it?"

His voice was fiercely protective. "You're going to be fine."

"And the baby?"

He hugged her as close as the IV would allow. "It's going to work out. Just wait and see."

You don't believe it, do you, Charlie? You're as scared as I am. She buried her face against his shoulder and thanked

God that for the first time in her life she didn't have to brave the unknown by herself.

THERE WAS SOME TALK about allowing Charlie to be in surgery for the delivery, but he hadn't completed the Lamaze classes and no one knew how he would handle it without adequate preparation. Besides, there was the very real danger to Caroline and their baby to consider.

Charlie didn't know what to do with himself. They said that, barring complications, the procedure would be over in less than a half hour, and he would be reunited with Caroline and the newborn before he knew it.

Thirty minutes passed.

Then thirty more.

He paced the floor of the waiting room, his gut twisting with a growing sense of dread. With each quarter hour that slid by, his hopes for a happy ending dimmed another degree.

Finally, a little before eight o'clock, Dr. Burkheit strode down the corridor toward him. Charlie stood perfectly still, as if someone had nailed him to the floor tiles. It was a good thing breathing was a reflex action because he doubted if he had the brain power at the moment to do it on his own.

Burkheit placed his arm on Charlie's shoulder. "Your wife is fine. She's tired but she's fine."

Charlie felt as though his knees were going out from under him and he willed himself to stay upright. "And the baby?"

A faint smile broke through Burkheit's fatigue. "A beautiful baby girl, just under five pounds. She's in respiratory distress, Charlie. We're doing everything we can."

An oceanic roar pounded in his ears. He vaguely heard Burkheit's talk of immature lungs and threat of pneumonia, but nothing made sense. He struggled to zero in on exactly what the doctor was saying.

" . . . in an isolette. We have the best neonatal care in the state right here. The next seven days will tell the story."

"Does Caroline know?"

Burkheit nodded. "She was conscious during the delivery."

"How did she take it?"

Burkheit considered the question. "You know your wife better than I. She's a strong woman."

AT THE MOMENT Caroline was feeling anything but strong. Pain from her incision tore through her middle but that was nothing compared to the pain slicing through her heart. A daughter. A baby girl. *Their child.* Somewhere in the bowels of the hospital her baby was all alone and frightened, taken from Caroline too early.

They promised she'd be able to see the baby very soon, but each instant was an eternity to Caroline. Her breasts ached for the child.

She struggled to sit upright in the hospital bed. If she could just see the baby, she would feel better. Grabbing onto the lowered railing for support, she swung her legs over the side. She was hooked up to an IV, but she'd noticed other women wheeling the trolley behind them like a shopping cart. She could do that. She *had* to do it even if the world was spinning around her like a child's top.

"What the hell?" came a familiar voice from the doorway.

"Charlie!" She swayed on her feet and he caught her before she had a chance to fall.

He cradled her in his arms, holding her tightly against his chest, careful not to dislodge the IV. "It's all right," he murmured. "I'm here. It's gonna be all right."

"I'm sorry," she said, sobs tearing through her body. "Dear God, I'm sorry."

"It's not your fault . . . it's not anybody's fault." He stroked her hair away from her face.

She cried until there were no more tears left. Her body ached from fear and sorrow. "I want to see her."

"You need your rest, Caroline."

"I have to see her. You can't stop me! I have to see where she is . . . if she's crying . . . I have to, Charlie!"

Charlie tried to convince her to rest but Caroline was adamant. He went off in search of a nurse. They needed a stretcher or a wheelchair or something to transport Caroline to the nursery, and the truth was, he prayed the hospital would put its collective foot down and tell Caroline she had to get some sleep before she saw the baby.

There weren't many things in life that scared Charlie. Seeing his newborn baby daughter in an incubator, fighting for survival, was one of them.

The head nurse on the maternity ward was less than thrilled with his request, but after speaking with his unstoppable wife, she relented. "Five minutes," she warned. "No more than that."

Charlie grunted his assent as he helped Caroline into the wheelchair. Her beautiful face was set in lines of pain. Each time he rolled the chair over a small bump in the tiled floor her sharp intake of breath tore at his gut. That was nothing, however, compared with the emptiness in his heart as he thought of the baby.

"You won't be able to see much," warned the nurse in charge of preemies. "She's in the isolette on the left, near the back."

He nodded. He didn't want to see much. Hell, he didn't want to see her at all. He didn't want to get to know his daughter only to lose her.

Caroline pressed her face against the glass, cooing soft, unintelligible words of love. Charlie looked at the ceiling, the light fixtures, the clock on the wall, but not once did he look at his little girl.

SAM, OF COURSE, was the first person they told about the baby's premature arrival. "How serious is it?" she asked Charlie while Caroline was being examined by Dr. Burkheit.

Charlie glanced toward Caroline's room, as if to make certain she wasn't standing in the doorway listening. "Pretty serious, Sam."

Sam's eyes closed for an instant.

He coughed to clear his throat. "Listen, I—it doesn't seem right that her family doesn't know about the baby. I mean, things might be over—what I'm trying to say is, I think we should tell her parents." He'd tried phoning his mother in London but her housekeeper said Jean was on the continent. He wondered what she'd think when she got the message.

"Do you want me to call them?" Sam asked.

"I guess that's the best way. They probably don't even know about me."

Sam patted his arm. "Don't take it personally, Charlie. It's a complicated situation."

"I figured that," he said.

She embraced him warmly. "Don't give up. Miracles happen every day."

"Yeah," he said. "So I've heard."

Caroline gained strength over the next two days; the baby, however, continued to struggle. "She's a fighter," said Dr. Burkheit. "That counts more than you know." They had a scare the first night when the baby stopped breathing in her sleep, setting off alarms at the nurse's station. Dr. Burkheit brought in a specialist from Philadelphia and was in phone contact with another from New York City. There was talk about a new treatment, a surfactant to lubricate the baby's lungs, that could be the answer to their prayers, but they had to track down the physician in Los Angeles who'd pioneered its development.

And all through it, she believed. In her whole life she had never believed in anything as wholeheartedly as she believed that their baby daughter would live. From somewhere deep inside her soul she discovered a wellspring of strength and hope that startled her with its intensity. All things are possible, a small voice whispered. Even being happy.

Charlie was at the hospital more often than not, but in body only. She knew his heart was far away. There was an empty look in his eyes, a hollowness that made her feel cold and lonely. She longed to hold him in her arms and tell him that everything would be fine, that their little girl would grow up to be healthy and strong, but she knew she hadn't the right. The baby's birth had signaled the close of their relationship, and she was acutely aware that the end was in sight. And she couldn't fault him. Not really. He had been there for her during her pregnancy. He'd been beside her during this crisis. It wasn't anyone's fault if reality was rearing its ugly head, reminding them that they were two separate people who had been brought together only to give life to this very special child. There would be no happy endings for them as a couple. Only as parents.

One miracle seemed all that was in the works for them.

She spent all her time gazing through the window of the nursery, praying for a sign that the worst was over. Charlie spent his time in the hallway, drinking coffee. He was keeping an emotional distance that made her ache with loneliness for those sweet months they'd shared as they prepared for the baby. Her optimism began to give way to a dark sense of foreboding that clouded her vision like a heavy fog.

Talk to me, Charlie, she thought as she watched him pace the hallway. *I can help you . . . we can help each other.* But Charlie maintained his distance and Caroline maintained her silence.

Sam popped up at the hospital a couple of times a day. Murphy and Scotty and Bill O'Rourke all showed up one night, three painfully self-conscious males without the slightest idea what to say. *You're not alone,* thought Caroline. *I don't know what to say, either.* She did her best to keep conversation light and breezy, dancing as far away from the topic of her baby as possible. Sam looked hurt, Scotty confused. Bill O'Rourke tried to bumble his way through with well-meant advice that his son, Murphy, quickly cut off at the pass.

Charlie was terse with his friends. Uncommunicative. She saw the way Bill's brow furrowed when he looked at his short-order cook, and the worried look on Scotty's face spoke volumes.

She'd spent the past six months as an almost-wife. Now her breasts were heavy with milk, but she had no child to hold close and nurse. All her life, it seemed, she had been struggling to be something that the fates had decreed she shouldn't be. In grammar school she'd wanted to be like the other girls. In college, she'd pretended to be from the leisure set. Self-confident. Flirtatious. Without a care in the world.

All lies. The ex-husband she'd made up from whole cloth simply to sound glamorous. The finishing schools. The trips to Europe and the exotic friends she'd invented just so she could fit into her chosen world. Same as she'd invented a family who loved her and cared about her future and supported her hopes and dreams.

She thought of the classes, the planning, the Lamaze breathing—ultimately none of it had mattered a damn. *You should have known better,* she thought with a bitter laugh. Of all people, she should have known family happiness wasn't in the cards for her.

She'd pictured herself and Charlie timing her contractions, the *I Love Lucy*-esque race to the hospital complete with a comical race to the delivery room. And, oh, how she'd wanted Charlie to rub her back and encourage her and be there to hear their baby's first cry. They'd shared so much these past months—good moods and bad moods, their hopes and their fears—and now that they could truly be a comfort to each other as their baby girl struggled for life, they were once again strangers.

Finally she felt strong enough to tackle creating a strong and wonderful family for herself and her daughter. A *real* family, not the product of her imagination but the product of love and hard work and commitment.

A family with Charlie right there at the center of it.

"Damn," she whispered into her pillow. "Damn, damn, damn."

"Caroline?"

She looked up to see Dr. Burkheit shadowed in the doorway—and a lump rose into her throat.

AS FOR CHARLIE, he was living in a state of suspended animation. He ate and slept like a normal human being, but he was operating on instinct, not intellect. He was numb inside. Cold as the dead branches on the trees outside his window. He knew he should say or do something to ease Caroline's pain but beyond spending his days at the hospital, he had nothing to offer her. An overwhelming sense of guilt overrode everything, even his fear.

He was glad he hadn't taken a good look at the baby. Glad he couldn't place a tiny face to the dreams and hopes he'd had for the future. Glad that he hadn't shared those dreams and hopes with Caroline only to see them turn to ashes before their eyes.

He swore softly and threw one of his running shoes the length of the workroom in the basement of his house in Rocky Hill.

"So now what?" he asked the empty room a week after the baby's birth. How did you go about dismantling a marriage that had never had a chance to begin with? Did he wait for Caroline to broach the subject or did he bite the bullet and get it out in the open now before it got harder to do? The christening, they'd originally said. After the christening, the deal was off. Now it was anybody's guess if the baby would even live.

He felt as if someone was cracking his rib cage open like a shell, exposing his vulnerable, beating heart to the world.

The best night of his life had been the one he'd spent with Caroline in that ridiculous makeshift fur vault in the back of her dress shop. Nothing in his privileged childhood or adventurous youth came close to the wonder he'd found in her arms. To think that out of that one impetuous—and, yes, irresponsible—encounter had come seven wonderful months. He'd give anything if he could turn back the clock to those days between Christmas and New Year's when he'd believed they just might have a chance.

But that chance was gone. All they had in common was that tiny bundle of humanity who struggled for life at the hospital, and if that small life flickered out—

The shrill blare of the phone upstairs jerked him back to reality. He took the rickety basement steps two at a time and grabbed the receiver on the fifth ring.

"Charlie?" It was Bill O'Rourke.

"Yeah, Bill." *You're a jerk, Donohue,* he thought. How could it have been Caroline when she didn't even know where he lived? "What's up?"

"I have a message for you from Caroline."

An iron fist grabbed him by the lungs. "The baby—?"

Bill hesitated. "I don't know. She just asked me to track you down and tell you to get to the hospital pronto."

"How did she sound?"

"Just go to the hospital," said Bill.

THE WONDER WAS he hadn't killed himself on the drive to the hospital. Regret ate at his gut like a cancer. Why hadn't he looked at their baby? Why hadn't he touched her cheek? Why had he let her brief time on earth slip by without acknowledgment?

He grabbed a spot in the parking garage then zoomed through the lobby full speed.

"Slow down," said a security guard. "You're running like the demons of hell are at your heels."

Charlie said nothing. The demons of hell had nothing on the pain of what might have been.

Caroline, dressed in slippers and a silky robe, met him at the elevator on the maternity floor. "Come with me," she said, taking his hand.

His fear downshifted into uncertainty. "Where are we going?"

"To the nursery."

He stopped in his tracks. "What's wrong? Don't try to soften it for me."

"Shut up and keep moving, Donohue." She walked slowly, thanks to the cesarean, but with determination and in moments they were standing in front of the glass window.

"That," she said, pointing to a tiny baby in the first isolette, "is your daughter." The pride and love in her voice were unmistakable. "You haven't looked at her before, have you, Donohue?"

He shook his head. *She's alive. You still have a chance.*

"You're going to look at your daughter," she ordered. "Right now. I'm going to make sure you do. She deserves better than this, and I'm not going to let you shortchange her another minute."

You don't know what you're asking, he thought. He wasn't brave or strong or any of the things a father should be. All he knew about fathering you could fit on the head of a pin. His own dad had skipped town the first possible moment. His stepfathers had been more interested in golf than going to Little League. The sum total of his parenting knowledge came from library books, *Father Knows Best* and *The Cosby Show,* with a touch of Hallmark cards, for good measure.

He took a deep breath then looked through the glass. At first his vision was all cloudy, as if he was peering through a scrim. He swallowed then blinked his eyes, taking in rapid-fire impressions. A shock of jet black hair like his. A tiny, perfect mouth like Caroline's. Froggy legs moving against the mattress to a rhythm all her own. "She's so small." His voice caught on the last word. "I could hold her in the palm of my hand." An exaggeration, perhaps, but he had never felt bigger—or more helpless—in his life.

"And perfect," said Caroline. "You forgot to say perfect."

"And perfect." He smiled for the first time in days. "Her eyes are blue like yours."

"All babies have blue eyes at first," she said.

"Is she . . . will she—" He couldn't form the words. The fear inside him was so great that it rendered him speechless.

"She'll be fine," said Caroline, tears glittering in her blue eyes. "The worst is over."

He heard the words as she told him about the wonders of modern medicine, about the strength of their baby girl. One day it would all make sense to him, but for now he could only nod and struggle to keep his heart on its sleeve where it belonged.

And that's when it hit him. A violent wave of emotion rushed over his body, washing away everything else but the intense, primal joy of knowing he had helped give life to the baby girl who looked at him through the glass. That delicate little face, that beautiful little girl, would be part of his heart and soul all the days of his life.

"Oh, God," he said, lowering his head to hide his tears. "She's going to be all right."

The sight of her big strong husband crying with joy over their baby girl was Caroline's undoing. Her tears flowed freely, and somehow she found herself in Charlie's arms, the two of them hugging and laughing—all the wonderful sharing and celebrating she'd imagined would be part of the birth of their baby.

"She's one week old, Charles," said Caroline, "and it's time we called her something besides 'the baby' and 'our daughter.'" *And it's time to talk about the future, Charlie, a future we can share together. . . .*

He couldn't think. He was pure emotion.

"She has the map of Ireland on her face," Caroline continued, nervous and hopeful both. "I was thinking that Erin is a beautiful name for a little girl."

Erin Bradley Donohue. The best of both of them was there, in that beautiful baby girl, for all the world to see.

There'd be time enough later to understand the hows and whys and the miracles of medicine and good genes. Glib old Charlie, everybody's pal, stood there without a thing to say.

This was it. The moment that could change the rest of their lives. Those hopes and dreams he'd entertained these past seven months flooded over him and washed away his fears. Now was the time to declare himself, put his cards on the table, ask her if what they'd had together on a temporary basis could be the foundation for something lasting, something wonderful, something—

"Son!" came a smoky voice from the doorway. "Isn't it time you introduced me to your bride?"

hard-working businessman...and if that meant...that his mother could spend every last dollar, pound and euro—and welcome to it. Money hadn't caused the

Endings and Beginnings

i

"It's bad enough I discover you're married via a hastily written Christmas card," the woman said, gliding into the room, all Givenchy and Gucci, "but to hide my first grandchild from me is unconscionable."

Caroline, mouth hanging open, frankly stared at this vision of sophistication. Tall, slender and somewhere in her sixties, this woman possessed the kind of soignée elegance that was found only in Europe. She looked from Charlie in his sweatshirt and faded jeans to the stylish woman standing before her. "Your mother?"

"You must be Caroline." The woman extended a perfectly manicured hand. "I'm not surprised he hasn't told you about me."

"You have me at a disadvantage, Mrs. Donohue," she said, shaking her mother-in-law's hand. She was shocked that Charlie's mother even knew she existed.

"The name is Jean. I won't even bother you with my last two married names." Charlie's mother launched into a spirited synopsis of her last two European husbands that left Caroline staring at her, dumbfounded.

This had to be a joke. The Charlie Donohue she'd married was a short-order cook. A regular guy who lived in some ramshackle Cape Cod in Rocky Hill. He drank beer and watched football on TV and thought cheeseburgers were manna from the gods. There was no way on earth he could have sprung from the womb of this woman. Why, Jean Donohue Whatever was everything Caroline had ever wanted to be: gracious, witty and to the manner born. Everything Caroline *pretended* to be. Why hadn't Charlie ever told her?

Jean was cooing over Erin, regaling Charlie with stories about himself as a baby. Caroline drew back and watched mother and son and granddaughter. She'd come this close to making an utter fool of herself. She had been so elated, so filled with hope and joy, when Dr. Burkheit told her that Erin was out of the woods, that she was ready to run to Charlie and tell him what was in her heart.

What had been in her heart for a long, long time.

Well, thank God she hadn't done anything so foolish. In a way she was glad Jean had shown up when she did. At least now Caroline had been spared the embarrassment of revealing her secret heart to Charlie and then having it broken in two.

Oil and water.

Chalk and cheese.

Why had she ever believed they had a chance?

JEAN ONLY LINGERED a little while. "I'm off to Miami," she said to Charlie in her inimitable fashion. "Your Uncle Peter is having a soiree and you know how terribly affronted he can be if one is late."

Charlie didn't have the slightest idea what his mother was talking about. He wasn't even entirely sure he *had* an Uncle Peter. "Thanks for coming by."

She looked at him, her pale brows arched in question. "You're welcome."

"I'm sure Caroline enjoyed meeting you."

"I have the feeling she was only slightly less surprised than you were, Charles."

"We—uh, we haven't gotten around to exchanging family histories yet."

"Still fighting your background?"

He shrugged. "Still living the way I want to."

She smiled. "And so am I."

"That about says it all, doesn't it? Thirty-five years of conflict summed up in two simple, declarative sentences."

She pressed a phone number on him. "Your Uncle Peter's private number. Do call when you've set a christening date."

He nodded and tucked the card in the back pocket of his jeans. Might as well have the whole family on hand for the breakup.

"I like her, Charles," said his mother as she climbed into her limousine in front of the hospital. "Hold on to her."

"I'll try."

"Be happy," Jean said softly. "If you can manage that, the rest will fall into place."

He started to say something flip and juvenile, one of the pat phrases he'd fallen back on in the past, but he saw the look in his mother's eyes, thought of Caroline and Erin and the whole mystical connection between families, and he leaned in the window of the limo and kissed her cheek. "I'll call."

"Good," said his mother.

The limo driver nodded and, gunning the engine, zoomed down Witherspoon Street away from the hospital.

"Okay," said Charlie, watching the car disappear around the corner. "So now she knows." Caroline had met his mother. She'd seen the fancy clothes and the fancy jewelry and heard the fancy phrases Jean draped over her conversations like so much tinsel. He was rich. Big deal. He was still Charlie Donohue, short-order cook. Who cared what his background was? All that mattered was the future.

He chuckled as he stepped into the elevator and pressed the button for the maternity floor. Charlie Donohue, short-order cook and heir to the fortune of the Donohues of Virginia.

Yeah, Caroline would see the humor in it.

CAROLINE COULD SEE them from the window of her hospital room. Charlie and his mother were talking intently, their dark heads pressed together. Talking about her, most likely. She could just imagine his mother's questions about her pedigree. Dear God, it was every bad dream she'd ever had. How dare he pretend to be a regular person when he was really anything but.

She pounced on him the second he stepped into her room. "You fraud."

He stopped halfway through the door. "What?"

"You fraud!" She socked him right in the center of his stomach.

"What the hell's gotten into you?" he asked. "I'm getting tired of being your punching bag."

She glared at him, enraged by his deception. "Your mother is rich."

"So what?"

"And I suppose you're rich, too?"

He grinned. Didn't he know he was taking his life in his hands? "Not according to my checking account."

"I met your mother, Charles. I saw those diamonds on her fingers."

"What does that have to do with me?"

"You come from money, don't you?"

"Is that a crime?"

"Go ahead, Charles, admit it. You were rich."

He straddled the straight-back chair next to the bed and looked up at her. "I was rich."

She socked him in the shoulder and didn't care that he looked as if he wanted to sock her right back. "I can't believe you never told me."

"Would it have made a difference?"

"Yes . . . no. Oh, damn it, Charles. You're not the person you said you were." *And who are you to talk?* asked an annoying little voice.

"Who did I say I was?"

She eased herself down onto the edge of the bed, her incision tugging at her belly. He tried to help her but she brushed him away with sharp, choppy gestures.

"You said you'd been in the Navy. You said you had some ratty old house in Rocky Hill. You said you were a short-order cook. You said—"

"You've seen me frying burgers at O'Rourke's. I'd call that primary evidence." He recited his Navy ID number and quoted his yearly property taxes. "I'll even show you my dog tags, if you want."

She wanted to hit him again.

"Don't even think about it," he warned. "I'm not entirely civilized."

"There you go again!" she cried, days of tension exploding inside her. "Jean said you went to prep school."

"Is that a crime?"

"Yes," she said. "It's a crime when you pretended you were a regular guy."

"What the hell does that mean? 'A regular guy?'"

"Regular guys don't go to prep schools."

"What else don't regular guys do?"

"You're making fun of me, Charles. I don't appreciate that."

"Look, you're working yourself up into a lather, Caroline. We have a lot in common, that's all. Why don't you get some sleep and we'll talk about it later."

"I don't want to go to sleep. I want to talk." Amazing how clearly you could speak through gritted teeth.

"I've heard of things like this," he said, foolishly pushing ahead. "Postpartum something or other."

"You say one word about hormones, and so help me I'll—"

"You'll do what? Divorce me?" He stood up and pushed the chair into the nightstand. The cork on his temper had finally blown and there was no turning back. "That's what this is all about, isn't it?" He stormed toward the door. "Don't worry, Caroline," he said over his shoulder. "As far as I'm concerned, the deal's still on."

"Good," said Caroline.

"Great," said Charlie.

"As soon as the baby is christened."

"Set the date," growled Charlie. "I'll be counting the days."

ERIN WAS GAINING WEIGHT. Her mother was losing it. The snow had stopped and the sun was shining. Caroline should have been a happy woman.

She wasn't.

What she was was miserable.

As luck would have it, Dr. Burkheit released her from the hospital the day after her gigantic blowup with Charlie. Erin, of course, had to stay on a bit longer. "Another five days at the most," said Dr. Burkheit. "She's doing splendidly."

It should have been one of the happiest days of their lives. Instead, that happiness was tempered with the knowledge that their time together was drawing to a close. Charlie drove her home in silence and after Sam arrived with one of her gourmet box lunches, he excused himself and went off to work at the bar.

"What's wrong?" asked Sam the minute the door closed behind him. "Did you two have a fight?"

"He's rich," said Caroline. "Can you believe it?"

"Charlie?" Sam started to laugh. "If you saw his house, you wouldn't say that."

Caroline told her best friend about Jean's visit.

"I don't believe it," said Sam.

"Neither did I," said Caroline. "But I saw it with my own eyes."

"You mean he was one of those snot-nosed rich kids with the fancy clothes and summer vacations in Europe?"

"Bingo," said Caroline.

Sam thought for a moment. "He must've fallen on hard times to end up working as a short-order cook."

"Ha!" said Caroline. "He didn't fall on hard times. He joined the Navy."

"That's great," said Sam, a big bright smile spreading across her face. "Now you can tell him all about yourself. Both of you were keeping secrets."

Caroline looked down at her hands. It was time for a new manicure.

"You *are* going to tell him all about yourself, aren't you?"

"Why?" asked Caroline. "What's the point?"

"Isn't that obvious?"

"Not to me." She rose from her chair, wincing at the tug from her incision, and walked to the window. "We have nothing in common, Sam. Now more than ever."

"But he's exactly the kind of man you've been looking for, Carly. He has the looks and the family background—not to mention the fact that he's the father of your child. It's a match made in heaven."

"Carly." She sighed. "I haven't been called Carly in years."

"Did I call you that?" Sam smiled faintly. "I haven't thought of you as Carly in a long, long time."

"Seems like another person, doesn't it?"

"I don't know," said Sam. "I still see that little girl peeking through your glamorous facade from time to time."

Caroline said nothing.

Sam cleared her throat. "I don't know how to tell you this, but Charlie asked me to call your mom and tell her about the baby."

"Oh, God." She leaned her forehead against the glass. "What did she say?"

"I didn't reach her. I told one of your sisters-in-law and she said she'd pass on the message."

"Right," said Caroline. "I'm sure passing on the news is number one on the Gretchner to-do list." She turned from the window and faced Sam. "How did it all get so complicated?"

"If I had the answer to that, I'd be on Oprah, not sitting here in your living room."

"I think it's too late for us now," said Caroline. "Too much has happened." Her anger with Charlie wasn't justified and she knew it. They'd studiously avoided discussion of family and past lives, but at least what he chose to share with her was on the up and up.

Not like her. She'd done too good a job of creating Caroline Bradley of Princeton. If she suddenly turned around and introduced Donohue to Carly, and to her past, how could he ever trust her? Like everyone else, he had bought the package in its entirety.

It hadn't mattered in the beginning, back when she'd believed their marriage would have more to do with law than love. She'd never expected him to become part of her heart, part of her life. How could she turn around and tell him that everything he believed her to be was false, a sham, part of a calculated attempt to be something she wasn't?

Admit it, she thought after Sam left. *You liked it when you believed he was an average guy who made burgers for a living.* She'd never felt uncertain around Charlie, or uncomfortable, or out of her league. He didn't have a degree from Harvard or Yale or Princeton. He didn't speak French or spend summers in the Hamptons or Martha's Vineyard. Although he'd believed her to be one of the privileged few,

Caroline had known the truth, and the notion that she and Charlie had been cut from the same bolt of cloth had bound her more closely to him than she'd ever wanted to admit.

Now it was over. Charlie wasn't really the Charlie she'd married. And Caroline wasn't the elegant lady dressed in Chanel, but the poor kid from Rocky Hill with the second-hand clothes and the family who didn't care. All Caroline and Charlie had in common was their little girl and the memory of a few months when, for a while, she'd believed she actually could have it all.

ii

Another blizzard swept over central New Jersey without warning and botched up plans to bring the baby home on Friday. Caroline thanked God she'd been expressing breast milk and supplying it to the nursery for Erin's nighttime feedings. At least she knew her little girl was being cared for properly.

Charlie's truck was in the shop and he got stranded at the bar and opted to spend the night there. "You okay?" he asked when he telephoned around eleven.

"Fine," said Caroline.

"Enough food?"

"Plenty."

"Call Angela next door if you have any problems," said Charlie. "She said she'd be in all weekend."

"I will," said Caroline.

They said goodbye formally, stiffly, and Caroline hung up the receiver feeling sad and very alone.

That was on Friday. The christening was set for Sunday afternoon, but it was anybody's guess if the weather would ease up enough to make their plans for a small party possible.

As it happened, the storm blew out to sea late Saturday morning, and within hours the road crews were on duty, trying to dig the county out from under. Caroline stood beside her window, watching the maintenance crew struggle to clear the parking lot of her condominium complex. "Go away," she said out loud. If they didn't clear the roads, there couldn't be a christening. And if there wasn't a christening, Caroline and Charlie were still bound by their original deal. Other women managed to have husbands and babies both. Why on earth was a happy family life the one goal that continued to elude her?

Funny thing. She had her sports car and her condo. Her fancy dress shop and fancier friends. They'd once seemed so important to her, so vital to proving she'd made a success out of herself despite the odds.

Now she knew she'd trade them all away in an instant if it meant she and Charlie and Erin could be together forever.

But it was too late now for happy endings. Maybe if she'd been honest from the start, they might have had a chance, but now with each day that passed she realized that the moment for truth was long gone.

CHARLIE FINISHED work on the cradle Saturday afternoon. Every inch of it had been lovingly sanded and stained and polished, and now it stood ready to occupy the position of honor in his daughter's nursery. Sam's mother had volunteered to outfit the cradle with the necessary goodies that Charlie knew nothing about, so he lugged it over to the Deans' house in Rocky Hill early that evening.

"What a treasure!" Betty Dean exclaimed as he set it down in their living room. "Erin's one lucky little girl."

Charlie beamed at the praise. "Why is it I feel like I'm the lucky one?"

"Just you wait until those two o'clock feedings, Charlie. You'll be wondering how lucky you really are!" Betty's words were teasing and Charlie didn't have to look far to see the absolute delight she took in everything to do with babies.

He glanced at the coffee table piled high with photos and clippings.

"Did I interrupt something?"

Betty motioned for him to take a seat on the sofa. "I'm putting together a family scrapbook for the little one." She held up a green leather volume and a cranberry one. "Which do you like best?"

He pointed toward the cranberry. "Birth announcement and that kind of thing?"

"Family *history*," said Betty, fingering some black and white photos. "So Erin knows where she came from. I'm alternating pages so if you could get together some of your favorites, I'll add them."

He nodded, drawn to a glossy color photo on the stack closest to him. "You have photos of Caroline as a little girl?"

"Why, of course, I do," said Betty as if it was the most natural thing in the world.

And as it turned out, it was.

LATE SUNDAY morning Charlie showed up at Caroline's apartment in Bill O'Rourke's Dodge.

"Ready to get the baby?" he asked, as if she wasn't already chomping at the bit to get to the hospital.

"Ready," she said, outwardly cool and calm.

Charlie negotiated the trip without hazard. The closer they got to the hospital, the louder Caroline's heart beat inside her chest. In less than one hour that tiny bundle of baby girl would be her responsibility. Helpless. Demanding. Beautiful and precious and deserving of so much. A full-time father, for one.

How on earth would she ever manage to be all things to that child?

"Cold feet?" asked Charlie.

"Of course not," she said. "It's chilly in here, that's all."

He said nothing, just raised the heat.

"Best of luck, Mr. and Mrs. Donohue," said the nurse fifteen minutes later as she placed Erin in Caroline's trembling arms. "She's a wonderful little girl."

Caroline bit back tears as she kissed the top of Erin's downy head. Charlie looked away, eyes downcast. The baby slept the sleep of the innocent. The nurse looked from the new mother to the new father and shrugged. Usually first-time parents were giddy with excitement, eager to race home with their precious bundle of joy. Caroline and Charlie stood in the middle of the lobby, Erin cradled in her mother's arms, and looked as if they had no place better to go.

"Well, best of luck," the nurse repeated. "I know you three will be very happy."

The noon siren sounded. Charlie brought the car around to the front. *Six more hours,* thought Caroline as they struggled to bundle the baby into the infant car seat Sam had sent along. In just six more hours the christening would be over. Party guests would be saying their goodbyes and when the front door closed behind the last one, Caroline and Charlie's marriage would come to an end.

JEAN DONOHUE had been unable to get a flight up from Miami, but she'd sent along a beautiful, lacy christening dress for Erin. It didn't come with a family history, but it did come from the heart, and even Charlie was touched. Caroline's family sent a card, which was more than she had expected.

Only Sam and Murphy, the baby's godparents, attended the church service.

"Oh, will you look at this little doll?" Sam crooned as she cradled her goddaughter in her arms. "She's the image of the two of you."

Caroline and Charlie made a point of avoiding each other's eyes.

"She has your hair, Charlie," said Sam, oblivious of the tension between them. "Dark as a raven's wing."

Murphy, however, seemed to pick up on the vibes. "Sam only gets poetic around babies."

Caroline forced a smile but Charlie seemed too jumpy to manage even that.

The ceremony was short and solemn, yet joyous. Charlie found himself laughing with tears in his eyes as the baby's little face wrinkled in a frown at the touch of the holy water on her forehead. Caroline, in one of her elegant Chanel suits, stood straight and proud near the baptismal font. She looked even more beautiful today than she had the first time he'd seen her, singing atop the piano at O'Rourke's Bar and Grill a lifetime ago.

He half expected a choir of angels to swoop down on them and touch the day with magic. Truth was, he might need exactly that.

They drove to Caroline's apartment slowly, easing their way over the ice-encrusted roads. Huge mountains of snow were piled on either side, giving the impression of driving through an enormous arctic tunnel.

The baby, of course, slept through it all.

Bill O'Rourke popped out on the balcony of Caroline's apartment as Charlie pulled up to the front door. "They're here!" he called out. "Let the party begin."

"I wish we weren't doing this," said Caroline as Charlie helped her out. "I'm not in much of a party mood."

"It won't last long," said Charlie. "I told Sam to skip the buffet and just bring over coffee and cakes."

Caroline swallowed past the lump in her throat. *Oh, Charlie,* she thought. *You can't wait to be free, can you?*

The birth certificate was signed, sealed and delivered. Erin had been baptized and blessed with godparents who adored her. The baby's parentage had been proudly proclaimed and documented. The only thing left was the party, and that would be over before they knew it.

"I WANT TO BE the first to toast the wee one," Scotty declaimed in his best professorial manner. "To a beautiful little girl who is surpassed only by the goodness in her parents' hearts. May you three lead a charmed life together."

"Oh, Scotty." Caroline hugged her dear old friend, struggling to control her tears.

"Now none of that," said Scotty, handing her his linen handkerchief. "This is a day for celebration!"

Involuntarily Caroline's eyes sought Charlie's, but he was deep in conversation with Sam's mom. There was something about the sight of Mrs. Dean talking with Charlie that gave Caroline pause, but she brushed her uneasiness away and edged closer to where they were standing.

"You should've seen her when the holy water dribbled on her chin. I'm surprised the whole town didn't hear her howls of indignation."

Betty laughed out loud then noticed Caroline. "So your little girl has made her presence known, has she, honey?"

"That she has, Aunt Betty." Caroline gave her surrogate mom a kiss on the cheek. "Her lung power is something to behold."

"Sammy was like that, too," said Betty with a shake of her head. "Afraid it's something she's never outgrown." Betty launched into a hilarious description of the differences between her daughter and her daughter's two children that had Charlie laughing uproariously.

Did Betty Dean have any idea how lucky she was to have a husband and children and grandchildren who loved her and shared in the good times and the bad? *Oh, Charlie,* she thought, holding the baby closer to her heart. *If only...*

"Would you excuse me?" asked Caroline. "I think she's tired. I'd better put her down."

She disappeared down the hallway with Erin. *You will not cry in public,* she warned herself. No matter how much it hurt, she'd keep her tears private.

The door to the nursery was closed. She shifted Erin and reached for the doorknob.

"Need a hand?"

She started as Charlie came up behind her. "The door," she said, gesturing with her head.

He turned the knob and the door swung open. There, in the middle of the room, was the pine cradle they'd bought on that other Sunday afternoon when life had seemed wonderful.

"Oh." Her breath rushed from her lungs. "It's...it's so beautiful, Charles. You put so much work into it."

"I wasn't sure what to put in it besides the baby," he said with a sheepish grin. "Sam's mom helped me with that."

"Mrs. Dean is a terrific seamstress," said Caroline stiffly. "Those coverlets are lovely."

"Should we put the baby to bed?"

Caroline's cheeks reddened. "I think she's hungry."

"I put the rocking chair near the window. I thought that would be a good place for you to nurse her."

"Thank you." *You look so serious, Charlie. Is it that hard to say goodbye?*

She settled herself in the rocking chair and he handed her two of the pastel towels stacked near the stuffed dogs. He squatted next to her and gently stroked Erin's petal-soft cheek. Despite the fact that they'd created the baby in her arms, Caroline couldn't bring herself to nurse in front of him. Once she'd dreamed of a scene like this, the sweetness and joy of it. Now it only made her feel exposed and vulnerable and terribly, terribly sad.

"I suppose I should start packing now," he said, as casually as you'd ask someone if they needed a loaf of bread from the store.

She struggled to keep her gaze focused on her daughter. "There's no rush, Charlie. Take your time." *Take forever please...*

"The moving men are coming next week. I have to get things ready."

Tears slid down her cheeks faster than she could blink them away. "I understand."

"I don't think you do."

Her backbone of steel snapped into place. "I'm a big girl, Charles. I took care of myself before, I can take care of myself and Erin now."

"Fine," he said with a lazy smile, "but wouldn't you be happier taking care of her in that big Victorian farmhouse we saw?"

She stared at him, wide-eyed. "The one where we found the cradle?" *That wonderful, family house?*

"That's the one."

"You bought that house?"

He nodded. "I bought it."

"When?"

"A week before Erin arrived."

"Without asking me?"

"I figured I'd take a chance, *Carly*."

It took a second for his words to sink in. "What did you call me?"

"Carly." He paused. "That was what they used to call you when you were a kid, wasn't it?"

"I—I don't understand. How could you possibly—"

"I was at Mrs. Dean's place picking up the stuff for the cradle. She showed me a photo album she's putting together for Erin."

"Baby pictures?"

"Childhood pictures." He took her hand. "Of you."

Her heart pounded violently, but she kept her tone cautious, measured. "So now you know."

"Why didn't you tell me you grew up near Rocky Hill?"

She struggled to seem casual but failed miserably. "You never asked."

"Sam's mom said you even spent a few years with them."

Her look was defiant. "Yes, I did. Funny thing, how forgetful families can be. I'm still waiting for train tickets to Ohio."

"I don't think you'll be needing them."

"I don't know if you can understand this, but here goes: I didn't go to the 'right' schools, Charles. I didn't grow up with servants and limousines and respect." Her laugh was bittersweet. "I didn't even have parents who cared whether I was with them or not."

"If you think that matters to me, then we have a bigger problem than where you grew up."

"This isn't funny," she managed. "If this is some kind of joke..."

She looked into his eyes and to her amazement she saw right into his soul. *He loves me,* she thought. Carly Bradley. The real woman behind the facade she'd worked so hard to create. The glitter didn't matter to Charlie; the grit in her soul did. *He loves me just the way I am.*

"That house is meant for us," he was saying. "There's a big room upstairs that would make a great nursery."

"I thought you didn't want to be tied down."

"I didn't," he said. "Not before I met you."

Her eyes closed for an instant. "No halfway measures," she said, cradling the baby against her. "It's all or nothing."

"I'll never let you go. You and Erin belong to me now."

"Say it, Charlie," she whispered. "Please say it." She needed to hear the words, feel them warming her heart, hold them close in memory for the rest of her days.

"I love you," he said. "I love your smile and your right hook and the way you've made something out of your life. I love the way you look at me when you don't think I know you're looking. And I love—" He said something intimate and she felt the heat in every part of her body. "Let's do it again, Caroline. Let's make those promises for real this time."

In sickness and in health until death do us part.... A promise that healed broken hearts and brought families together. A promise that cast light into the darkness of the future and made the present a thing of wonder and joy.

"I love you, Charlie," she said, as their daughter slept blissfully in her arms. "More than you'll ever know."

"Forever?" His voice was husky, low with emotion.

She looked into his beautiful green eyes and saw the pattern of her future reflected in them, and that future made her heart sing.

"Oh, Charlie," she said softly as he pulled both mother and child into his strong arms. "For always."

Back by Popular Demand

Janet Dailey
Americana

A romantic tour of America through fifty favorite Harlequin Presents, each set in a different state researched by Janet and her husband, Bill. A journey of a lifetime in one cherished collection.

In July, don't miss the exciting states featured in:

Title #11 — HAWAII
Kona Winds

#12 — IDAHO
The Travelling Kind

Available wherever
Harlequin books are sold.

You'll flip . . . your pages won't!
Read paperbacks *hands-free* with

Book Mate · I

The perfect "mate" for all your romance paperbacks
Traveling • Vacationing • At Work • In Bed • Studying
• Cooking • Eating

Perfect size for
all standard
paperbacks,
this wonderful
invention
makes reading
a pure pleasure!
Ingenious
design holds
paperback
books OPEN
and FLAT so
even wind can't
ruffle pages—
leaves your
hands free to do
other things.
Reinforced,
wipe-clean vinyl-
covered holder flexes to let you
turn pages without undoing the
strap . . . supports paperbacks so
well, they have the strength of
hardcovers!

Pages turn WITHOUT
opening the strap

SEE-THROUGH STRAP

Reinforced back stays flat.

Built in bookmark

BOOK MARK

BACK COVER
HOLDING STRIP

10" x 7¼" opened.
Snaps closed for easy carrying, too

Available now. Send your name, address, and zip code, along with a check or
money order for just $5.95 + .75¢ for delivery (for a total of $6.70) payable to
Reader Service to:

Reader Service
Bookmate Offer
3010 Walden Avenue
P.O. Box 1396
Buffalo, N.Y. 14269-1396

Offer not available in Canada
*New York residents add appropriate sales tax.

BM-GR

**THIS JULY, HARLEQUIN OFFERS YOU
THE PERFECT SUMMER READ!**

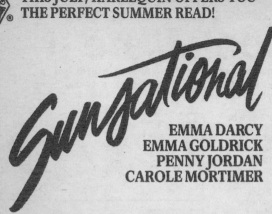

**EMMA DARCY
EMMA GOLDRICK
PENNY JORDAN
CAROLE MORTIMER**

From top authors of Harlequin Presents comes
HARLEQUIN SUNSATIONAL, a four-stories-in-one
book with 768 pages of romantic reading.

Written by such prolific Harlequin authors as Emma Darcy,
Emma Goldrick, Penny Jordan and Carole Mortimer,
HARLEQUIN SUNSATIONAL is the perfect summer
companion to take along to the beach, cottage, on your
dream destination or just for reading at home in the warm
sunshine!

Don't miss this unique reading opportunity.

Available wherever Harlequin books are sold.